Reg...
den...
Superintendent Dalziel and DCI Pascoe. Their appearances have won him numerous awards including a CWA Gold Dagger and the Diamond Dagger for Lifetime Achievement. They have also been adapted into a hugely popular BBC TV series.

By the same author

REGINALD HILL

BORN GUILTY

HARPER

This novel is entirely a work of fiction.
The names, characters and incidents portrayed in them are
the work of the author's imagination. Any resemblance to
actual persons, living or dead, events or localities is
entirely coincidental.

Harper
An imprint of HarperCollins*Publishers*
77–85 Fulham Palace Road,
Hammersmith, London W6 8JB

www.harpercollins.co.uk

This paperback re-issue 2010
1

Previously published in paperback by
Collins Crime 1995

First published in Great Britain by
Collins Crime 1995

A catalogue record for this book is
available from the British Library

ISBN 978-0-00-733481-0

Set in Meridien by Palimpsest Book Production Ltd
Grangemouth, Stirlingshire

Printed and bound in Great Britain by
Clays Ltd, St Ives plc

Mixed Sources

Product group from well-managed
forests and other controlled sources
www.fsc.org Cert no. SW-COC-001806
© 1996 Forest Stewardship Council

FSC is a non-profit international organisation established to promote the responsible
management of the world's forests. Products carrying the FSC label are independ-
ently certified to assure consumers that they come from forests that are managed to
meet the social, economic and ecological needs of present and future generations.

Find out more about HarperCollins and the environment at
www.harpercollins.co.uk/green

1

This all started when Joe Sixsmith came sneaking out of a small side door at St Monkey's.

The reason he was in St Monkey's was to rehearse Haydn's *Creation*.

The reason he was sneaking out was that on arrival his Aunt Mirabelle had seized his arm in a grip like a council bailiff's and said, 'What's this I've been hearing, Joseph?'

Only the impatient rattatooing of Mr Perfect's baton saved him from immediate grilling.

Joe had no problem guessing what it was Mirabelle had been hearing. Galina Hacker, that's what. Normally his aunt, a firm believer that any bachelor butting forty and not an alto needed a wife, would have been delighted to hear her baritone nephew was keeping company. But in this case, as well as being an affront to her own preferred candidate, Beryl Boddington (who gave Joe a little wave from the sopranos as they took their place), rumours about Galina must have hit the Rasselas Estate like word of Mrs Simpson reaching Lambeth Palace.

Joe, a reasonable though not always a rational man, could see how it might be a shock to the auntly system to learn he'd taken up with a spiky-haired seventeen-year-old with a stud in her nose, no bra, and a skirt like a pelmet. But he saw no reason to explain himself. On the other hand, he saw every reason to avoid interrogation.

If the Boyling Corner Concert Choir had been on its home ground, he wouldn't have stood a chance. Mirabelle had the few exits from the square-built chapel more tightly covered than a nun's nipples. But the choir's growing reputation had led to an invitation to join with the South Bedfordshire Sinfonia and St Monkey's Chorale in a performance of the oratorio to mark the five hundredth anniversary of the granting of Luton's Royal Charter. After token resistance from some of the older members, Boyling Corner had agreed that it made sense for the performance to take place in St Monica's (known to impious Lutonians everywhere as St Monkey's). Its advantages were obvious. Better acoustics, central situation, more seating space. And, less obvious, but best of all to a desperate man, a much greater variety of escape routes.

Joe waited for the final Amen. He glanced towards the contraltos. Mirabelle's eyes were fixed firmly on Mr Perfect's – that is to say, the conductor, Geoffrey Parfitt's – raised baton. As it came down, he took a step backwards into the taller men behind him. His heel came down on someone's toe and a voice shot up an anguished octave.

'Sor-ry!' sang Joe.

Then he was off like a whippet. He'd spotted an outer door in a small side chapel. He'd no idea if it would be open, but if you couldn't trust God in a place like this, what's a heaven for? As he reached the door he heard the conductor saying, 'Not bad, but still a way to go. Wrap up well. It's a raw night and we don't want any sore throats, do we?'

He grasped the handle, turned it, felt resistance, said a prayer, and next moment he was safe in the darkness of the night.

Mr Perfect was right. The air was cold and dank, but Joe sucked it in like draught Guinness. His first instinct was to turn left and head for the bright lights of St Monkey's Square from which it was only a short step to the real Guinness at the Glit. But that could be a fatal error. For a woman of her age and bulk, Mirabelle was no slouch over fifty yards. Better safe than sorry. He turned right and headed into the gloomy hinterland of the churchyard.

Though it had a Charter, Luton didn't have a cathedral. The rich burghers of the last century had set about compensating for this oversight by commissioning the erection of the largest parish church in the country. The money ran out before it quite reached that stature, but it was big, and *The*

Lost Traveller's Guide, the famous series devoted to places you were unlikely to visit on purpose, described St Monkey's as 'a splendid example of the controlled exuberance of late Victorian Gothic'.

Joe, like most Lutonian kids, had found its cypressed grounds and the dark nooks formed by its many buttresses very convenient for the controlled exuberance of early sexual adventure. But that had been a good twenty years ago, before the sand got in the social machine and civilization started grinding to a halt.

First the druggies had taken over till nightly sweeps by the police had driven them to further, fouler venues, like the infamous Scratchings. Then the new homeless, expelled by commercial indignation from the comparatively warm doorways of the shopping centres, had moved their boxes here. The police had started their sweeps again, leaving the Reverend Timothy Cannister teetering uneasily between his duty of Christian charity and the demands of the uncharitable Christians who made up most of his congregation. Vincent, his Visigothic verger, had no such doubts. Set your cardboard box up in St Monkey's and you could be rudely awoken by a bucket of dirty water.

But still they came. Create a society which didn't offer help to the helpless or hope to the hopeless, and where did you expect them to go?

So mused Joe as he made his way cautiously along the dark flagstones between the church wall and the graveyard. A gust of wind tore a hole in the seething clouds to permit a welcome glimpse of the moon. In its chill bone-light he glimpsed a little way ahead, in the angle of the great corner buttress which marked the far end of the building, one of these pathetic boxes. Over it stooped a figure.

Joe hesitated, unwilling to risk disturbing the poor devil. Anyone desperate enough to brave the verger's wrath deserved as much peace as he could find. Except that this figure didn't look like it was preparing to kip down. More like it was leaning into the box to . . .

Suddenly light stabbed into his eyes, cutting off further

speculation. And a woman's voice cried, 'You there! What do you think you're doing?'

Joe threw up his hand to catch the glare. The torch beam swung away to the box just in time to catch the figure taking off, dodging away between the headstones to the high boundary wall and going over it with the ease of fear.

Then the light came drilling back into his eyes.

'All right. Who are you? What are you doing here?' demanded the woman. But there was a note of uncertainty there too. She sounded like what Aunt Mirabelle designated *a real lady*, and Joe guessed that the first thing real ladies learnt at their real ladies' seminaries was, you meet a black man in a black churchyard, you run like hell!

'My name's Joe Sixsmith,' he said, pulling a battered business card out of his pocket and holding it up in the beam.

'Good Lord. A detective. You here on business?'

'No, ma'am. I've been in the church rehearsing, and I was just taking a short cut . . .'

'Me too,' she said. 'Listening, I mean, not singing. I just crept in and sat quietly. Lovely music, isn't it?'

'It surely is,' said Joe, a long admirer of the English upper-class ability to indulge in small talk in any circumstances. 'Listen, that guy who ran off . . .'

'Yes. Who was he, do you think? Did you get a good look at him?'

'Not really. Could be he's one of those derelicts who sleep in cardboard boxes . . .'

'Ah yes. Dreadful, isn't it?'

He couldn't make out from her tone what precisely she found dreadful. He went on, 'Only he moved a bit nimble for a down-and-out. And he looked more like he was looking into the box than *getting* into it.'

'You think so? Perhaps we'd better take a look.'

She began to move forward, the torch beam running over the flags and up the side of the box. It had once contained an Alfredo fridge freezer. Joe wondered about warning her that if there was anything in it now, it was unlikely to be white goods. But he didn't fancy trying to take a torch off a *real lady* so he could have first look.

She reached the box and peered in.

'Oh Lord,' she said.

And Joe, coming to stand beside her, saw that it had been white goods after all.

'You all right, mate?' said Joe.

It was a redundant question but at least it showed you didn't need to attend a seminary to pick up the vernacular. If a Brit tourist had stumbled on the Crucifixion, first thing he'd probably have said was, 'You all right, mate?'

There was no reply. He didn't expect one. The figure curled at the bottom of the box was male, blond, hazel-eyed, young – fifteen to twenty maybe – and not going to get any older.

Gingerly he reached in to confirm his diagnosis. The boy's left hand was folded palm up against his shoulder, as though in greeting. Or farewell. Something was written on the ball of his thumb . . . a long number faded almost to invisibility except for the central three digits . . . 292 . . . at least it wasn't tattooed like in the death camps . . . The association of ideas made Joe shudder.

'Is he dead?' demanded the woman impatiently.

I'm just putting off touching him, thought Joe. Boldly, he grasped the wrist. Temperature alone told him what he'd already known. Waste of time looking for a pulse. His time, not the boy's. He had no more to waste.

'I'm afraid so,' he said.

The torch beam jerked out of the box and she cradled it against her chest, letting him glimpse her face for the first time. Fortyish, fine boned, slightly hook nosed, with her skin more weather-beaten than an English sun was likely to cause. Lit from beneath, the face looked rather more cadaverous than the boy's in the box, except that her narrow blue eyes had the bright light of intelligence in them.

'Listen, we ought to get help, the police, an ambulance . . .'

'Yes. You go. You know the ropes and you'll move faster . . .'

'We'll both go.'

'No. You'll move faster without me. To tell the truth, I feel a bit wobbly. It's just beginning to hit home . . . that boy in there . . . he is no more than a boy, is he? . . . I've a son of my own . . . What is the world coming to?'

'An end, maybe,' said Joe. 'OK, I'll go. You sit down over here. I won't be a minute.'

Leaving her perched on a plinth of monumental masonry under a weeping angel, he hurried away.

Naturally, because even in a churchyard, God's Law and Sod's Law are only a letter apart, he was just in time to meet Mirabelle coming out of the main entrance arm in arm with Rev. Pot of Boyling Corner Chapel, and the Reverend Timothy Cannister of St Monica's.

'Where've you been, Joe?' she cried, hurling aside the pastoral pair and seizing him with both hands. 'I said I wanted a word with you.'

'Not now,' said Joe. 'I've got to go.'

'What's so urgent you can't talk to your old auntie?' she demanded with the indignation of one who knows there is no possible answer.

Except one.

'Death,' said Joe. 'Excuse me, Vicar. You got a phone in the vicarage I could use?'

2

It must have been a quiet night on the mean streets of Luton because by the time Joe finished his phoning and came out of the vicarage, a police car was already belling its way into the square.

Out of it leapt a fresh-faced young constable he didn't know followed by a fat-faced one he did.

His name was Dean Forton and he rated the Sixsmith Detective Agency lower than Wimbledon FC.

'What the hell are you doing here?' he said ungraciously as Joe approached.

'I found the body.'

'Must have tripped over it then,' said Forton. 'OK, let's take a look at it.'

He seemed quite pleased at the prospect. First on the murder scene can get a chance to shine. But when he realized it was just a dosser, his enthusiasm faded.

'More bother than they're worth,' he said to his younger colleague. 'Here, Sandy, seeing we've got him in a box in a boneyard, why don't you whip back to the car, get a shovel, and we'll save everyone a bit of time and trouble.'

'You're a real riot, Dean,' said the youngster, his Scottish roll of the r's exaggerated by a slight tremor as he looked down at what Joe guessed was his first corpse.

'All right then,' said Forton. 'At least keep the ghouls off till the girls get here.'

The ghouls were a growing group of spectators led by Mirabelle. The girls, Joe guessed, were CID. Forton hung his emergency lantern on the outstretched arm of the weeping angel under which the real lady was no longer sitting.

In fact, she was nowhere in sight. Joe wasn't too surprised. Not getting involved was a kneejerk reaction of the English upper classes, particularly when what you weren't getting involved with was a dead dosser, a black PI and Luton's finest in a cold and gloomy churchyard.

The girls arrived led by DS Chivers, another old acquaintance and even less of a fan than Forton. Joe gave him a bare outline of his discovery of the body, not bothering at this juncture to complicate matters with reference to the woman. He was immediately punished for this economy by her reappearance.

'Ah,' she said, cutting across Chivers's questioning. 'You came back then.'

Joe felt she was stealing his lines. Chivers felt she was undermining his authority.

'Who the hell are you?' he asked irritably.

She gave him a look which would have stopped an assegai in full flight. The image popped into Joe's mind fully formed and he realized it came from a certainty that this was a good old-fashioned English colonial lady. Her dun-coloured skirt and shirt derived from the practical rather than the fashionable side of safari, but it was her complexion which was the real giveaway. That could only come from long exposure to the sun which used never to set.

She said to Chivers, 'Kindly don't interrupt. Mr Sixsmith, after you left, it struck me the quickest way to summon help would be to use my car phone, therefore I made my way round to the Cloisters and phoned Emergency.'

This told Joe a lot.

First, it explained the speed of the police response.

Second, it confirmed the woman's status. The Cloisters was a paved area at the back of the church. Folklore claimed it was all that remained of the original medieval abbey. Archaeology proved it was merely a pavement laid down by the Victorian contractors to stop their material and machines from sinking into the Lutonian bog. Now it provided space to park a few cars, a convenience in the gift of the Reverend Timothy Cannister and only doled out to top people. Joe didn't anticipate being invited to park his Morris Oxford there.

Third, he recognized the explanation as apology. Perhaps her houseboys hadn't been big on civic responsibility. Whatever, she'd doubted if he'd go near a phone and this was her way of saying sorry without admitting there was anything to be sorry about.

He said, 'That was good thinking. Sometimes they need a couple of calls to get them out of the canteen.'

She rewarded him with a not unattractive smile, then overpaid him by turning to Chivers and saying, 'Now, Constable, why don't you trot off and fetch one of your superiors?'

Chivers went red as a radish, but before he could explode into real trouble, a voice cried, 'Mrs Calverley, I thought it was you. I do hope you haven't been inconvenienced.'

The Reverend Timothy Cannister had broken past the young Scots constable. Known to the compulsive punsters of Luton as Tin Can because of his fondness for rattling one in your face, his reaction to the woman confirmed she belonged to the cheque-in-the-post set rather than the coin-in-the-slot class.

Also the name meant something to Chivers whose indignant response withered on his lip.

'No inconvenience, Tim,' she said cheerfully. 'I'm just helping this constable with his enquiries.'

'It's sergeant, ma'am, and at the moment I'm senior officer present. So if you could just spare a moment . . . ?'

'Why on earth didn't you say so? Let me tell you all I know about this dreadful business.'

It took less than a minute of admirably terse narrative. Chivers didn't interrupt or ask any questions, and then Mrs Calverley accepted Tin Can's invitation to step into the vicarage for a warming potation, though she winced visibly at his preciosity.

'All right for me to go and get one of them too?' asked Joe.

'Not before you answer a few questions, Sixsmith,' snarled Chivers.

'Nothing I can add to what the lady says.'

'You're supposed to be a detective, aren't you? How about trying to give me a description of the perpetrator?'

'What perpetrator?' asked Joe. 'Perpetrator of what?'

'Don't get clever with me, sunshine. There's a body in that box, remember?'

'I know. And I think you'll find he's been dead an hour or so.'

'How do you know?'

'Because I felt for a pulse and he was cold enough not to have died just that minute,' said Joe.

'So what was this guy you spotted doing then?'

'Maybe the same as me, checking the kid's pulse to see if he needed help.'

Chivers snarled a laugh and said, 'Do you think Immigration knows about all these Good Samaritans flooding into the country? More likely he was one of those weirdos who get their kicks beating dossers up. So, a description.'

Joe gave him what he could. Finally Chivers said, 'All right. Sod off. We'll be in touch.'

'And thank you too, Sergeant, for your courtesy. I'll be sure to mention it to Mr Woodbine. I was real pleased to hear he's been made up to superintendent.'

It was a low blow. Willie Woodbine disliked Chivers almost as much as Joe did, plus the new detective superintendent hadn't been hindered in his elevation by the help Joe had somewhat fortuitously supplied in solving a recent big murder case.

Chivers was a nifty counter puncher and now he said, 'You'll be going to the celebration party at his house next Sunday then?'

He knows I've as much chance of being invited there as I have of being invited to stand for the Cheltenham Tories, thought Joe.

'Hope I can make it,' he said. 'If I do, I'll see you there, shall I?'

He saw the dart draw blood. Chivers and the CID girls might get a drink down the pub, but no way was Willie Woodbine going to take them home!

He took a last glance at the cardboard box before he walked

away. No one should end up in a thing like that, especially not someone so young.

His musing on death's indignities made him forget life's perils.

'There you are, Joseph Sixsmith. Now what you been up to?'

It was Aunt Mirabelle, lurking in the portico. At least her eagerness to be brought up to date made her forget Galina. But she showed more pertinacity than Chivers by suddenly asking, 'What you doing sneaking out of that side door anyway?'

Time to go. He glanced at his watch which had stopped and said, 'Auntic, we'll talk tomorrow, OK? I got an appointment. Business.'

'At this time of night.'

'Crime doesn't keep office hours,' he tossed over his shoulder.

He'd seen that on the letterhead of a security firm he'd failed to do business with. He'd thought at the time it was a pretty crappy slogan. Now he got Mirabelle's vote.

'Don't give me that clever dick crossword stuff,' she yelled after him. 'You never went to no college. Joseph Sixsmith, you get yourself back here!'

Joe had made it to the square. Freedom was at hand but old habits die hard and he'd been obeying Aunt Mirabelle's commands as long as he could remember. He hesitated on the edge of the pavement. He who hesitates is sometimes saved. A dusty blue Range Rover came shooting out of the narrow lane that led to the Cloisters car park and swept by him at a speed that would probably have exploded his vital organs if he'd taken another step.

He glimpsed Mrs Calverley's angular profile above the wheel. She gave no sign that she'd noticed him. Well, he supposed she'd had a nasty shock. And so had he.

There were two ways of taking this near miss. One was that God had used Aunt Mirabelle's voice to save his life. The other was, a man who's just been so close to death needs a drink.

He weighed the alternatives judiciously. On the whole,

he reckoned that after all the eighteenth-century praise and thanksgiving God had been getting tonight, He wouldn't be averse to a bit of modern secular music for a change.

Deafening his ears to Mirabelle's unceasing commands, he set off for the Glit.

3

From time to time, Dick Hull, who runs the Gary Glitter public house in Luton, gets an acute attack of conscience. It seems to him that despite all he has done by way of decor, music and memorabilia, he is failing in his priestlike task of celebrating the one and only supernova of the British pop firmament.

Whenever this black mood comes upon him, he seeks solace in The Tape.

This is a recording he made at one of Gary's legendary Gangshows by hurling a cassette recorder on to the stage and reclaiming it later under a savage assault by three stewards. Miraculously, the tape had kept on recording. The resulting sound in Hull's ears was more than hi-fidelity. It was the truth, the whole truth and nothing but the truth. Played full belt on the Glit's PA system, it took him back to that glorious night in Glasgow, and all his self-doubt faded away.

It was playing tonight. Joe heard it several streets away. Legend had it that when fog blanketed Britain so bad that most airports were packing up and going home, at Luton planes still landed, homing in on the Glit.

Joe didn't altogether believe this. But he did wonder how a God accustomed to the gentle murmurings of Hallelujah choruses might feel about this level of decibels.

Happily, he was able from long experience to detect that it was approaching its climax. This was not, great though it was, Gary's valedictory rendition of 'I'm the Leader of the Gang (I am)' but the voice of a steward shouting 'Awafokyer-selyerweedickheed!' and Hull's respondent scream as a size eleven army surplus boot came down on his hand.

The scream peaked as Joe entered. No one was talking. Even the new generation of kids brought up in a sound environment which made the machine room Joe had worked in most of his adult life seem like a forest glade, couldn't compete with this combination of frantic fans, stroppy stewards, and personal pain.

Then it was over. For a second there was a fragment of that rarest of things at the Glit, perfect silence.

In that moment Joe's gaze met Galina Hacker's across the crowded bar, and his heart sank. She'd been at the Oxfam shop again. At least the seventies flared trousersuit she wore covered those provocative legs (how could anything so skinny be so sexy?) but she'd given the tunic a bit of pazazz by cutting off the sleeves, and even from this distance Joe could see she was wearing nothing beneath it. The flesh missing off her legs had been redistributed up there with equally disturbing results.

First things first. He gestured to the bar and shouldered his way through, giving and returning greetings. Next best thing to anonymity for a PI was a place where everyone knew you, especially when it meant your pint of Guinness was already waiting, neat and welcoming as a vicar at a wedding.

'Thanks, Eric,' he said.

Eric, a young man whose habitually worried expression clashed strangely with the brash assertiveness of his diamanté-studded waistcoat, watched in respectful silence as Joe downed five inches, then said, 'No Whitey?'

'No. I've been rehearsing. He doesn't care for Haydn.'

Whitey was his cat. No way you could get him into the chapel. Rev. Pot reckoned he'd got enough on his plate dealing with human crap. But St Monkey's larger spaces had tempted Joe to bed Whitey down on a hassock in a remote pew at the first united rehearsal. He'd been all right through the introductory Chaos and the piano entry of the choir. But when they reached *let there be light, and there was* LIGHT, and the voices and instruments exploded in that most glorious of musical exultations, Whitey had shot upright and started a howling which had persisted long after the music had died away.

Most people had been amused. Aunt Mirabelle was not most people. According to her, Joe had let down himself, his family, Boyling Corner Chapel, and every decent Christian soul who'd ever had the misfortune to come in contact with him.

Memory of Mirabelle was so strong that when a hand grasped his arm he jumped guiltily and almost spilt some stout.

'Thought you wasn't coming,' said Galina accusingly.

He turned and looked at her. Despite apparently being assaulted by a mad sheep-shearer and a myopic action painter, she was still a beautiful girl. But why not? Blacked out teeth and a raggedy suit hadn't stopped Judy Garland of immortal memory from being the loveliest swell walking down the avenue.

'Hello, Gal,' he said. 'Got a drink?'

For answer she held up a bottle. Joe winced. It wasn't just the contents, winceable though they were, being something called Luger which the ads claimed 'blows you away'. It was the way these young girls drank straight from the bottle that offended something deep down. When he'd mentioned this to his friend, Merv Golightly, his distaste had been submitted to a long and deeply unflattering sexual analysis. But so were most things that tugged at Merv's consciousness, from Luton's performance in the FA Cup to the way that John Major walked. As a taxi driver, Merv was used to a captive audience. An American visitor had once hired him to drive her to Leeds and back twice a week for a month. 'It's cheaper than my analyst,' she said. 'And it does me more good.'

'Let's sit down,' said Galina.

She led him to a table where a bunch of her mates were protecting a couple of empty chairs by smashing their bottles down on any hand foolish enough to grasp them. They greeted Joe with their customary silent incredulity that one of his advanced years could still be moving with no apparent mechanical aid, then went back to their conversation which consisted of an interchange of staccato screams. The only alternative was to lean forward so that your lips were almost touching your interlocutor's ear. This was the mode preferred by Joe and Galina, and if Aunt Mirabelle could have seen them in this position, the worst case scenarios hypothesized by her spies would have been positively confirmed.

A tape of the conversation would have been more puzzling.

'You got anywhere yet?' said Galina.

'Give me time,' said Joe.

'It's been a week.'

'Six days,' said Joe firmly. 'I said it would need to be slow else you could end up getting what you're trying to avoid.'

'Yeah? Maybe publicity's what we need, get it out in the open, make them show their hand.'

'We've been through all this,' said Joe gently. 'If they've nothing to show, all you're doing is giving the loonies a feast. There's no such thing as good publicity. You see a headline saying: BISHOP NOT BONKING CURATE'S WIFE, it doesn't stop rumours, it starts them. Get a hint of this in the papers, makes no matter how innocent they say your granddad is, there are enough loonies out there to give him and you and the whole family a really lousy time. Is that what you want?'

'Of course it's not,' said the girl. 'Only I hoped . . .'

Her voice tailed off, though he could still feel her breath warm on his ear lobe. He knew what she hoped. That in bringing her worries to him, she'd be told in no time flat that she had nothing to worry about. That's what people often wanted, and they had a nasty habit of blaming him when he couldn't give it to them.

She said, 'He's been round at the club again, asking questions. I got a proper description this time.'

She took a piece of paper from an inner pocket. It was warm from her breast. On it she'd scribbled: *5'8"–5'10" (bigger than me but not too much) reddish hair. Blue eyes. Swollen nose. Big feet. Olive-green jacket.*

Joe said, 'This sound the same as the one who got talking to your mum?'

'Yeah, except she didn't say anything about his nose.

Maybe someone's hit him since then. Gets in my range, it'll be more than a swollen nose he ends up with!'

Joe regarded her gravely and said, 'You're not stupid enough to do that, are you, Gal?'

In fact, he knew she wasn't stupid at all. And the more he talked to her, the brighter she seemed. He'd known her for a long time without really knowing her. She was a cashier at the Luton and Biggleswade Building Society where Joe stashed what little money he managed to save from his erratic income. She was pleasant and personable and always greeted him by name and passed the time of day as she updated his book.

He'd never seen her outside the building society except for one night he'd been invited to the Uke, the local Ukrainian Club, by a client and he'd spotted her sitting with a middle-aged couple and an older white-haired man. She'd given him a wave and he'd gone over and been introduced to her parents, George and Galina Hacker, and her grandfather, Taras Kovalko. Joe's client had filled him in later. Taras was one of the numerous displaced persons who found refuge in the UK after the war. He'd settled in Manchester, married an English girl, had one daughter he called Galina after his own mother. She had married George Hacker, a salesman, and they'd gone to live in Luton. Widowed and retired, Taras had come to live with them a couple of years ago.

Joe, who'd hitherto guessed that the girl's unusual name was merely one of those Anglo-Saxon flights of fancy which filled the classified 'Births' with Clints and Garths and Meryls and Kylies, was pleased to know it had a real meaning. He believed in families. Blood was thicker than water, though he wasn't so sure about Guinness.

Then about a week ago, when he visited the building society to draw out a little of the little that was left, the girl had asked in a low voice if she could see him professionally.

'Sure,' he said. 'When?'

'It's my half day today,' she said.

'Fine,' said Joe, smiling at her. In her M & S cardie with minimal make up and straight brushed hair, she looked about fourteen. He didn't fancy making her walk down the rather seedy street which housed his rather scruffy office, so he said, 'How about four o'clock in the Sugar 'n' Tongs?'

The Sugar 'n' Tongs was the kind of place people took their grannies, very safe, very central.

'OK,' she said.

He'd got there early so she wouldn't feel uncomfortable arriving by herself. He realized he stuck out like a sore thumb among the mainly formidable female clientele. But he'd been united with them in conversation-stopping surprise when a spiky-topped alien in a skirt like a guardrail above a dizzying drop, and a halter straining like a tops'l in a Force Ten gale, had come through the door. The unity had been shortlived. From being a spectator he became part of the spectacle as the newcomer headed straight for his table and from that vermilion mouth came the words, 'Hello, Mr Sixsmith. Good of you to see me.'

Though the noise level here was decibels below the Glit, they set the pattern for future conversations by leaning close together to thwart the straining ears.

What was said would probably have disappointed the would-be eavesdroppers, but Joe it deeply dismayed.

'I was down at the Uke last week helping with the refreshments. It was a ladies' social night, Mum's really keen, it was her actually that got Grandda started going, he's never been a one for living in the past, but since he joined he's been really enjoying it. And I got talking to Mrs Vansovich, you may remember seeing her, little old lady, about the size of a garden gnome and she looks a bit like one too. The men make a joke about her, Vansovich always a witch, very funny ha ha, but she is a bit of a gossip, no denying. She started telling me about this man who'd been asking questions, said he was trying to contact someone called Taras something beginning with a K. He said his grandmother had got to know this Taras after the war when she was a driver for some colonel in charge of dealing with displaced persons in southern Germany. He said his grandmother was bedridden now and would like to see this Taras again, but she couldn't remember his second name except that it began with a K, and she thought he came from Vinnitsa which is where

Grandda was born, and Mrs Vansovich knows this because she was born there too and is always wanting to talk about it.'

Tea arrived and she paused for breath. When the waitress had gone, Joe said, 'Galina . . .'

'Gal. My friends call me Gal. Or Gallie.'

Joe, conscious of the presence of some of the sharpest observers in Luton, didn't think this was a good time to offer her the familiarity of calling him Joe.

He said, 'Gallie, if you could get to the point . . .'

'Sorry. It's not easy, not without telling you all this. The upshot was that old Vansovich must have told this man everything she knew about Grandda, and he said it might be the same one but he wasn't sure, and could she please keep quiet about it till he was, as he didn't want to embarrass anyone with talk of an old flame. He went off then, leaving Vansovich convinced there's been some great romance. She's a bit frightened of mentioning it to Mum, I think, but me being young, she thought I'd be interested.'

'And were you?'

'Yeah, it sounded a bit of a giggle really, Grandda and the colonel's lady driver! I dropped a few hints to him, taking the mickey like I often do. Usually we have a good laugh but he got quite ratty. So I thought, hello, Vansovich has said something and it's something he doesn't want to talk about, so I let it drop. I did begin to wonder if maybe this thing had gone all the way and that maybe this jerk-off asking the questions was some sort of cousin of mine. Then Mum brought Grandda back from the club a couple of days later and I could see he was upset. I asked Mum about it and she said she'd called in at the supermarket on the way home, and when she came out to the car park, there was this guy talking to Grandda through the car window. Mum said he was holding the glass down with his fingers while Grandda was trying to wind it up inside. Mum heard him say, where's the harm in a few facts, Mr Kovalko, if you've got nothing to hide? Then Mum asked him what the hell he was playing at? And he said sorry, he was just asking for directions, and took off. Since then, Grandda's hardly been out of the house.'

She paused, picked up a teacake, examined it, put it back on the plate.

Joe said, 'So what do you want me to do, Gallie?'

'I should have thought that was obvious,' she said. 'I want you to find out who this guy is, what he's after.'

Joe said gently, 'But it sounds like your grandfather's got some idea who he is and what he wants. Why not just ask him?'

'Because . . . because he won't say anything! He doesn't want to tell me.'

'In that case . . .' said Joe.

He was beginning to have a suspicion what this might be all about, but he'd learned the hard way about looking before he leapt. If the girl didn't tell him what was on her mind, no way he was going to play guess-guess.

'I think he's frightened, and I don't like people going around frightening my grandda,' she said fiercely. 'I want him stopped!'

'So have a word with the police,' he said.

'You're joking!' she said with a dismissive scorn. 'Listen, Mr Sixsmith . . .'

She put a hand on his, and looked him straight in the eye. It probably looked like uncontrollable passion to the lynx-eyed tea drinkers, but Joe could see she was bringing herself to the point of telling him the truth. He found himself hoping she wouldn't make it.

But she was there.

In a flat, rapid voice she said, 'I know it sounds stupid but I was reading in one of the supplements about this debate whether they should prosecute old war criminals. And the article said there were half a dozen they were pretty certain of living in this country, and several more they suspected, and a lot of them were eastern Europeans, Ukrainians and others, who'd served in those concentration camps and came here as displaced persons after the war . . .'

Her voice dried up as though articulation had made her fully aware for the first time of the enormity of what she was saying.

He said, 'Hey, look, I don't know much about it, but there

24

must be thousands of people like your grandda came here to settle after the war. They were victims, they needed help. Why should anyone suddenly start thinking . . . I mean, there must be a hundred other explanations . . .'

'That's what I want you to do. Find one,' she said. 'But if there's someone out there trying to pin something like this on Grandda, I want the bastard sorted out!'

She spoke with a fierce intensity that took him aback. This was mainly why he said he'd help. He had the feeling that if he didn't, she might look elsewhere for assistance in taking more direct action against the inquisitive stranger.

He'd got a description. Young, red-haired, nice smile, really charming (the last two were Mrs Vansovich's), medium build, big feet, blue check jacket, black trousers, lime-green windcheater (he'd had this on in the car park), some kind of accent (Irish/Scottish?). And now a swollen nose.

He'd changed their meeting place to the Glit after that first encounter. The friends she sat with confirmed Joe's suspicions that she mightn't be short of assistance if she decided to have a pop at this guy herself, though every time he saw her in the building society, he couldn't believe what he was believing!

But he had no difficulty in believing after that first all too public encounter in the Sugar 'n' Tongs that, as sure as the fall of a sparrow is known to the living God, not even the protective cover of the Glit could hide their further meetings from Mirabelle.

'So how are things going?' she now breathed in his ear. 'Any progress?'

He said, 'I've got one of my operatives working on a lead in London. I'm expecting a report any time. Can you call round my office lunchtime tomorrow and I'll let you know if anything comes up.'

Anyone who dared go out dressed like Gallie had nothing to fear from his mean street, and it was as far out of the public eye as he could hope to get.

'OK,' she said.

She leaned away from him, tipped her head back, stuck

25

the bottle in her mouth and drank. It was the kind of shot TV advertisers sold their souls for.

Won't wean me off Guinness, thought Joe, but I get the subliminal!

On the other hand, by the time he left the pub an hour later, he'd completely forgotten the name of the drink.

4

The following morning as Joe pushed open the door of the Bullpat Square Law Centre, he recalled his phrase 'one of my operatives' with a certain unease.

Truth was, Joe had operatives like politicians have principles – he latched on to whatever was free, useful, and handy. It wasn't guilt that caused the unease, just fear that somehow the woman he was going to see might discover how she'd been categorized.

It was only eight o'clock but the Centre didn't keep social hours.

'Morning, Joe,' said the young man at the reception counter.

'Morning, Harry,' said Joe cautiously. He had difficulty differentiating the tribe of young helpers.

This one seemed happy with 'Harry' so Joe went on, 'Butcher in?'

'Here when I arrived,' said Harry proudly. 'Got her first punter too.' The helpers, drawn in roughly equal numbers from idealistic law students and the unemployed, adored Butcher. The Centre's motto was: *Law helps not hurts* which drew the odd wry grimace from those who'd had their legs chopped off by Butcher in full flight, but she didn't draw blood except when necessary. A Social Security snoop who'd been foolish enough to hack into the Centre's accounts in an effort to prove 'unemployed' helpers were getting paid more than out-of-pocket expenses had found himself teetering on the edge of a career-ending court case. The cheers as his head dropped into the basket would have been heard in Hertfordshire. But Butcher had held back, and now the man came in on his day off to give advice on knotty benefit cases.

It was this capacity for making friends in unlikely places that had got her elected as 'one of Joe's operatives'. Casting around for ways of discovering whether in fact there was any official interest in Galina Hacker's granddad, he'd recalled Butcher's wet Wykehamist. This was a Tory MP who'd been damp enough to be sacked from a junior ministerial post under Thatcher and too intelligent to be offered another under Major. Even with these pluses, it was still difficult to see the common ground on which he and Butcher (who dated the new Dark Ages from 1979) might meet. But meet they did from time to time, and out of Government didn't mean that Piers (*Piers*!) was out of touch.

Joe had mentioned his problem. Butcher had said she would be going to town in a couple of days and might bump into Piers and if so she might mention Joe's problem too. For a consideration.

'What consideration?' Joe had asked.

'We'll consider that when we see what I get from Piers,' Butcher had replied.

Now Joe sat down to wait till Butcher was free, but the door to her office opened almost immediately.

'Thought I recognized that grainy grunt,' said the woman who appeared in the doorway. 'For once your timing's perfect. Step inside. Someone I want you to meet.'

'Oh yes. Who's that?'

'Your consideration,' said Butcher with a wicked grin.

Joe didn't like the sound of this. He'd been hoping Piers would have drawn a blank, which would have been good news for Gallie and also kept him out of Butcher's debt. Nevertheless he rose, trying to look like a man without a care in the world. One good thing (one of many good things) about Butcher was she was small enough for even a short man to loom over, a rare pleasure in a country which free antenatal care seemed to have peopled with giantesses. Perhaps this was the secret agenda of the Tories' anti-health service policies – no woman allowed to be taller than Queen Victoria. It would certainly get the short PI vote!

In the office, piled high with the files which resulted from working a twenty-hour day and brumous from the strong cheroots Butcher used as a substitute for sleep, sat a girl, fourteen or fifteen, shoulder-length dark brown hair, tall (another giantess in the making!) with a sallow complexion and dark suspicious eyes. She was wearing the combination of grey skirt and blue blouse which was as close as they got to uniform at Grandison Comp, and a book-stuffed sports bag at her feet suggested she was on her way there now. Or rather out of her way, as Grandison lay on the far side of town.

'Mavis, this is Joe Sixsmith I was telling you about,' said Butcher.

'Hello,' said Joe.

The girl didn't reply but looked him up and down dubiously.

'Doesn't look much like a private detective to me,' she said.

'Would he be much good if he did?' wondered Butcher.

The girl considered Butcher's logic then said, 'Sorry. I'm dead stupid till morning break.'

'So what do you reckon?'

'What?'

'Do you think he'll do?'

'Well, if you recommend him and there's nothing else on offer . . .'

Joe said, 'Hey, wasn't there some guy you told me about called Wilberforce or something got slavery off the statutes a few years back?'

'Sorry, Joe, but you put yourself in the marketplace, you've got to expect punters want to handle the goods. OK, Mavis, why don't you tell Mr Sixsmith your problem?'

Joe looked expectantly at the girl who said, 'Well, it's not really my problem, it's this friend of mine, well, she was a friend, Sally Eaglesfield . . . look, this is really embarrassing.'

'I'm not embarrassed,' said Butcher kindly. 'You embarrassed, Joe?'

'Not yet,' he said.

'Well, I am,' said the girl spiritedly. 'Can't *you* tell him?

29

He'll probably pay more attention to you. Besides, I've got to scoot else I'll miss assembly. See you.'

She was gone, moving with the awkward grace of a young deer.

'So what is her problem?' asked Joe.

'You heard her. Not her's. Her best friend's.'

'In my experience, when folk come to me weighed down with their friends' problems, it's usually just a way of telling me their own.'

'That's quite sharp for you, Sixsmith,' said Butcher. 'But in this case, you're wrong. Only problem Mavis has got is she's fallen out with her best friend.'

'Happens all the time, tell her to get a new best friend.'

'Suddenly you're an expert on adolescence too,' mocked Butcher.

'When I was a kid, we were too poor to have adolescence,' retorted Joe who found Butcher's company provoked him to PI wise-crackery. 'So who's she blaming?'

'Sharp,' complimented Butcher. 'There's a teacher at Grandison, invites kids home to little soirees, you know, listen to a few discs, drink coffee, talk about the world. An elite little group.'

'To which the friend got invited, Mavis didn't, so she's crying foul?' guessed Joe.

'Mavis, despite her name, is not musical. Sally plays the clarinet. She's good enough to play in the South Beds Sinfonia, as does the teacher. Another bond.'

Joe tried to conjure up a picture of the Sinfonia's clarinettists without luck. Choristers didn't pay much heed to instrumentalists so long as they didn't get above themselves and drown the singing. Not much chance of that with the Boyling Corner Choir. Even the famous Glitterband would have found it hard to compete.

'So what's Mavis saying?'

'She reckons there's something going on at these soirees.'

'Sex, you mean?'

'Je-sus! The man with the tumescent mind. Yes, possibly, but not uniquely. Not even necessarily physically, though we should never discount that possibility. There's all kinds of corruption, Sixsmith . . .'

'No, hold on!' said Joe. 'These are allegations from one teenage girl about something that may be happening to another . . .'

'I'm no teenage girl,' said Butcher sharply. 'And I think there may be cause for concern here.'

'Yes, OK,' said Joe, unhappily acknowledging that if Butcher was worried, there might be something in it. 'How come you got in the act anyway? Who is this kid?'

'Glad to see you show some curiosity about your client at last,' said Butcher. 'Mavis Dalgety, younger child of Maude and Andrew Dalgety of 25 Sumpter Row, Luton. Her brother Chris is doing law in London. During the vac he helps out sometimes in the Centre, and Mavis would tag along, so we got acquainted. She was hanging around here this morning when I arrived. Said it was an accident, just passing, but I could see there was something wrong. Besides, you don't just pass Bullpat Square on your way to Grandison.'

'Still don't sound the kind of thing you go running to a lawyer with,' said Joe.

'I think all she wanted was a sympathetic female ear,' said Butcher. 'Look at the alternatives. Parents? Teenage kids do not confide in their parents. The school? They'd close ranks faster than the Brigade of Guards. So what does that leave?'

'The police?' suggested Joe.

Butcher gave a savage laugh.

'Oh no. Definitely not the police. No way!'

Even for Butcher, who thought of the police as funnel-web spiders to keep down the flies, this was a bit vehement.

'So where do I come in?' he asked.

'Through that door with perfect timing. I can't help this kid, Sixsmith. I can give her advice, but the practical side of investigating this thing I don't have the training for and I don't have the time for. I tell her this. And I'm also telling her that I do happen to know this PI who owes me a big favour. And at that very moment I heard your dulcet tones on the morning air. Bit like St Joan hearing the bells.'

'She the one got barbecued?' said Joe hopefully. 'Listen,

Butcher, before we go any further, let's just establish how big this favour is. Do I gather you got something from good old Piers? I mean something more than a very good time. Looks to me like you've come straight from the station.'

His detective sensors might not be state-of-the-art, but he'd registered that instead of her normal working uniform of jeans and T-shirt, Butcher was wearing a nifty green and orange dress which clung above, and stopped not much short of Gallie Hacker's plimsoll line below. Just the job for a cosy supper with a wet Wykehamist.

She lit one of her foul cheroots, perhaps to hide a blush, and said, 'Sixsmith, with those attitudes, I'll get Piers to put you up for the Carlton.'

'As a target, you mean,' said Joe. 'OK. So let's have the pillow talk.'

'You be careful,' she said. 'OK. Here it is. This war criminals in Britain thing has been rumbling on for years now. Since way back when, a combined task force from the Home Office who've got the records and the Yard who've got the investigatory know-how, has been digging deep to see if in fact there is anyone living here it would be safe to prosecute. Opinion both in and outside the House is divided between those who think that no prosecution could be safe, either legally or ethnically, and those who think the bastards should be pursued to the ends of the earth or their lives, whichever comes first.'

'How do you feel?' asked Joe.

'Let's save that for sometime when I've got some time,' she said. 'For the moment, as one of your great predecessors said, just the facts, Joe, just the facts. Of course, as this is an official government enquiry and highly classified, it's got more leaks than a Liberian tanker. It seems they've got it down to three main groups. First is a handful of highly probables. Second is a larger number of pretty possibles, and the third is a still larger group of could-be-worth-a-closer-looks.'

'And Taras Kovalko's on one of these lists?' said Joe unhappily. 'Which one?'

'Just the third,' said Butcher. It should have sounded more reassuring than it did.

'And it's definitely him?'

'Piers's informant says there's a Manchester address crossed out with a note, *moved to Luton area*.'

'Can't be very important if they don't have the exact address,' said Joe.

'Don't fool yourself. There'll be a file with the Hackers' address in it somewhere.'

'A file? Hey, that makes it sound real heavy. Surely no one's that bothered about this third list?'

'You're right, that's what Piers says. But he also says if someone official has decided to take a closer look at your Mr Kovalko, that bumps him right up out of list three into list two at the least. Sorry, Joe. And that's all Piers was able to get with a couple of phone calls. Any more will be word of mouth in the Turkish baths stuff. So, have we got a deal?'

'I suppose so,' said Joe in a depressed voice. 'I mean, yes, of course we have. I make a bargain, I stick to it. Don't know how I'm going to set about it but I'll try to take a look at this randy schoolmaster of yours.'

'Ah,' said Butcher. 'Didn't I say? Not a school*master* exactly.'

It took Joe a moment to register this.

'You mean, a lady teacher?' he said aghast. 'But women don't do things like that!'

Butcher sighed and said, 'I'd need notice of that remark to decide if it's sexist or not. Listen, Joe. Don't be deceived. Anything a man can do, a woman can be cleverer at, and this Georgina Woodbine is a real operator. Couple of years back there was a Grandison girl, Eileen Montgomery, fell off an edge during a school expedition to the Peak District. There were rumours of emotional upset, suicide attempt, and so on, but the teacher in charge, deputy head Georgie Woodbine, came out squeaky clean. So take care. It's the same in a comp as in any business. You don't get to the top without knowing how to cover your tracks with other people's careers.'

But only one word of all this was really registering with Joe.

'Woodbine?' he said. 'You keep on saying Woodbine. Nothing to do with . . .'

He didn't even like to voice the idea. But Butcher had no such qualms.

'Oh yes,' she said cheerfully. 'Georgina Woodbine, dearly beloved wife of Detective Chief Inspector, no, I beg his pardon, *Superintendent* Willie Woodbine. Didn't I mention it? Sorry, Joe. It must have slipped my mind.'

5

Luton on a bright autumn morning, with the impartial sun gilding the tower of St Monkey's, the dome of the Sikh temple, and the Clint Eastwood inflatable above Dirty Harry's, was not a bad place to be, but Joe felt little of his customary filial pride as he drove to the office.

'Whitey,' he said, 'there has to be something better than investigating things I don't want to investigate for clients who ain't going to pay. What say we run away to sea?'

The cat sleeping on the passenger seat opened the eye in the white eye patch which, luckily or unluckily depending where you got your hangups, stopped him from being completely black, and fixed Joe with a gaze which said, you're on your own, sailor!

Maybe I set my sights too high, thought Joe. Maybe if I devoted myself to begging packets of cheese and onion crisps and ashtrays full of beer down the Glit, I'd be happy too.

Whitey yawned widely. The message was clear. You don't have the talent for it. Stick to what you know.

A little while later they arrived at the office which was housed in the kind of building where small businesses went to die.

Joe picked up his mail. It was junk except for *Pius Thoughts*, the journal of PIU, the Private Investigators' Union. Ignoring the tiny lift which Whitey, who valued his skin above rubies, refused to enter, he laboured upstairs after the cat. In the office, he went through the ritual of checking his answerphone and his desk diary. No calls, no appointments. He wrote *Galina Hacker 12.30* in the diary. It looked better, but he preferred the blank page.

Next he filled his kettle in the tiny washroom, plugged it into the skirting board socket and nudged it on with his foot. While it boiled he improved the shining hour by cleaning out Whitey's litter tray, a job too long postponed. The cat watched with the idle interest of a man in a bus queue watching a navvy dig a hole. Then, when Joe had finished, he stepped daintily on to the pristine litter and crapped copiously.

'Why do you always do that?' demanded Joe. 'Time for that is *before* I clean things up.'

Whitey gave him a look which wondered how an intelligent being, or even a human, could imagine he was going to use a soiled tray, jumped into the bottom desk drawer and went to sleep. Joe flung the windows open, cleaned the tray again, made a pot of tea, and settled down in his chair with *Pius Thoughts*. There was an article on 'Combating Stake-Out Fatigue Syndrome' which looked interesting. He got through two paragraphs and fell asleep.

He was awoken by Aunt Mirabelle's voice and looked around for her in disorientated panic till he realized he'd forgotten to turn off his answerphone.

'I know you're there, Joseph. I can feel it,' she was declaiming. 'So you come out from behind this ungodly machine and speak to me plain.'

There was no point in pretending. He picked up the phone.

'Morning, Auntie,' he said.

'Good morning to you, Joseph. How long is it since you seen Beryl?'

'Saw her last night at the rehearsal, remember?'

'Not likely to forget, the things you got up to, am I?' retorted Mirabelle. 'I mean, seen to talk to, take out? You've been neglecting that girl.'

'Auntie, what's to neglect? Beryl and me's just friends, not a couple, courting or anything like that . . .'

'Courting? You don't know the meaning of the word! But that's no reason not to be polite and pass the time of day instead of sneaking off to that sin-hole of yours to meet that trollop you're making a fool of yourself with!'

He'd been right. Even in the Glit, Mirabelle's agents kept their eternal vigil.

'Auntie, the Glit's a pub, the girl's a client . . .'

'You her client, more likely! Joseph, you stick with Beryl. If it's little Desmond who bothers you, he's a nice kid and once you get two, three more of your own, you'll hardly notice him!'

'Auntie, I've got to go out. On business . . .'

'Business? What business? Only business you and that cat have got is lying around all day seeing who can sleep the longest. Tell you what. You can pick me up, drive me to rehearsal tonight. Give me a chance to have a good close talk without you running off somewhere.'

Joe desperately tried to think of an acceptable excuse.

'Auntie, I'm not sure I can make it tonight . . .'

He was saved the agony of invention by Mirabelle's outrage.

'You not thinking of missing rehearsal, I hope, Joseph? That voice of yours gets so rough from all that profane singing you do down that hellhole, it needs all the rehearsing it can get!'

'Yes, Auntie,' said Joe meekly. 'I'll pick you up. Bye.'

He put the phone down and cleared his throat and tried a couple of notes. That wasn't so bad, he thought. What did she mean, rough? He had a tape of *The Creation* in his radio cassette and he switched it on now. At first he only joined in the baritone line of the choruses, then he thought, guy who's modest when he's by himself must be really stuck up! And he started joining in the male solos too. When he got to Uriel's words – *with beauty, courage, strength adorned, to heaven he stands erect and tall, a man* – an inbuilt sense of irony made him break into the little soft shoe shuffle which had them beating the tables at the Glit on Karaoke Nite.

He wondered which would offend Mirabelle more – the outrage to religion or to music. Himself, he felt they were both big enough to take anything he could throw at them. But when he reached *the partner for him formed, a woman fair and graceful spouse,* his thoughts turned to Mirabelle's attempts to marry him off, and to Beryl Boddington.

It wasn't that he didn't like her. In fact, of all Mirabelle's candidates for his hand, she was way ahead of the field. Not that this meant much when you considered many of the others didn't even make it out of the starting gate!

Thing was that Mirabelle's hopes for his happiness, plus her real affection for him, plus her family pride, didn't combine to dull her sense of reality.

'Joe's the kind of catch a one-armed woman might be glad to get a hold of,' she opined to her coven of confidantes.

And whenever a woman came her way who seemed in need of a man and not well placed to be choosy, Mirabelle pounced.

Beryl's 'disability' in Mirabelle's eyes was the existence of a young son, Desmond, without benefit of clergy. In Joe's eyes her only 'disability' was being elected by Mirabelle which, coupled with his own 'disability' of having got pretty near forty without getting caught, made him naturally wary.

'Getting caught' was, he knew, a deplorably politically incorrect way of looking at marriage, but it had been the received wisdom at Robco Engineering where he'd spent the first twenty years of his working life, and that was an indoctrination harder to throw off than a Jesuit education.

To be fair, Beryl had shown little sign that she was interested in getting caught either, and so far their occasional dates had ended with nothing more than the swooning softness of a good night kiss, leaving him to soothe his frustration with the thought that once more he'd pulled back from the brink. Except of course there was no escaping the fact that it was her push rather than his pull which kept him from falling!

Nevertheless, a relationship undoubtedly existed. He tried to imagine how he'd feel if Beryl took up with some other fellow, found he didn't care for the feeling, so switched it off.

Sometimes it wasn't such a bad thing not having one of those creative minds.

Galina was dead on time. As soon as he saw her Joe felt guilty. Last night he'd had no compunction about asking her to come to the office. But back in her building society mode she was a very different kettle of fish from the exotic alien of the Glit, and he came over all avuncular.

Gallie wasn't having any of that, however.

She refused a cup of tea, settled down with the apple and low fat yoghurt she'd brought with her for lunch, and said, 'OK, I've not got much time. This operative of yours find out anything?'

'Something,' said Joe.

Omitting any reference to Piers or Butcher, he told her about the lists.

She listened intently, her yoghurt ignored. Her face gave nothing away but Joe could feel the pain inside. She must have been hoping even more than him for an official blank.

'So what's it all mean, Mr Sixsmith?' she asked.

'My operative reckons the third list's just there to make the numbers up,' said Joe.

'Why should anyone want to do that?'

'It's the civil service mind,' he said. 'Everything by threes.'

'So there's nothing to worry about?'

He was desperate to give her reassurance but knew he mustn't go further than the facts warranted. He'd fallen into that trap before.

'We can't get away from the fact someone's asking questions,' he said. 'But there's still nothing to say for sure it's got anything to do with these lists.'

It was the best he could do but he could see it was far from enough.

'Just coincidence, you mean?' she said doubtfully.

'It happens,' he said. 'And even if it is connected, well, if there's nothing to find out, then this guy will just give up and go back and say so.'

'*If?*'

Building society mode or exotic alien, the look she was fixing him with was cold enough to kill.

You stupid git! Joe accused himself. Putting up the possibility that all her certainties are calculated to hide.

He played dumb. It wasn't difficult.

'Yeah, you know, there's no mileage in these guys making something up. He probably found out day one there was nothing to find and he's been spinning it out a bit for expenses. He could be back in Whitehall now wondering who to bother next.'

She shook her head.

'I don't think so, Mr Sixsmith,' she said. 'I think he's still around and he'll keep on digging and digging till something shows up. I've read about these people. They don't ever give up.'

Joe looked at her with a heart-squeezing pity he didn't dare show. It was herself she was talking about as much as the nosey stranger. Apart from lying in permanent ambush, Joe didn't have a clue how he might get a line on him or what he could do if he did. But that didn't matter. The real focal point of all this trouble was old Taras and the way he was reacting. That was where the doubt whose existence was too terrible to admit had started.

He said, 'It might help if I could get into the club, socially, I mean. Chat to Mrs Vansovich without making her curious.'

'That friend who brought you there last time . . .'

'A client, rewarding me with a drink,' said Joe. 'If I ask him to invite me back, that would really make him suspicious.'

She frowned, then her face cleared.

'There's a family night day after tomorrow. Mum's told Grandda he may not feel like going out, but he's jolly well going to that! People often bring friends. I can invite you.'

'As a friend?' said Joe, thinking how most parents he knew would react to their little girl bringing home a 'friend' who was black, balding, and twice her age.

'Why not? You are, aren't you? Besides, people do turns. You're a singer. Everyone down the Glit thinks you're great. There you are. A performer, an important customer from the society, and a friend! Dead natural I should invite you, isn't it?'

She spoke with utter conviction. Oh the youth of the heart, thought Joe. All that innocence which loving parents think is at risk when their daughters go out into the world and start painting their faces and flashing their flesh. But guilt, like charity, begins at home. It's in the genes. It's an hereditary disease.

'Yeah, dead natural,' smiled Joe.

6

Aunt Mirabelle's favourite reading in the Good Book was the Lamentations of the prophet Jeremiah, and she had his style off to a 't'. On their way to St Monkey's that night, Joe could not but admire the way in which his lousy job, his squalid lifestyle, and his terrible driving, were woven into a seamless whole.

The flow didn't halt till the car did in St Monkey's Square.

'What you doing?' demanded Mirabelle.

'I'm going to drop you here then go find somewhere to park,' he explained.

'What's wrong with that parking place back of the church?'

'The Cloisters? I think that's reserved for special permits.'

'And I'm not special? You drive round there, Joseph. Good Baptist's more special than a good Anglican any day!'

There was one space left. As Joe backed in, the Visigothic verger appeared, wearing an expression that fell a furlong or so short of Christian welcome. But when Mirabelle eased her bulk out of the car and greeted him with a hearty 'Good evening, brother!' he remembered urgent business elsewhere.

Pity he hadn't been so conscientious the previous night, thought Joe. If the boy in the box had been found a couple of hours earlier, there might have been time to save him.

No sign of Mrs Calverley's Range Rover tonight. Maybe her peep over the edge had dulled her appetite for eavesdropping on *The Creation*. He guessed she might have a reputation for toughness, but last night's experience had visibly upset her.

The rehearsal went fairly well. As he sang, Joe studied the clarinettists and tried to guess which of the two young women was Mavis Dalgety's ex-friend, Sally Eaglesfield. He settled for the smaller, darker girl who studied her music with unblinking intensity as though fearful it might blow away. He didn't know what instrument Willie Woodbine's wife played and as the Sinfonia was an equal opportunities orchestra with women puffing and banging and scraping everywhere, there wasn't much hope of picking her out. Maybe the girl he thought was Sally would identify her by making a beeline for her after the rehearsal was over.

He was distracted from this bit of great detectivery by Mirabelle, who materialized at his side while the last Amen was still trembling on the air. He guessed the little side door was probably nailed up too.

'Now look who's there,' she exclaimed in a tone of surprise that rang as false as a cracked bell. 'Beryl. We were just talking about you.'

'Hi, Mirabelle. Hi, Joe. Sorry, can't stop to talk. I'm on my way to work.'

She was a nurse at the Royal Infirmary and, cap apart, was already kitted out in her uniform.

Mirabelle said, 'Joseph was just saying he'd run you there, weren't you, Joseph? All them attacks, you don't want to be walking round there by yourself.'

There'd been a couple of recent incidents with a flasher in the hospital grounds and the police were advising extra caution till the intruder was caught.

'Well, that's very kind of you, Joe . . .'

'No trouble at all,' assured Mirabelle. 'Now excuse me, I want a word with Rev. Pot.'

She moved off and Joe found Beryl regarding him quizzically. He returned the look with pleasure. She was . . . he sought for the right word and all he could come up with was *sturdy*. This was why he had to invent answers for crossword puzzles and make up his own clues to fit them. On the other hand, what was wrong with *sturdy* when it expressed not just a physical but a spiritual characteristic? Strong, self-reliant, dependable, trustworthy . . .

'What are you staring at, Joe?' she asked.

'You. You look great,' he said. Smooth talker he might not

be, but he knew better than to offer *sturdy* as a compliment. Not that sturdiness meant lack of shape. And those wide brown eyes and full red lips . . .

The full red lips opened to show strong white teeth in a moist pink mouth as she yawned.

'Sorry,' she said. 'Nothing to do with you.'

He looked even more closely at her and saw that as well as *sturdy* and *great* she looked tired.

'You getting any sleep?' he asked.

'Surely. Between getting home in the morning, doing the chores, and picking Desmond up from school at three, I usually manage to snatch a couple of minutes,' she laughed. 'Are you serious about this lift?'

He led her out to the Cloisters.

'Going up in the world, aren't we?' she mocked. 'I thought only the nobs got to park here?'

'I'm Tin Can's token PI,' said Joe.

She laughed. He liked making her laugh.

In the car he said, 'You so tired, why don't you let your sister pick Desmond up?'

'Already she gives him his breakfast, drops him off at school. If I'm not there to pick him up, he's going to start thinking I'm his auntie, Lucy's his ma.'

'At least you could duck the odd rehearsal till you're off nights.'

She let out a gasp of mock horror.

'You want Rev. Pot to nail me to his penitent stool? No, the singing's no sweat. In fact, when I hear that music and open my mouth, it's about the only time I stop feeling tired. Gives you a bigger hit than ganja, don't you feel that, Joe?'

'You wouldn't expect a clean-living boy to know anything about that, would you?' said Joe.

'This the same clean-living boy who's running around with the Mutant from Planet X?'

'Beryl, let me tell you about Galina . . .'

'Joe, it's OK,' she said. 'I'm only joking. It's none of my business. Just like what's mine is none of yours, OK? This'll do.'

Obediently he stopped the car and she was out of the door

before he realized they weren't at the Infirmary's main gate but at a side entrance which ran between the path labs and research blocks. Beyond these buildings she could either follow the service road to the main block or take a tree-shaded pathway which curved through the grounds to the nursing wards, cutting off several miles of corridor.

He didn't doubt which way she'd go, and he didn't doubt which way Mirabelle would go if she heard he'd let Beryl loose unaccompanied.

'Hold on!' cried Joe.

From beneath his seat he took a heavy steel spanner about a foot long, with tape bound around the handle to provide a firmer grip. This had been a present from Merv Golightly whose constant companion in his taxi was a monstrous lug wrench called Percy. The mere sight of Merv's lanky figure twirling Percy like a conductor's baton was usually enough to subdue most troublemakers. In Joe's line of business, a similar aid was very necessary, opined Merv, and Little Perce had been the result. Joe, who found violence either coming from him or aimed at him very scary, had never found occasion to use it. But there wasn't much point offering himself as Beryl's defender if all his defence consisted of was warding off blows with his head.

Fearful of the woman's ridicule, however, he took the precaution of slipping Little Perce up his jacket sleeve before pursuing her.

'Joe, what are you doing here?' she demanded as he caught up with her.

'I promised Mirabelle I'd see you safe,' he panted, thinking maybe he should take up Merv's invitation to start working out with him at the Hoplite Health Club.

'Now look, Joe,' she said, beginning to sound angry, 'I can look after myself . . .'

'*You* can, maybe,' he interrupted. 'What about me? You want I should be more afraid of you than of Mirabelle?'

She shook her head, laughing.

'Joe, sometimes you're so down to earth, I can't see how you can bear to keep on playing this PI game. You must be able to see you're not cut out for it. Most of the time you make no money, so all you're doing being so-called self-employed is stopping your entitlement to benefit.'

'You think I'd be better sitting on my butt, waiting for my giro?' he said fiercely.

'Could be. In any case, things are getting better, or so they keep telling us. There'll be jobs to go for . . .'

'You taken a good look at me lately, girl? Jobs will come slow and I'll be way, way down the queue. Also, what do I want with another job so I can punch a clock for a few more years always wondering when it'll punch back and tell me I'm surplus to requirements again? Leastways, being my own boss, my so-called friends can *tell* me I'm useless, but they can't dump me for it!'

They strode on, each so deep in a confusion of feeling that they could probably have run a whole gauntlet of flashers without noticing. When they reached the buildings, Joe stopped and said, 'I'll be on my way now.'

'You still here, Joe?' she said with a good affectation of surprise. 'Well, thanks for the lift.'

'Yeah, well, that's OK,' said Joe, feeling both wretched and indignant. He turned to go but had only taken a few steps when she caught his arm.

'Hey, don't I get a farewell kiss?'

He aimed at her cheek. She gave him her lips, briefly but fully.

As she stepped away she said, 'Friends don't think you're useless, Joe. They just worry about you. That's what friends are for. You fall out, then you kiss and make up.'

'Don't think I'm quite made up yet,' he said, moving towards her again.

She turned away, laughing.

'Only way to get another kiss here is have a heart attack, Joe,' she tossed over her shoulder.

Could be that's what I'm doing, thought Joe, watching her go. The way her body moved beneath the blue and white skirt, *sturdy* was no longer the word that came to mind.

He wandered back beneath the arching trees, letting his fancy drift at will. No harm in *thinking*, was there? But he was no sadist, so why was his fancy making Beryl scream as he unbuttoned her uniform?

Suddenly he was out of his imagined embrace and back in the real black autumn night with a chill wind rustling the dead leaves at his feet and somewhere to the left of him where the darkness was deepest the tail end of a long scream fading away into the night.

'Oh shoot!' said Joe.

Then he was off running, he had no idea where. He just hoped that the sound of his approach might scare any attacker off. Ahead loomed a clump of trees, blacker lines against the blackness. He swerved to skirt them, then one of the black lines moved and hit him so hard in the stomach he collapsed on the grass retching.

A moment later he was dragged to his feet by his collar and a torch beam shone in his face.

'Gotcha!' said a voice. 'Hey, don't I know you?'

There was something familiar about the voice . . . an accent . . . and in the light spilling back from his own face to his captor's he made out just enough to trigger his memory.

'You're Forton's mate,' he croaked. 'Sandy . . . last night . . . St Monkey's . . . Joe Sixsmith . . .'

'That's right. Deano warned me about you but he didn't say you were into this!'

'Into what?' gasped Joe. 'I've just been up to the hospital . . . one of the nurses . . .'

He made the mistake of gesturing with his arm in the direction of the hospital. There was a dull thud as Little Perce shot out of his sleeve and hit the ground.

'And what's this? A prescription?' demanded the constable, scooping it up. 'Sixsmith, you're nicked!'

7

In *The Lost Traveller's Guide*, a page and a half of Luton's ten-page entry is deservedly set aside for the Central Police Station. Designed by the same hand that conjured up St Monkey's, it is as much a monument to secular law as the church is to divine. No citizen can pass by that imposing façade without feeling the safer for it. No criminal can pass beneath that blue-lamped portico without feeling the sorrier for it.

Lutonians are proud of their police station, but it must be admitted it wouldn't have survived the bulldozing sixties if some foresighted councillor hadn't got it registered as a listed building. From time to time plans are still put forward to build a glass and concrete blockhouse on a few acres of green belt and turn the old building into a heritage centre or DIY supermarket or something. But the City Fathers, aware that cold, draughty and damp conditions produce a certain desirable cast of mind in crooks and cops alike, wisely refuse to be moved.

Joe Sixsmith, as a good citizen, approved their wisdom. Seated in a barred-windowed, cracked-panelled, flaking-painted, musty-smelling interview room which not even the presence of a piece of hi-tech recording equipment could drag out of the Middle Ages, he felt ready to confess to anything.

What PC Sandy Mackay wanted him to confess to was being the Infirmary flasher. Joe was the young man's first significant collar and he was reluctant to let him go without a result. In this he was actively encouraged by Detective Sergeant Chivers who, though less deeply persuaded of Joe's guilt in this particular instance, had a somewhat *démodé* belief that all things evened themselves out before the Great Chief Constable in the sky, and low lifes like Joe got away with so much that sending them down for anything was a kind of wild justice.

An hour's hard questioning had reduced even Chivers's hoped for options.

'Whatever happens, we'll do you for carrying an offensive weapon,' he assured Joe.

'Defensive,' said Joe.

'Offensive,' said Chivers grimly. 'That's what I reckon you are, Sixsmith. And that's what I reckon anything to do with you is.'

The door opened. Willie Woodbine's head appeared. He said, 'Sergeant, a word.'

Chivers noted the suspension of the interview and the time on the tape and switched it off. Then he followed Woodbine out into the corridor.

The door which looked like it had been used as an interrogation aid in the unreconstructed past didn't fit properly and eased back open an inch. This was enough to permit Joe and PC Sandy to overhear what was being said.

'What the chuff's going on in there?' demanded Woodbine.

Chivers explained, or tried to.

Woodbine interrupted, 'This nurse who was flashed at tonight, the one who screamed, you've talked to her, I presume?'

'Yes, of course . . .'

'And did she say it was a black man or a white man who did the flashing?'

'Well, it was pretty gloomy . . .'

'Come on, Sergeant, she's a nurse. First thing they learn is to tell the difference between a black dick and a white dick. Which did she say it was?'

'White, she thought, but . . .'

'And this nurse Sixsmith claims he was escorting to the wards, she confirms his story?'

'Yes, but she's his fancy woman, isn't she? Say anything to get him off the hook . . .'

'That's right. And do anything too, you'd say? Well, I'll tell you what she's done, Sergeant. She's rung that bitch Butcher, and that bitch Butcher's rung me and demanded to know if we're holding her client Joseph Sixsmith, and has he been arrested, and on what charge? And she says this isn't the first time her client has been harassed by my officers and this time she's going to see he sues the arse off us. And she's on her way now, Sergeant, and what am I going to tell her?'

'Well, there's always the offensive weapon, sir . . .'

'Offensive weapon? That's Joe Sixsmith you've got in there. You may not like the man, and maybe you ought to ask yourself why you don't like him, but please reassure me, you're not so far gone you don't know he's not violent! Offensive weapon? If you gave him a sub-machine gun, he'd probably try to get Radio 2 on it! No, you want violence, you ought to listen to that bitch Butcher! Get out of my way!'

The door swung fully open. Joe and Sandy who'd been sitting looking at each other expressionlessly turned their heads to see Woodbine smiling down at them.

'Joe, how've you been? It's good of you to help us out like this again. Sorry we had to put you in here while I was on my way, but I don't leave Chivers the key to the executive washroom, you with me? Come on upstairs now. Sergeant, rustle us up some coffee, will you? And I daresay I can find a drop of the Caledonian Cream to keep the cold out.'

Two minutes later Joe found himself in a deep armchair in Woodbine's office. Here the oak panelling shone with a deep sheen, the broad windows were covered with rich brocaded curtains, and the paintwork was as smooth and perfect as a model's make-up.

'Now, take me through it again,' said Woodbine, putting on an expression of fascinated interest.

'Er, through what, exactly?' said Joe.

'Through your very brave attempt to apprehend this weirdo who's been terrorizing those poor nurses,' said Woodbine.

So Joe took him through it again. When he reached the

point of his arrest, the superintendent sucked in his breath and said, 'Silly lad. But he's young, Joe. And Scottish. You've got to make allowances. I'll see he apologizes. Some more Scotch? No? So how's life treating you, Joe? Anything I can help with, you've only got to ask.'

Well, you could tell me about your wife's sex life, thought Joe. No, perhaps not. His eye ran over Woodbine's untidy desk. There was a file open on it, and some photographs.

Joe said, 'That boy in the box at St Monkey's. Anything on him yet?'

'What's your interest?' said Woodbine sharply.

'Well, I found him, didn't I?' said Joe defensively.

The smile which had vanished from Woodbine's face returned and he said, 'So you did. Can't stop running into trouble, can you, Joe?'

'Thought I wasn't in trouble,' said Joe.

'Of course you're not. As for the boy, can't tell you anything, sorry. Not my department really, not unless it turned out to be murder, which I doubt.'

As he spoke, he swept the papers on his desk together and closed the file.

And Joe, though he couldn't be absolutely sure upside down, wondered why, if it wasn't Woodbine's department, the super happened to have what looked very much like a photo of the dead boy's face in front of him?

There was a tap at the door and Chivers's head appeared.

'Miss Butcher to see you, sir,' he said.

Butcher was only five-two and built like a Third World waif, but she came in like the Queen's Champion at a trial by combat.

'You OK, Joe?' she asked. 'Superintendent, I'd like a word alone with my client.'

'By all means,' said Woodbine. 'We're finished here anyway. Thanks again for your help, Joe. By the way, I'm having a little do Sunday lunchtime to celebrate my promotion, say thanks to everyone who's helped and encouraged me. It wouldn't be complete without you. Do try to make it, midday, very informal, bubbles and a bit of a buffet is what my good lady's got in mind. Do try to come.'

He put his arm across Joe's shoulders and urged him gently to the door.

'Yeah, well, thanks a lot, Superintendent . . .'

'Make it *Willie* on Sunday, eh?' breathed Woodbine in his ear. 'Keep the formality for in front of the troops!'

'Yeah sure,' said Joe. 'Willie on Sunday it is. Goodbye now.'

As they walked down the ornate Victorian staircase, he said, 'Hey, thanks for coming.'

'Don't know why I bother; Woodbine's obviously got you all dusted down and gift wrapped. So fill me in. Just what happened to put you into bed with that smarmy fascist?'

'He's OK, really,' said Joe. He described the evening's events which Butcher listened to with much shaking of her head.

'Sixsmith,' she said, 'you've got such a talent for being in the wrong place at the wrong time, I bet you were born in a different hospital from the one they took your mother to.'

This was a touch too subtle for Joe so he let it go.

Outside, he found his car parked in front of the station with Little Perce on the passenger seat. Butcher headed for hers which was parked in a space marked *Chief Constable*.

'Hey, I'm sorry you got dragged out like this,' he called after her.

'That's OK. It was worth it. Sight of me made him ladle on the old pals act so much, you got an invite to his party. Now you'll be able to take a real close-up look at Mrs Georgie, won't you?'

'Hey, no,' said Joe in alarm. 'I'm going to no party . . .'

'You don't, I'll go and I'll say you sent me,' she retorted. Then she began to laugh.

'What?' said Joe.

'*Willie on Sunday it is*!' she gurgled. 'Sixsmith, one way or another, you may yet be the death of me!'

8

Saturday night came and Joe found he was greeted at the Uke with much less hostility from Gallie's parents than he'd expected.

As he helped the girl carry a round of drinks from the bar, she whispered in his ear, 'By the way, I told Mum you were gay. You know how they worry.'

'You *what*?' said Joe, but she just laughed and then they were back at the table. So much for innocence. Now he'd have to find a way of disabusing the Hackers. Not because he felt demeaned or anything. Nothing wrong with being gay. If you were, that is. But if you weren't, and the Hackers found out he wasn't, they might start thinking he'd told their daughter he was to lull her into a false sense of security before he pounced. Or was he being paranoid?

Whatever, here and now wasn't the time, not till they'd got to know him a bit better. But he was dismayed to find himself checking his speech and gestures for anything camp!

A native Lutonian, George Hacker was easy to get on with once he discovered in Joe a shared interest in the ups and downs of the town's football club. Galina, his wife, eyed Joe much more warily at first. She was a broader, less angular version of her daughter and still retained the strong Manchester accent of her youth. She hit Joe with a volley of probing questions which he answered with an openness as natural as her curiosity till Gallie said, 'What's up, Mum? Think Joe's an illegal immigrant or something.'

'Don't be daft!' said her mother flushing. 'I just like to know about folk. I'm sure Mr Sixsmith is just as interested in knowing about us.'

'Course I am,' said Joe, seizing this heaven-sent opportunity. 'You from the Ukraine yourself then, Mrs Hacker?'

'Not me,' she laughed. 'Manchester born and bred. My dad settled there after the war, isn't that right, Father?'

Taras Kovalko took enough time to give the impression this was a question needing serious consideration before he nodded his head. It was a fine head with a strong-featured, deep-lined face beneath a crown of unruly white hair. His daughter had inherited his shrewd watchful eyes, but while her gaze had the unselfish wariness of a mother concerned for her daughter, the old man's had more of the suspicious cornered animal in it . . .

Steady, boy, thought Joe, uneasy at this sudden flight of imagination. You'll be writing poetry next.

'Must've been hard, settling down in a new country like that, Mr Kovalko,' he said.

'You say so? How did you find it?'

The overlay of Lancashire on his native accent gave a rather comic effect, but it would have taken a braver as well as a ruder man than Joe to show amusement.

'I was born here in Luton,' explained Joe. He'd already told the daughter this and the old man had been listening keenly. So was his reply an attempt at diversion?

He said, 'You ever go back home? To the Ukraine, I mean? Vinnitsa, isn't it?'

The mention of the city brought the eyes into direct contact with his for a moment, then they dropped to the half empty spirit glass before him.

'No,' he said. 'There is nothing for me there. No family, no friends. My life is here now. Has been here for nearly fifty years. I am an Englishman now. Like you.'

He tossed back the rest of his drink and put the glass on the table with an emphatic bang.

'English he might be but he still likes the old firewater, isn't that right, Taras?' laughed George Hacker. He picked up the glass and headed for the bar.

Joe said, 'You still come here though, to the Uke.'

Kovalko shrugged.

'Old parents need a place to go so they are not always

under their children's feet. This is as good as any other place.'

'Must bring back memories, all the same,' said Joe. 'Just hearing the old language for instance.'

Kovalko said, 'Look around, Mr Sixsmith. How many here speak the old language, do you think?'

'How many's it take to have a conversation?' said Joe. 'In any case, aren't there more people coming now from the old country, especially since it got its independence back?'

'Independence? From what? They lose one yoke, they will rush to put on another,' said Kovalko cynically. 'Pray to God they can do it without finding an excuse to fight each other.'

'I didn't know there was any chance of that in the Ukraine,' said Joe.

'We are talking about human beings. Violence is always a possibility. All that the good society can do is minimize opportunity, either to perform it or provoke it. But absolute control is impossible. There must be streets and pubs even in Luton that you will not visit alone after dark, Mr Sixsmith.'

'Because I'm black, you mean?' said Joe. 'Yeah, well, maybe . . .'

I'm being diverted again, he thought.

He said, 'I don't say I wouldn't run for cover if the Nazis ever took over here. But doesn't history show that in the end they always get beaten because there's more inside most people that wants to live in peace with other people than wants to fight them? Shoot, you must know this better than anybody. Must have been times when the Nazis took over your country and started shipping off the Jews to the extermination camps and folk like yourself to the forced labour camps that you felt this was it, the end, nowhere else for the human race to go. But we won, and you're here, and you've got your family, so the best is always possible as well as the worst. Nothing for you to feel guilty about.'

'Guilty? What do you mean, guilty?' demanded Kovalko, the hand on the table clenching into a fist.

'Hey, it's all right. All I meant was, people can get to feel guilty 'cos they made it through bad times while a lot of other folk didn't. But it's OK. What you've got here, you got for all those others too. They didn't make it, sure, but the

Nazis didn't make it either. You're here. The guys who ran the death camps aren't. They're long gone.'

This was pushing it, but there might not be another chance to push so hard and test a reaction. There was none, unless absolute stillness, almost to the point of catalepsy, counted. Then George came back with the drink which he put down in front of his father-in-law with a cheery, 'There you go, Taras.'

The clenched fingers uncoiled, seized the glass and tossed the drink down in a single movement.

'Hey, you must really have needed that,' said George. 'You in one of them moods, we'd better buy you a bottle!'

A sudden explosion of microphone static removed the need for Taras to reply. A small man in a plum-coloured jacket had appeared on a dais alongside the door to the kitchen. When finally he got the relationship between his mouth and the mike right, he said, 'Good evening, ladies and gentlemen, nice to see so many of our members here with their families and friends. As you know, tonight's the night when we entertain ourselves and hopefully each other. Everyone will get a chance, but to start with we have a very old favourite of us all with a song from the old country, your friend and mine, Yulia Vansovich!'

There was an outburst of applause which didn't altogether conceal a heartfelt groan from certain quarters. Then Mrs Vansovich, wearing a folksy skirt and blouse which Joe assumed to be traditional, was helped on to the dais. Clutching the mike in both hands, she began to sing in a pretty fair soprano voice, accompanied by a pianist who made up in flamboyance what he lacked in accuracy. The song was a nicely strophic melody with a foot-stomping chorus, which at least half the audience joined in.

Taras wasn't one of them.

'What's she singing about?' Joe asked.

'Some nonsense about a boy driving geese to the market and selling them to the butcher's lovely daughter for a kiss,' said Kovalko scornfully.

Just when it seemed the song was set to go on forever, Mrs Vansovich had a fit of coughing. A glass of something long and red restored her, but by this time her place had been taken by a melancholy bass, and despite her game efforts to remount the dais, she was finally persuaded back to her chair. After the bass, the emphasis shifted from ethnic to pop. Gallie and her mother returned from the kitchen and the elder woman said, 'I believe you sing a bit, Mr Sixsmith. Going to give us a turn then?'

Joe made a few modest protests, but Gallie's urging, plus the good smells coming from the kitchen which reminded him how badly he sang on a full stomach, persuaded him to step forward.

Knowing from experience that no singer ever got booed off a popular stage for being too sentimental, he said to the pianist, 'You know *Two Little Boys*?'

'No, but I can get you a big fat tart if you're desperate.'

After that, Joe didn't confuse the issue by suggesting a key, but started singing and after a while was pleased to hear the piano scattering a few notes in the general direction of the melody.

At the end he got enough applause to encourage an encore.

'I'd like to dedicate this song to the lady who started off the entertainment tonight,' said Joe. 'We haven't met, but I thought she sang real beautiful.'

And fixing his eyes on Mrs Vansovich, he sang *Silver Threads Among the Gold*.

The applause at the end of this was augmented by the MC's announcement that food was now ready for collection next door. The middle-aged couple sharing Mrs Vansovich's table rose instantly and made off, leaving her alone. Joe stepped down from the dais and went towards her and shook her hand.

'Lovely song you sang,' he said. 'Did you once do it professionally?'

She laughed and shook her head.

'But it is flattering to hear you say so,' she said. 'You too sing very well, Mr . . . ?'

'Sixsmith. Joe Sixsmith,' he said, sitting down next to her.

'You were here once before, I think,' she said.

'That's right,' he said, thinking she didn't miss much. 'Just for a drink.'

'And tonight you are with the Hacker family and Mr Kovalko.'

'Yeah. Nice people. I gather you and old Taras come from the same town.'

'Vinnitsa. Yes. He told you that?'

She sounded doubtful. Joe took the hint and said, 'No, it wasn't him, now I come to think of it. One of the ladies mentioned it when I was asking about the lovely lady with the gorgeous voice.'

This made her raise her thin pencilled eyebrows. She must in fact have once been very pretty, thought Joe, regarding the highly made up, finely boned face. And if that steady querying gaze was any indicator, she wasn't stupid either, so back-pedal on the flattery!

He said, 'The song you sang, is it traditional?'

She said, 'Oh yes, an old song my grandmother used to sing. She was a peasant woman. I was a girl of the city and I wanted to be modern and I scorned such songs when I was young. But now I am older, they are the ones that come back to me when I think of that time before the Germans came.'

'Will you go back to Vinnitsa now things are easier over there?' asked Joe.

'Yes,' she said. 'I would like to, once, before I die.'

'You still got family there?'

'No. No family,' she said. 'My grandmother who sang the song was Jewish. They took her, of course, within a few weeks of arriving. My grandfather too, though he was not Jewish. And later they came for my parents because some neighbour had written to say that my mother was the daughter of a Jewess. I had just married. My parents, who had been worried about me seeing my boyfriend because they said I was too young, now encouraged this marriage. I understood later my father wanted me to change my name and move away from my home.'

Oh shoot, thought Joe. He'd sat down with the old lady (whom he now realized was not so old, still in her sixties, he guessed) in order to pump her about Kovalko. Now she was no longer just an old gossip who might be useful, but a real live woman with a history that made his own life and background seem cosseted and secure.

She went on, 'When my husband was rounded up with all young men for forced labour, I went with him, thinking we might stay together. It was not possible. I heard later he died of hunger, sickness, some such thing, while working under the Nazis.'

Suddenly she laughed and squeezed his hand.

'But here come my friends with the food. In any case, I do not think you want to talk about these sad things, Mr Sixsmith. I think you would like to know whether Mr Kovalko and I talk about the old Vinnitsa. The answer is, no, we do not. He says he remembers nothing of the old days, but he was so ill when the Americans found him that the first part of his life had been wiped almost clean. Such things happen. We all have things we would like to forget ... to be forgotten. But some things can never be wiped clean. Never!'

She squeezed his hand fiercely then let go. Joe thought, I got it wrong. He'd assumed they called her Mrs Once-a-witch because she was a silly old gossip. But the disconcerting ease with which she'd spotted his real motives in talking to her suggested another reason.

Not that it was all that clever, he reassured himself as he made his way back to the Hackers. She'd probably not been able to resist mentioning the nosey stranger to Kovalko and his reaction must have roused her curiosity. Now here was another stranger, and a PI at that (Joe didn't doubt she knew all about his background).

And to these people, probing questions about that terrible time in their lives must always come back to one thing. How did you survive?

'Mr Sixsmith, sit down, eat!'

There was food on the table, slices of thick round sausage and little dumplings, potatoes flecked with pepper, all giving off a strong garlicky smell which made Joe glad he didn't have a date.

Though the number of dates I do have, he thought glumly, I could eat garlic most nights of the week.

'Liked the songs, Joe,' said George. 'Old Vansovich beating your ear?'

'Interesting old lady,' said Joe.

'Old fool!' snarled Kovalko.

George hadn't been joking about getting a bottle. It stood by the old man's plate and was already a third empty. He refilled his glass. His daughter said, 'Now, Father.' His answer to this mild reproof was to down the liquor and fill the glass again.

Not a man to cross, thought Joe. In or out of drink.

He concentrated on his food for a while. It was very tasty and he said so, aiming at being complimentary without sounding surprised.

Mrs Hacker looked pleased but her father snorted contemptuously.

'You like this stuff, you must be used to swill,' he said. The bottle was down to the halfway line.

'Father!' said his daughter indignantly.

Gallie came in as peacemaker.

'Grandda was a chef,' she said to Joe, half apologizing, half boasting. 'He's very good, but it means his standards are too high for the rest of us. Isn't that right, Grandda?'

The old man drank another glass of vodka and smiled at his granddaughter. There was real warmth between these two, a depth of affection which underlined the pain the girl must be feeling if, as Joe suspected, no matter how tiny and unacknowledged, a grain of suspicion had got lodged in her heart.

'Well, I think these little dumpling things are really tasty,' said Joe.

Kovalko's gaze turned to him. There was no warmth there now.

'You think so? Well, I tell you, when I was at the Hotel Pripyat learning my craft, if I had produced *vareniki* like these, old Leonid, the head chef, would have said, "Who has been out in the countryside gathering these sheep droppings?"

And I would have been there till after midnight, mixing dough until I got it right.'

'Must have been a hard life,' said Joe. 'Lousy hours. Did you always want to be a chef, Mr Kovalko?'

The old man shrugged and said, 'Take no notice of what I say. No longer my business. The *vareniki* are fine. Now I am artist of the pallet not the palate.'

'Eh?' said Joe.

'One of his old customers in Manchester made that joke,' said Mrs Hacker proudly. 'Father paints pictures, you see, just as a hobby, and this chap when he found out said he was an artist of the pallet as well as the palate. Not bad, eh? That's one of his there.'

She indicated a strong watercolour of a curving river which hung beside the bar.

'Very nice,' said Joe.

'Order, order, please,' cried the MC. 'I hope you're enjoying your supper but there's still a lot of people who haven't sung for it!'

The show got under way again. Kovalko relapsed into a dull silence, but any idea that he'd drunk himself stupid vanished when he got up to go to the gents and made his way across the room steady as a gymnast.

Joe said, 'I ought to be going. Busy day tomorrow. I've really enjoyed it. Thanks for inviting me along, Gallie.'

'Thanks for coming. And for singing,' said the girl.

'Good night,' said Joe to her parents. 'Say good night to Mr Kovalko for me.'

As he passed Mrs Vansovich's table he paused and said, 'Nice to meet you.'

'You go so early?' she said. 'Well, come again.'

'Oh, I will,' said Joe. 'By the way, do you recall a hotel in Vinnitsa called the Pripyat, or something like that?'

She thought then shook her head.

'Sorry, no.'

'There's a Hotel Pripyat in Kiev,' said the male half of the couple sharing her table. 'Big old place. I saw it when we were visiting our cousins there last year. You'd be better off trying the Dnieper or Moskva, I reckon.'

'I'll bear it in mind,' said Joe. 'Thanks anyway. Good night.'

As he turned away, he saw that Kovalko had come out of the toilet and was standing in the doorway, watching him. He waved his hand.

The old man didn't wave back.

9

'My oh my,' said Merv Golightly as Joe got into his taxi. 'It's a dressy up party, is it? Have to hurry, don't want you to be any later.'

'I'm not late,' protested Joe.

'Oh yes, you are. About thirty years in that suit, I'd say!'

Merv, who appreciated a good joke, especially his own, laughed at this one for the first five minutes of the journey. Even Joe had to admit there was a real point to it. What to wear at Willie Woodbine's party had exercised his mind greatly. The balding cord jacket was obviously out, though he had hopes if it got much smoother, it might eventually pass for a blazer in the dark with the light behind it. This left either the casual look, which meant his blue leather jerkin over a Gary Glitter T-shirt; or the formal look which meant his funeral, wedding, and choir performance suit.

It was a good suit. He'd had it so long it had come back into fashion twice, and there was hardly a mark on it. Unfortunately, with its broad lapels, slanting pockets, triple-buttoned jacket and seventeen-inch trousers with a two-inch turn up, it was at the bottom of its fashion cycle just now.

Also, since he'd bought it, he'd put on a bit of weight. His belt covered the fact that the top button of his trousers wouldn't fasten, but the jacket presented a greater problem. Fastened, he could hardly breathe. Unfastened, it flapped open to reveal to an amazed world a flash of the technicolour dreamcoat lining which had so taken his young fancy all those years ago.

But having decided Willie Woodbine's party demanded formal, it had to be the suit.

The other problem had been whether he should take something. Bottle of vino might be a bit naff, suggesting Willie couldn't afford to provide booze for his guests. Flowers for the lady was the thing, and he'd inspired little Miss Leaf at the flower shop to lewd speculation by buying a big Cellophane-wrapped bunch of chrysanths.

Finally resolving that the reward for all this effort was going to be gulping down as much of the promised bubbly as he could lay his lips on, he'd ordered Merv's cab.

Now at last he was on his reluctant way to Willie Woodbine's house on Beacon Heights.

The Heights is Luton's premier residential area, a fact which did not escape comment.

'You ever wonder how come a poor underpaid pig gets enough money to live on the Heights?' enquired Merv.

'Superintendent must make a good screw,' said Joe.

'He ain't been a superintendent more than two minutes,' rejoined Merv. 'And he's been living up there ever since he got married, so they say, when he was still just a big-hat beat bobby. Now whose trough he got his nose in, do you think?'

'I think he's honest, if you must know,' said Joe.

'You say so?' said Merv as they began their climb of the Heights. 'Then he's really out of place living round here. See that purple brick job with all the hysteria? He's wrecked more companies than Colonel Custer. Always rises from his clients' ashes. Been bankrupt so many times, that telly Watchdog programme is offering him a series. Now that place there with the turrets, they're artistic. All free love and slap it in the blancmange, Julian. Come the hot weather, they run a chopper every hour from the airport, twenty-five pound a trip, money back if you don't spot at least three bare-back bonks in the shrubbery. Guy next door made his money in the Golden Triangle and I don't mean the Chinkie takeaway in Tongtown. Very close family. Well, the wife and kids are very close anyway, sharing a single cell in a Thai jail. He got away but it shook him up. Now he just stays home and tends his garden. They say when he has a bonfire, any bird lucky enough to fly through the smoke comes out the other side upside down and whistling *Fly me to the moon*. Up ahead, whitewashed paella type job, we're into the toe-chewing set . . .'

Joe clutched his chrysanths like a talisman and let it all flow over him. Merv's unquenchable cheerfulness had helped him through too many bad times to start complaining now. Made redundant together, it had been Merv's determination to give the bastards the finger by flourishing like the green bay tree that had helped turn his deep hidden fantasy about being a detective into reality. At least it felt real to him, despite Mirabelle's unshakeable conviction it was a delusion induced by something they put in the drinks at the Glit.

'. . . and there it is at last, before your very eyes, Luton's answer to South Fork, Willie Woodbine's pig farm!'

It was a fairly conventional looking house, not a mansion, but not a prefab either, with a good class of car parked in the horseshoe driveway.

'You want I should pick you up, Joe?'

'Only if I fall down,' said Joe. 'No, look, if I need you, I'll give you a ring and set off down the hill, OK? It's a lovely day for a nice walk.'

'Then you won't need a taxi,' laughed Merv. 'Guy like you walking round a neighbourhood like this, you'll be down town before you can say civil liberties. Take care of yourself, baby!'

He did a noisy U-turn and swept away down the hill, leaving a trail of rubber and bubbly laughter. Joe watched till the taxi was out of sight, then began to feel very lonely. Also very hot. Like he'd said, it was a lovely day with the autumn sun deep into nostalgia, and the sturdy suit was clinging to his form like oven foil to a rib of beef.

No point hanging around here like a nervous kid at his first dance, thought Joe. Let's go and party!

He set off up the drive past the line of cars. Good pickings here for a bold car thief, he thought. But no one was going to be that bold, not within spitting distance of a houseful of cops.

Except that the nearer he got to the house, the less full of anything it seemed, though he could actually hear a distant buzz of voices and clinking of glasses and a ring-a-ding of music.

Of course, they had to be round the back, tempted into the open air by the Indian summer. Well, entering a crowded garden was marginally less daunting than entering a crowded room.

Taking a deep breath, he pushed open a wrought iron gate and set off down the path which led to the rear of the house.

Here, on a paved terrace running down to a beautifully kept lawn where a marble nymph poured water from an unemptying pitcher into an unfilling pool, and a trio of young women played a selection from the Shows, he found the party.

He saw instantly that he'd got it wrong. While the Gary Glitter T-shirt might've been a bit garish, it would at least have been a step in the right direction. Expensive informality was the order of the day. Nearest thing he could see to male dressing up was a couple of old geezers in striped blazers and cravats.

He took half a step back, contemplating a full retreat before he was noticed. Then a rather striking woman in early middle age, perhaps, but still with jet black hair and a body which fitted not too absurdly into a contour hugging catsuit, came towards him smiling.

She said, 'For me? Thank you,' as she took the flowers from him. Then turning to her friends she went on, 'I wonder who they can be from?'

She thinks I'm delivering them! thought Joe.

He'd heard footsteps come up behind him and stop. He knew he was blocking the way but, despite the fact that his whole instinct was for flight, his feet weren't taking orders.

The black-haired woman turned back to him and said, 'I can't find a card. Wasn't there a card?' And then from cool inquisition of a possibly errant inferior, her tone and expression glowed to warm welcome of a much desired guest.

'Dora! You made it. How lovely to see you. Do come through. Would you mind? You're blocking the way.'

Joe re-established contact with his legs and moved aside.

But instead of going by him, the new arrival took his arm and said, 'Mr Sixsmith? I thought it was you. Dora Calverley, remember? I'm so glad we've met again. But of course. I might have guessed you'd be here where all the best detectives are. Georgina, how are you? Lovely . . . er . . . suit.'

The change was just as marked, from genuine enthusiasm to formal courtesy.

Georgina Woodbine registered the parody and for a split second let it show in a narrowing of the eyes and a flaring of the nostrils. Then she was all smiles again as she advanced, saying, 'Mr Sixsmith, of course! How silly of me. Edgar told me you were coming. I don't know what I was thinking of.'

Oh yes, you do, lady, thought Joe bitterly. You were thinking let's have a bit of fun with this lowlife PI that Edgar's (*Edgar!*) wished on me.

His hostess's attention was now returned to Mrs Calverley.

'Dora, did some fellow with a plebby accent get on to you? I felt guilty afterwards in case he was some sort of salesman. Let me get you something to drink and we can really get down to the trivia.'

'No, I've had no contact with anyone, plebeian or patrician, who admitted contact with you,' said Mrs Calverley smiling. 'Please, don't abandon your friends. I'm sure Mr Sixsmith and I between us can sniff out the bar. *À bientôt!*'

The hand on his arm pushed Joe forward irresistibly. At least, he didn't resist till they were out of Georgina's range and not yet within anyone else's. Here he halted and said, 'Thanks, Mrs Calverley.'

'For what?' she asked, those shrewd blue eyes watching him from that sun-sallow face.

'For getting me past the guard dog,' he said.

The woman laughed and said, 'No sweat. I was brought up not to be rude to my hostess till the party was over and I'd left the house. You helped me not to disgrace my upbringing.'

'Have you known Mrs Woodbine a long time?'

'Long enough. We were once . . . close. But it's years since I came to this house. I see Georgie's taste has not deserted her.'

The words came out flat enough for irony as her gaze

moved over the pink and white flagged patio, the marble nymph, the syncopating trio, and the Victorian-style conservatory with its heavily curtained door.

'It's her house then?' said Joe, digesting what she'd just said.

'Indeed. Her father was a builder. Barnfather's – you must have seen their sign. Used to be big but they overstretched themselves in the eighties boom, I believe, and are now feeling the pinch. Happily for Georgie, Tom had rather traditional notions of a woman's role and when he died, his son got the business and Georgie got the house and a tidy lump sum.'

'But she stayed on teaching? Must be dedicated,' said Joe, happy to tap this unexpected source of info.

'To education? Perhaps. To the sense of power being deputy head gives her, certainly. It must have become increasingly important as Edgar soared upwards.'

'Pardon?'

'To marry a police constable which is what he was when they met, must have given a strong-willed woman like Georgie a sense of control. I do not doubt she pushed him onward and upward. Sergeant, inspector. But the trouble with helping to launch people is that eventually they take off and fly of their own accord. Chief inspector must have put him almost out of her reach, and I fear she can take no credit whatsoever now he's reached the dizzy heights of superintendent.'

No, thought Joe, that one's down to me!

A young woman passed by with a tray laden with glasses of champagne and also of that fizzy orange mixture which Merv, who liked a good Spoonerism, called Fuck's Biz. Mrs Calverley took two glasses of the latter and handed one to Joe.

Correctly reading the disappointed look on his face, she said, 'You'll thank me later. Long experience of drinking in the midday sun has led me to this wisdom. Maximum liquid, minimum alcohol.'

'Spend a lot of time in the tropics then?' enquired Joe.

'Or have I just overdosed on the sunbed, you mean?' she laughed. 'Getting on for twenty years in Zimbabwe. Still

Rhodesia when I went there, just. But you don't want to hear about my life and hard times, do you? Heard anything more about that boy we found in the box?'

'Nothing,' said Joe. 'There'll be an inquest, I suppose, when they identify him.'

'*If* they identify him,' she said heavily. 'I rang up a couple of times. No one knows much, and what's worse, no one seems to care.'

'But you do?' said Joe. He tried not to sound surprised but didn't make it.

'Didn't take me for a bleeding heart then?' she said, regarding him quizzically. 'Well, I'm not, believe me. But something about that poor kid's face, I don't know . . . perhaps it reminded me of Fred – that's my own boy, about the same age. Anyway, I haven't been able to get that face out of my mind, and I keep on thinking, there has to be someone somewhere who knows and cares, or if they don't, maybe they can explain how a young life came to end like that!'

She stopped abruptly, as if embarrassed, then said, 'Anyway, idle curiosity apart, I thought today's party might give me a chance to buttonhole Edgar Woodbine and see if I can get some sense out of him. Remarkable what a man will come up with if you grab him in front of his boss. And there he is. And that must be Richard Draycott, the new chief constable. Perfect.'

Joe followed her gaze to where Willie Woodbine was talking with a slightly built man in slacks and a polo shirt, who looked young enough to be his son.

Mrs Calverley said, 'Wish me luck. Oh, and if I may be personal, Mr Sixsmith, wouldn't you be a little more comfortable if you took that rather original jacket off and loosened your tie?'

Joe watched her head towards Woodbine and cut expertly into the male conversation.

One of the tray girls approached. Joe said, 'Hold on a second,' put his glass on the tray, took off his jacket and removed his tie. Much better. But just because Mrs C. had been right on this didn't mean she was right on everything.

He picked up a glass of bubbly, downed it in one, took another and said, 'Thanks a lot.'

'Just wave when you want some more,' grinned the girl.

Joe emptied the second glass and said, 'I'm waving.'

To give the impression he wasn't simply boozing, he wandered over to the trio and put on his listening-to-the-music face. The trio comprised violin, viola and clarinet. The clarinettist looked familiar. It was the dark-haired girl he'd identified as Gally Eaglesfield in the Sinfonia. Her appearance here confirmed the guess.

They finished playing a selection from *Carousel* and Joe led the applause, then said, 'You play in the Sinfonia, right?'

'Yes,' she said, regarding him rather warily.

'I'm in the choir. You know, *The Creation*.'

'Oh yes.'

This was real probing stuff.

He said heartily, 'Earning a bit of pocket money?'

'Oh no,' she said shocked. 'I wouldn't expect Mrs Woodbine to pay, I owe her so much. Oh, hello, Mr Dalgety.'

A tall slim man with elegantly waved, becomingly greying hair had arrived at Joe's shoulder.

'Sally, I thought it was you. How're you doing? We haven't seen you for ages. You and Mavis haven't fallen out, have you?'

His eyes twinkled as he spoke. Must have a little battery up his nose, thought Joe at the same time as he flashed a thank you beam to the god who looked after balding black gumshoes for sending along Mavis Dalgety's dad to ask the questions Joe could see no way of getting round to.

'No!' said the girl a tad over vehemently. 'Just that it's a busy time, school work, and the orchestra, and everything. Excuse me. I said I'd help in the kitchen.'

She moved swiftly away towards the house and disappeared through the conservatory door.

Dalgety glanced at Joe and made a wry face.

'Nice girl,' he said. 'Awkward age. You have any children Mr . . . er . . . ?'

'Sixsmith. Joe Sixsmith,' said Joe taking the proffered hand.

'Andrew Dalgety.' The man's grip was firm and dry. He was very like a US senator in the movies, the lean rangy northern type, not the plush *you-all*ing southern variety.

'No, afraid not,' said Joe.

'You're probably lucky. I've got two. Boy's reaching an age of discretion, thank God. But my girl . . . well, same age as Sally. With the ladies, you don't know what they're thinking at any age, but between twelve and nineteen I swear *they* don't know what they're thinking either. You work with Edgar, do you?'

Trying to place me, thought Joe. Sussed out I'm not likely to be on Georgie's list so reckons I must be a cop. But even that's a problem 'cos this is a chief inspector and over do, not a pint and pie CID booze up!

He let the champers do the talking for him and heard himself saying, 'Ed and I occasionally work together, but no publicity, know what I mean?'

'Oh yes. Indeed,' said the man, clearly baffled. 'Haven't noticed a loo in your travels, have you? Must be one in there somewhere. Excuse me.'

Joe grinned as he watched him head into the house, then helped himself to another passing drink. What a swell party this is! he hummed. A finger tapped on his shoulder. He turned smiling. But the smile flickered as he found himself looking into the eyes of his host who returned his gaze in most unhostly fashion.

'There you are, Willie,' said Joe. 'Swell party.'

'What have you been saying to Dora Calverley, Sixsmith?' demanded Woodbine.

'Nothing. Well hardly anything. I was listening to her mainly . . .'

'Don't give me that crap,' snarled Woodbine. 'I saw you beating her ear earlier and now the blasted woman's making my life a misery about that dead yob in the churchyard. What the hell do you think you're playing at?'

With the quiet dignity of a man who's downed about a

litre of champagne, Joe said, 'Sorry, didn't realize when you invited me I wasn't meant to talk to the other guests. Maybe I should just leave.'

It was a speech to melt a heart of stone, but Joe didn't really anticipate it doing much to a detective superintendent. It was with some surprise, therefore, that he realized the hand Woodbine was placing on his shoulder was in friendly embrace, and his teeth were being bared in a rueful smile, and the voice wasn't reciting his rights but saying, 'Sorry, Joe. Pay no heed to what I say. Pressure of work. We're here to relax and enjoy ourselves, aren't we? Mr Draycott, sir, there you are. This is Joe Sixsmith you were asking about. Joe, have you met Dick Draycott, our new chief constable?'

All was explained as Joe turned to find himself facing the new chief constable, accompanied by Georgina Woodbine who was wearing a smile so frozen, it looked like it might fall off if she moved her head too quickly.

'I'm delighted to meet you, Mr Sixsmith,' said Draycott. 'Edgar speaks well of you. I've always believed there's a role for the private sector so long as its members acknowledge its secondary status.'

Georgina was finding the smile hard to maintain. She said, 'I must pop inside and check that all's well there. Excuse me.'

Woodbine gave a sigh of relief as she vanished into the house and had to turn it into a cough. Poor sod was terrified she might blow his inter-communal credentials by headbutting me, thought Joe.

For the next five minutes or so, Joe and the chief constable made polite conversation about football and other important things. The trio reduced to a duo by the continued absence of Sally Eaglesfield had started up again. Mrs Calverley, still nursing her Buck's Fizz, strolled by, giving Joe a slightly ironical smile as she took in his company. Then Andrew Dalgety came up to Woodbine and murmured in his ear, 'Edgar, Georgie says it's chow time so could you get the show on the road?'

'Fine. Excuse me, sir,' said Woodbine, touching Draycott's arm.

They made their way to the steps in front of the conservatory where Georgina Woodbine was standing.

She clapped her hands together and in a voice accustomed to carry across the inattentive vastnesses of school assembly halls, she said, 'Ladies and gentlemen, Edgar and I are truly delighted to see so many friends and colleagues gathered here on this lovely day, though it does give one cause to wonder, who's directing the traffic?'

Genteel laughter. She went on in this vein a little longer, then introduced the chief constable as guest of honour. Draycott made a fluent and well-practised speech, saying how delighted he was to get the chance to meet so many important people, but of course the most important of them all today was the man whose well-merited promotion they were celebrating. And finally Willie Woodbine strutted his stuff, striking a nice balance between grovelling gratitude to the new chief for turning up and crowing kiss-my-assery at his old colleagues for being left behind.

Long applause, then the stage, or rather steps, were left to Georgina who said, 'Well, that was very nice. But the really important news is that the buffet is now ready for investigation by the serious food squad.'

She drew the curtains obscuring the doorway aside to reveal a trio of tables laden with enough grub to fill a relief lorry.

Someone cried, 'Bravo!' and started applauding. Others joined in.

What the shoot are we clapping about, wondered Joe, who felt strongly that only the starving should applaud food.

But feeling Willie Woodbine's eyes upon him, and being a good guest, he decided there was no harm in a token ironic clap.

He raised his hands and brought them together, like a major-domo signalling to the servants.

The result was devastating.

From somewhere in the middle of the house came a dull booming noise accompanied by the sound of shattering glass and a mighty rushing wind which tore through the conservatory to pick up great handfuls of the carefully arranged buffet and hurl them across the patio at the astonished guests.

And Joe, falling backwards with the remnants of a salmon mousse wrapped around his face, thought appreciatively, 'Now that's what I call service!'

10

In an emergency some people keep their heads like draught Guinness while others are losing theirs faster than lukewarm lager.

On the Guinness side were Dick Draycott and Dora Calverley who rapidly began to move around among the guests checking for damage. Woodbine was rather more lagerish, running around like a man trying to impress a promotions board, crying, 'Don't panic! Don't panic!'

Joe's first inclination after checking he'd lost neither his head nor anything else, was to head away from the house in case there was any plan to offer seconds. But that stupid little git who squatted in his mind right next to that dear old instinct for self-preservation was crying, 'You saw Sally Eaglesfield go in there and you ain't seen her come out!'

'Oh shoot,' said Joe and headed for the conservatory.

Someone was by his side. It was Andrew Dalgety.

Joe said, 'I think Sally's still in there.'

'Oh God. I hope not,' said Dalgety. At that moment Georgina Woodbine, who had stood miraculously unscathed and apparently unmoved as her gourmet buffet blizzarded by her, came running forward screaming in delayed hysterics and collapsed into Dalgety's arms.

On your own again, thought Joe, and stepped fearfully into the wrecked conservatory.

His reward was instantaneous. A groan drew his gaze to the floor just inside the door. The girl lay there, eyes open, looking more frightened than hurt.

'What happened?' she asked in a bewildered voice. 'I was coming out then I heard them all making speeches . . .'

'It's OK,' said Joe. 'Gas leak, maybe. Let's have a look.'

He ran his hands over her body, thinking such familiarity would probably have got him lynched in Louisiana or Cheltenham.

'Any pain?'

'No, nothing. Oh God, look at the mess. Georgie will be furious. Where is she? Is she OK?'

'She's fine. Let me help you out of here.'

He raised her up and bearing most of her slight weight on his arm, he led her on to the terrace. Dalgety had similarly escorted Georgina to the lawn and was lowering her on to the grass. The sight seemed to reassure Sally who now pushed Joe aside and said, 'Really, I'm fine. What's happened to my friends?'

Just at this moment the other members of the trio came hurrying up and Joe was able to leave Sally in their care with a clear conscience.

At least, it was fairly clear. Ever since childhood he'd had a morally debilitating sense that he was at least partially responsible for any disaster which occurred in his vicinity. Perhaps Aunt Mirabelle's habit of saying whenever she dropped a stitch or slopped her tea, 'Now see what you've made me do, Joseph?' had something to do with it. No way he'd caused this explosion, of course. On the other hand, he was here, and he had clapped . . .

'Come on, make yourself useful,' snapped Willie Woodbine, who'd got over his don't panic routine. 'Let's check for fire.'

You want to check for fire, you call the brigade, thought Joe. But he followed the superintendent into the house and didn't protest when a small fire extinguisher was pushed into his hand.

The source of the explosion was easy to find. It was the kitchen, which was a wreck. There was still a strong smell of gas in the air, confirming Joe's initial diagnosis. There was a lot of smouldering debris but no actual fire.

'Just had it done,' said Woodbine. 'Everything fire resistant, thank God. Look at that bloody thing! I told her it was useless, all style, no function. Built to leak!'

He was referring to the huge hi-tech oven unit which even in ruins looked as if it had been built to explore the stars rather than cook the Sunday joint.

'Must've been some leak,' said Joe as Woodbine sprayed foam around.

'Buy something that pricey, you don't expect little holes,' growled Woodbine. 'Come on. Let's have some work from you.'

'I was just trying to save you having to replace this one,' protested Joe, holding up his extinguisher.

'Don't be a nana. I won't be replacing it. Insurance will. There you go. Always hated that thing.'

Woodbine had sent a miraculously preserved tall blue coffee pot crashing to the ground with a well aimed jet.

'At least check if that phone's still working,' he ordered.

The wall phone was in an alcove formed by a tall cabinet and the fridge freezer. He got the dialling tone.

'Yeah,' he said.

'Fine,' said Woodbine. 'Dial Emergency. That's 999.'

'I know what it is,' said Joe. As he dialled, his eyes ran down the kitchen wall calendar pinned alongside the phone. It was covered with scrawls indicating appointments, reminders, and messages in what was presumably Georgie's elegant scrawl. One caught his eye partly because it was ringed, partly because it seemed an unlikely message, reminder or appointment for a policeman's wife. *Rob Vicar*? He suddenly recalled he was supposed to be investigating Georgina Woodbine's alleged double life. Perhaps it was a triple life!

The phone answered.

'Which service?' enquired the operator.

'Well, police,' said Joe uncertainly.

The policeman who came on didn't seem much interested in the explosion, assuring Joe he should have got the fire brigade.

'Give us your phone number and I'll pass it on,' he offered.

'7829267,' read Joe. Something about the number struck him as familiar which was odd as he'd never had occasion to ring Woodbine at home. Neither it seemed had the officer he was talking to, for there was none of the anticipated upgrade of urgency.

'What's happening?' demanded Woodbine, returning from heaven knew what demolition exercise in a walk-in closet.

Joe explained.

'Give that here,' snarled Woodbine. 'Who the hell's that?'

Time to go, thought Joe, who didn't like blood, not even at the other end of a phone line.

He went down the passage which ran off the entrance hall. Not too much damage here. The arrangement of doors must have channelled most of the blast backwards towards the conservatory. The glass panel on the front door was cracked. Way Woodbine was going on, probably the whole thing would be off its hinges by the time the assessor got here. He opened the door and went out into the garden. You could tell this was a high-class neighbourhood. Anywhere else a bang like that would have had the neighbours thronging the streets in search of excitement. Nothing here to disturb the Sunday calm except a black and white mongrel trotting by in search of some pedigree pooch to ruin.

'There you are,' said Dora Calverley coming round the side of the house. 'Unscathed, are you?'

'Yeah. And you?'

'Fine. And most of the damage back there is sartorial, I'm glad to say. This would be a rather good time to steal away, I think. Where's your car?'

'Came by taxi. But we can't just bunk off . . .'

'What else do you propose? Look for someone to give the kiss of life to? Or enquire politely of your hostess what time lunch will be served? Which reminds me, I'm starving. Come home with me, I'm sure I can rustle up a sandwich. And I've got a proposition I'd like to put to you.'

'Yeah, but . . .' said Joe, still feeling guilty at the thought of just sneaking off like this. 'What about my jacket? I dropped it back there when the bang went off.'

'Anything in it? Money? Credit cards?'

'No,' admitted Joe, who always carried what little he had in his back pocket.

'Then you're better off leaving it and claiming off Edgar's insurance. Pity you couldn't dump the trousers too.'

This sounded dishonest to Joe, moulded in the Mirabelle school of morality. On the other hand, he was pretty peckish.

He said, 'This sandwich won't have anything salmony in it, will it?'

'Not likely,' laughed Mrs Calverley.

'Then let's go,' said Joe.

On their way down the Heights, they met the emergency services coming up.

'Bet you don't get service like that on the Rasselas Estate,' said Mrs Calverley.

'Don't have too many police superintendents living there either,' said Joe.

It wasn't till fifteen silent minutes on that his detective software turned up the menu containing the question he should have responded with. By this time they were somewhere to the north east of the town, belting along a narrow country road.

Joe said, 'How come you know I live on Rasselas?'

The woman suddenly swung the wheel violently in what seemed at first a suicidal desire to drive them straight into a hedge. But at the last minute the branches parted in a narrow opening through which they plunged into a long straight green lane.

'I asked a few questions,' said Mrs Calverley. 'Like to know who I'm hiring.'

Ahead the lane ended in what had presumably been a gateway. There was no gate now but an ancient rusty cattle grid between two massive columns, one of which had slipped out of the vertical and teetered drunkenly towards the other. It did not seem possible to Joe that there was room for the Range Rover either vertically or laterally, but Mrs Calverley showed no inclination to decrease speed.

Joe closed his eyes. Mirabelle would have been glad to hear the fervour of his prayer. When he opened them again, quite ready for heaven, he found they were racing at undiminished speed up an unevenly gravelled drive towards a tall black house.

'Hire for what?' said Joe aiming at aplomb.

'Let's have a drink first,' she said. 'You look like you need it. Welcome to Hoot Hall.'

It wasn't in fact a very welcoming place. Maybe once it had been, with hordes of servants scooting around serving cocktails while far below relays of peasants stoked the boilers. Heat was of the essence with walls thicker than an Immigration officer's skin. But the days of peasant stokers were long gone and in the high-ceilinged drawing room he was led into, damp was flaking the paint and bubbling the paper and the air was tinged with a miasma of swamp. Joe sat gingerly on the edge of an ancient sofa and looked up into the quizzical brown eyes of a young Jack-the-lad smiling at him from an ornate gilt frame hung above the empty fireplace.

'Dickie,' said Mrs C. to his unasked question. 'My late husband, painted by a fond student when he still had hair and charm.'

'Student . . . ?'

'He taught at the Varsity till circumstances and the lure of colonial riches persuaded him to leave.'

She spoke with a faintly amused cynicism which mocked both the dead man and her own, by implication, disappointed expectations. He looked once more at Dickie Calverley, this time with sympathy. Mrs C. was not a woman he would care to disappoint. So softly, softly . . .

'Let's get out of here,' she said, shivering. 'Just because the job I've got for you involves dead bodies, there's no need for us to suffer mortuary conditions, is there?'

She led him to a cavernous kitchen where an Aga took some of the chill off the air. Here she produced a bottle of Scotch and a couple of glasses which she filled.

'Health,' she said, knocking hers back. 'Cheese OK for your sandwich?'

'Fine,' he said. 'This job . . .'

'It's that boy in the box,' she said, sawing at a loaf of bread which seemed to have the texture of an oak log. 'As I said, I can't get him out of my mind. Ah, that sounds like Fred.'

Her ears were better than his. He had no sense of anyone

approaching till the back door was suddenly thrown open and a young man entered. He was seventeen or eighteen, dressed in a long waxed jacket and carrying a shotgun. He had a narrow, unhealthily pale face, his mother's dark blue eyes and long brownish hair which the light wind had wrapped around his neck.

Hair colour and skin tone apart perhaps, Joe could see no resemblance between him and the boy in the box, but mothers, he knew, see with different eyes.

'This is my son, Fred,' she said. 'Fred, this is Mr Sixsmith.'

'Oh yes?' said the youth indifferently.

'Pleased to meet you,' said Joe.

'Where've you been, dear?' asked his mother.

'Potting a few crows,' said the youth. 'Black bastards get everywhere this time of year. I'm off for a shower, now. Hope there's some hot water.'

He strolled away whistling. Joe watched and waited to see if his mother would try to dilute his rudeness. She didn't.

Shoot, thought Joe magnanimously. Everyone needs someone to love them, even little twerps like that.

Even boys found dead in boxes.

'What's the deal?' he said.

'I'd like you to find out who he is, who he was.'

'But the police . . .'

'They're doing nothing!' she exclaimed, emphasizing her point by banging a lump of cheese on the table with a crash that suggested it came from the same tree as the bread. 'Edgar Woodbine says there's nothing to go on. The boy had nothing on him, his prints aren't on record, there's no missing person description which fits. They're ready to bury him and forget him. Worse, I get the impression that they don't really want to find anything that might help. More trouble than it's worth.'

'I'm sorry,' said Joe, 'but if the police can't help, I don't see what I can do . . .'

'Do you always turn away business like this?' she asked.

'I don't take money for sitting on my thumb,' he said.

'That does you credit, though it can't do much *for* your

credit,' she said. 'But you must have channels the police can't use.'

'There's still got to be a starting point,' he replied.

'How about the man you disturbed? What do you think he was up to? Mouth to mouth resuscitation?'

'Checking out if there was anything worth lifting is my guess,' said Joe.

'And if he found something, a wallet say, couldn't there have been some pointer to the boy's identity in it?'

'Yeah, could be,' said Joe, thinking, I should have thought of that! Presumably the cops had. He went on. 'But won't the police . . . ?'

'They say the description you gave could fit almost anyone between the ages of thirteen and thirty.'

'I only got a glimpse,' protested Joe. 'You saw as much as I did.'

'But I don't have a trained eye,' she said. 'Look, isn't it worth a try? A few hours nosing around? Suppose I give you a cheque for a hundred, and when that's finished, you let me know?'

He hesitated a moment longer, then thought, what the shoot am I doing? She needs the gesture, I need the cash.

'OK,' he said. 'I'll give it a go. On one condition.'

'What's that?'

'I don't have to eat that sandwich,' said Joe Sixsmith.

11

That same Sunday evening, Joe was watching a thriller in which the detective had been beaten, shot, tortured and lost his wife, but still looked set to get everything right, when the phone rang.

It was Aunt Mirabelle.

'Joseph, someone's been telling me you almost got yourself killed. Thought I might see you at the chapel this evening after an experience like that.'

'Yeah, well, thought I'd better take it easy . . .'

'That's your trouble. Taking things far too easy for your own good,' she said sternly. 'I spoke to Rev. Pot about you. He wants to see you first thing tomorrow. That means before nine. You be there!'

Joe returned to his film just in time to see the detective having his clothes stripped off by a whore with a heart of gold.

'I wish,' he said enviously. But as the music swelled and the bodies writhed, his mind drifted off in contemplation of how Mirabelle could be pissed off with him for simultaneously putting his life at risk and taking things easy.

'Women, eh, Whitey?' he said. 'No problem thinking two, three different things at the same time.'

The cat gave him the one-eyed look which said this was rich coming from someone who found it hard to think one different thing at the same time, then went back to sleep.

Joe, who'd had a hard day, was not long in following his example.

Next morning he overslept by half an hour. Monday was laundry day so he shoved his dirty linen in a pillow case, made do (much to Whitey's distress) with a cold sausage sarnie for breakfast, and on the dot of nine he pushed open the doors of the Boyling Corner Chapel. The Reverend Percy Potemkin, known as Rev. Pot wherever in South Beds the Word of the Lord was heard in sermon or in song, was tidying up.

'What's this, Joseph?' he said. 'You know I don't do prodigals till after lunch.'

'Mirabelle said you wanted to see me urgent, Rev.,' said Joe.

'*Wanted* is fanciful,' said Rev. Pot climbing on a stepladder to take the hymn numbers off the board. '*Urgent* is fiction. Here, hold this thing for me. It shakes like a soul in torment.'

'What's Auntie been saying, Rev.?' asked Joe, steadying the ladder.

'She says you're wasting your time in a nothing job for which you've got no talent anyway. Now, I tend to agree with her. On the other hand, I told her, the boy is happy. Positive capability he may not have, but negative capability he seems to have got in plenty.'

'Is that good?' asked Joe cautiously.

'Well, it means you may not have much idea what you're doing, but you're not going to let it fret you into a breakdown.'

This negative capability sounded OK to Joe, like that other 'ity' some old lady had laid on him, what was it . . . ? *Serendipity*. Finding things out by accident. Except of course if a man keeps on being in the right place at the right time, who's to say it's always an accident?

'So what's the message, Rev.?' he asked.

'From me? Avoid mixed drinks and carnal thoughts. Never be late for rehearsals. And remember the eleventh commandment.'

'What's that?' asked Joe.

'It's the one says, honour your auntie and keep her off your pastor's back; didn't you learn anything at Sunday School?'

'Praise the Lord. Ye heavens adore him,' said Joe.

'Joseph, you're not having a revelation, I hope?' said Rev.

Pot. 'I can't stomach revelations before I've had my coffee.'

'No, it's hymn number 292,' said Joe, looking up at the one remaining number on the hymn board.

'So it is,' said Rev. Pot, removing it. 'And if we'd had the pleasure of your company last night we could have enjoyed hearing that beery baritone of yours singing it. Take heed, Joe. One day you *will* have a revelation, and you may not much care for what is revealed. You'd better believe it.'

'Oh I do, I do,' said Joe fervently. And he did, he did. For he'd already had it and, like Rev. Pot said, he didn't much like it.

292, the hymn number, was also the readable remnant of the number inked on the dead boy's hand and was also the centre of Willie Woodbine's telephone number. 7829267. So what? It meant nothing. And it was just his stupid imagination that was now confirming that the other almost invisible digits on the dead boy's thumb were 78 and 67. Except, of course, as was often pointed out to him by his detractors, he didn't have a stupid imagination. And also, as had been pointed out by Mrs C., Willie Woodbine seemed not only uninterested in but positively opposed to efforts to discover the dead boy's identity . . .

For a moment Joe felt sick to his stomach, but the old negative 'ity' soon got to work and shoved the troublesome revelation into a limbo file, and he was able to sing *The heavens are telling the glory of God* as he drove on to the office to see what else this unpredictable world might have in store for him.

What it had was a ginger-headed young man in a lilac anorak leaning up against his office door.

'Joe Sixsmith?' he said. 'Hi, I'm the *Bugle*'s crime reporter.'

'No, you're not,' said Joe. 'Not unless you've had a hair graft and lost forty pounds.'

'What? Oh, you mean Tony Sloppe? No, I'm Tony's assistant. Well, not assistant exactly. I do most things on the paper, but I'm hoping to make crime my speciality and Tony lets me help out. Can we talk?'

There was an engaging frankness about the young man which, coupled with the kind of Scots accent which sells whisky rather than threatens mayhem, had Joe beginning to agree before he recalled the first rule of his profession: Trust God, and only on Sundays.

'You got ID?' he asked.

'No!' said the young man indignantly. 'Oh, sorry. You mean identification. Hang about.'

He started a search of his multi-pocketed anorak which involved unfastening half a dozen zips before he found the right compartment.

'Here,' he said triumphantly, producing a press card in the name of Duncan Docherty. 'My friends call me Dunk.'

'Come inside, Mr Docherty,' said Joe.

He took his seat and put on his best steely expression but the effect was spoilt by Whitey rubbing up against Docherty's legs and purring like this was love at first sight. The young man looked immensely flattered as he stooped to stroke him.

'Bet he does this to everyone, eh?' he said, inviting the disclaimer which would make him special.

'You got your lunch with you? Cold pork sarnies maybe?' Docherty's hand flew to a bulge in his anorak.

'Hey, that's real Sherlock Holmes stuff,' he said admiringly.

'No trick,' said Joe. 'Whitey can smell a packed lunch at two hundred metres.'

Secretly he felt rather pleased about the pork. Tesco's had been pushing rolled shoulder, fifty pence off, on Friday, and he'd guessed that most of Luton's landladies would be serving it up as the traditional Sunday roast.

'So what can I do for you?' he asked.

'It's about this explosion up at Superintendent Woodbine's house yesterday. You were there, right?'

'What makes you think that?' asked Joe.

'We've got our sources,' said Docherty smugly. 'Now, what did you make of the explosion, Mr Sixsmith?'

Joe thought a moment, then said, 'Bang!'

'Yeah, funny. But what do you think caused it?'

'You talked to Mr Woodbine yet?'

'Tried, but couldn't get near him,' said the youth. 'There's an official handout says it was a gas leak.'

'So what's the problem?' said Joe.

'First thing you learn in this job is, always look beyond the official statements,' said Docherty confidently.

'That's the first thing, is it?' said Joe. 'When do you get on to the second?'

The young man looked hurt.

'I'm just trying to get at the truth,' he protested.

'So how come you're asking me when there's all those other guests?' demanded Joe.

'Well, they're all police brass and establishment figures,' explained the youth. 'You're different, sort of, well, different. And with your training and experience, if it was a terrorist attack, you'd be the one most likely to spot it.'

Joe wanted to laugh but he'd been brought up not to tread on people's susceptibilities long before this crazy political correctness stuff made rudeness a hanging offence.

He opened his mouth to disabuse the boy but instead he said, 'The Cally!'

'What?'

'I bet you're a member of the Cally.'

Back in the sixties when MacMurdos, the Kilmarnock shoemakers (By Appointment, Cordwainers to the Queen), had built their new factory in Luton, presumably to be a bit nearer to the royal feet, there had been a large influx of Scottish workers, partly for their expertise, partly because in those long past, never-had-it-so-good days, there was little surplus workforce in the south east. Like all good Celtic exiles they had felt the need of a place to be properly homesick in, and thus the Caledonian Club had been formed. Thirty years on, its race base had spread, and Joe's rendition of 'My Luve is like a Red Red Rose' last Burns Night had brought cheers and tears in equal floods. But it never lost its basic Scottishness and was the first place any new arrivals from the North headed for.

'Aye, sure I am.'

'And Police Constable Sandy Mackay, I bet he's a member too.'

He saw he'd hit the bull. The cold pork and now this. Maybe he'd cracked this deduction business at last!

'Yes, the name's familiar . . .' said Docherty trying to recover ground.

'Come on,' said Joe. 'First thing you'd do when you got this half-baked notion in your head was contact your police contact, i.e. Constable Mackay, and ask him if he'd heard anything funny. And he said, no, looks like a gas leak, but I do happen to know that this weird PI fellow was at the party, so he might be a good bet to check it out with. Right?'

'Yes, all right. Something like that. So if there was anything . . .'

'Does your editor know you're groping around asking questions like these? Or Tony Sloppe?'

'No. It was my own idea . . .'

'Thank God for that,' said Joe. 'It was a gas leak. I was there. I saw the kitchen. Nothing suspicious . . .'

Except that how many gas taps did you need turned on for a cold buffet? A picture of the mangled oven console had flashed across his mind, and on it all the taps . . . He shook his head. Forget it. Overactive imagination disease must be contagious.

He concluded, '. . . and if you're going to start getting up Willie Woodbine's nose, you could end up being sneezed all the way back to Scotland. Fancy a cup of tea?'

It wasn't just his natural hospitableness which made him put the kettle on. Joe would never have admitted to being superstitious but he knew beyond doubt that existence was like a huge Persian carpet. Looked at from close up, your little square might just seem a mess, but stand back far enough and you'd see for sure it was all one carefully patterned weave. Trouble was, like a photographer on a cliff, it was hard to get the right focus without falling off. But God was good and gave you little nudges, like things going in threes. He'd had the pork and the Cally. The third was due. It had something to do with Dunk Docherty, so make the tea and wait for inspiration.

'Take sugar?'

'No, it's bad for you.'

'You sure are full of stupid ideas,' laughed Joe. 'Your body's a dynamo, needs all the energy it can get to generate electricity for the brain.'

'Is that so? Maybe that's why I'm dogsbody on the *Bugle* instead of editor of *The Times*,' grinned Docherty.

He had a nice grin. In fact he was a very good looking boy, despite a certain puffiness about the nose . . .

Oh shoot! thought Joe. Here it was. Number three.

Galina Hacker's last description of the man bothering her granddad had included the details, red hair, busted nose, lilac jacket, and big feet. He threw a glance at Docherty's feet. Even allowing for the magnifying properties of modern trainers, these looked like at least elevens.

Now, Joe, he admonished himself. Don't go rushing at this thing. It all fits, sure – nosey (ha ha) young reporter looking to make a name for himself, right description and all – but how many sure things have you seen nosedive at the final fence? So go easy, be subtle.

Whitey looked up from his saucer of very sweet tea and made a noise which an anthropomorphist might have interpreted as a disbelieving groan.

'Is your cat OK?' asked Docherty anxiously.

'Yeah. He just bolts his food. I mean, your food. Gets dyspepsia. You a boxer or something, Dunk?'

'No. Why?'

'Just you look like you do a bit of fighting. You know, the nose.'

'Hey, you're doing it again, this Sherlock thing,' said Docherty admiringly. 'I think Tony Sloppe's got you figured all wrong.'

Joe knew better than to enquire how Sloppe had characterized his detective abilities.

He said, 'So you do a bit of boxing then?'

'No, but I'm thinking of taking it up. You need to be able to take care of yourself in our game,' said the youngster disconsolately. 'Ask a few polite questions and some folk are more ready to give you a knuckle sandwich than a nice cup of tea.'

He raised his cup in acknowledgement of Joe's humanity.

'So what happened?' asked Joe, offering his last Kit Kat

and feeling guiltily relieved when the reporter refused it.

'I had this idea for a piece about homelessness, the bottom end I mean, people sleeping rough, that sort of thing. And there's a growing problem here, you know. You get the local input, plus, as the Smoke gets more crowded, a lot of folk are spreading out into surrounding centres where compassion fatigue hasn't reached such a level and there's still some hope of making a living begging . . .'

He was getting launched into his proposed article. Joe didn't have time to be rehearsed on, so he interrupted, 'So you got duffed up for your trouble?'

'Aye, that's right. I was just asking this guy in the park a few questions and suddenly he busts my nose. Just like that. Made me feel homesick for Cowdenbeath, I tell you.'

Joe, still not able to see a way of bringing up Taras Kovalko without arousing suspicion, was suddenly struck by another idea.

'Did you finish this piece?'

'Not yet. A couple of other things came up, so I put it on the back burner.'

'But you must have made a few contacts.'

'As well as fists, you mean? Yes, I suppose so. Why?'

'You heard about the dead kid they found in the box outside St Monkey's?'

'Aye. I did the story. Could have been OK too, but the editor didn't care for the picture.'

'A picture? You mean you've got a photo?'

'Aye, one of the snaps the polis took. Only he looks a wee bit dead on it and my editor says this is a family paper, we don't have pictures of corpses in it.'

'Well, that could be very useful,' said Joe. 'You see, Dunk, I want to find out who this kid was.'

'Why so?'

Joe saw no reason to mention Mrs C. so he said, 'It was me who found him. I feel sort of responsible.'

'You found him? Hey, you don't need to advertise, do you? Work just comes looking for you!'

'That's one way of putting it,' said Joe. 'Now, there was no ID on him, but I saw someone running away from the box. Don't go misty eyed, he was long dead. But this guy might have lifted whatever he had in his pockets. Find him and maybe we can get a lead to the boy's identity.'

'And you'd like to use my contacts?' said Docherty, making it sound like he ran the Luton Mafia. 'So what's in it for me?'

'Could be a story.'

'Dead youth named? Real Pulitzer stuff,' he scoffed.

'And I'd owe you a favour,' said Joe. 'If there was anything you're working on where an extra pair of hands or a new face might come in useful . . .'

He said a little prayer and waited.

'Well, there might be,' said the reporter. 'But you'd need to keep it under your hat till I'm ready to publish.'

'My first duty's always to the client,' said Joe, jesuheritically as Aunt Mirabelle liked to classify any form of misleading speech.

'OK,' said Dunk Docherty, leaning forward and lowering his voice. 'There's a chance, just a chance, I may be on the track of a World War Two concentration camp guard who settled down here in Luton.'

'Now that,' said Joe, 'is really amazing.'

12

It wasn't all that amazing actually.

The leaked lists referred to by Piers, the Wet Wykehamist, had reached among others the desk of an old mate of Tony Sloppe's on the *Sun*. His attention was naturally focused on the short 'A' list. His assistants were delegated to do some deep checking of likely names on List 'B'. And the 'C' list was relegated to a bottom drawer. Sloppe, hearing of the investigation and wanting to know if there was anything in it for him, was told that the only name in his area was on the 'C' list. Deciding it wasn't worth wasting his own precious time upon, he gave it to the eager beaver, Dunk Docherty.

Dunk had plugged into the Gaelic mainframe which he confidently asserted controlled most of the English media.

A friend working for Radio Manchester had checked out Kovalko during his long stay up there. As a chef, a citizen and a family man, his record was excellent. But a friend of the friend who was a member of the local Ukrainian Club recalled that sometime in the seventies there'd been a couple of grey suits (which meant official snoopers) asking questions of and about Taras.

'And?' said Joe.

'And nothing. Seems it's not too rare for naturalized foreigners and no one takes much notice. Anyway, I passed it all on to Tony who told me not to waste any more time on it.'

'But you ignored him. Like with the gas leak. It'll get you into trouble one day.'

'Oh aye, but it might get me on to a national too,' laughed Docherty. 'Anyway I just worked at it in my own time. I got the idea from this guy in Manchester. Why not try the Uke Club here? So I did. And I hit it lucky.'

His luck had consisted of making contact with Mrs Vansovich who had been happy to retail to him Kovalko's story of his loss of memory and her own failure to stimulate its recovery by throwing recollections of Vinnitsa at him.

'She clammed up when I went to see her a second time,' admitted Dunk. 'I think maybe she was beginning to smell a rat.'

A whole nest of them by the time I got to her, thought Joe.

He said, 'So what else have you got?'

'Well, I spoke to the guy himself. He lives with his daughter and she left him in a car park while she went shopping so I took the chance and confronted him. I told him I was doing a piece about displaced people who'd settled here and would be interested in hearing about his background.'

'And what did he do? Confess to being Martin Bormann?'

'No, but he certainly looked worried.'

Joe said, 'I was taught to be worried if strange men spoke to me in car parks. So are you going to keep on harassing the poor sod? How old is he? Over seventy?'

'Now hold on there,' said the reporter indignantly. 'I'm not harassing anybody. If he's got nothing to hide, he's got nothing to worry about, has he? And if he has got something to hide, what difference does it make how old he is? At least he's lived long enough to get old.'

'OK,' said Joe. 'But you've got to watch the innocent don't suffer too, like the Hackers.'

Shouldn't have said the name, he thought instantly. Docherty hasn't mentioned it. But the youngster was too heated to notice.

He said, 'The victims who died in those camps, they were innocent too. And their families. Don't we owe something to them?'

'Sure,' said Joe. 'But we're ahead of ourselves. You were going to say how I could help.'

'Oh aye. Look, I do want to tread carefully till I see where

93

I am. The trouble is, I'm known now and I think next time I show, it could get confrontational.'

'Which you're not ready for,' said Joe.

'Not yet. But there's something there,' said Dunk obstinately. 'What would be great would be if you could somehow get a line on the family, find out what he's told them about his past. Maybe he's got some souvenirs, that sort of thing . . .'

'And how do you propose I'm going to manage that?' asked Joe.

'Hey, I thought I saw something about detective on the door,' grinned the young man. 'And meanwhile, I'll be out on those mean streets seeing what I can dig up about your boy in the box. Deal?'

Joe considered uneasily the moral implications of all this. Ethics were a maze. Secret of a maze was keep turning left. Or was it right?

Oh shoot! Ethics could look after themselves.

He said, 'Deal.'

After Docherty had left, Joe picked up the phone and dialled the Bullpat Square Law Centre. He got through to Butcher surprisingly quickly.

'So you're still with us,' she said. 'I hear the party went off with a bang.'

'Fairest way of sharing a buffet I ever did see,' said Joe.

'You really OK?'

'Fine, apart from mousse stains all over my shirt. And I may have lost a jacket. How will I be for insurance?'

'If it's the one with the sickbag lining, you should pay them.'

'It's OK for rich lawyers with toyboys. Talking of which, is your friend Piers good for another favour? Or are you rationed to one a visit?'

'Don't push it, Sixsmith,' she said warningly.

'Sorry. Look, do you think Piers could find out why Kovalko was on that list?'

'I explained all that to you,' she said patiently. 'List "C" is the barely possibles, the ones who make up the numbers.'

'Yes, but there has to be a reason why he figures even as

a barely possible. This interest in him isn't official, by the way, I've found out that much.'

'Really?' she said. 'Sixsmith, you don't catch the service bus but somehow you still get there.'

'We all have our own methods,' said Joe. 'There was some official interest way back though. In the seventies. Be nice to know what that was all about.'

'I can't promise anything but I'll ask. You're obviously on a burn, Sixsmith. So how're you doing with old Kiss-the-girls?'

'Sorry?'

'Georgie Porgie pudden 'n' pie kissed the girls and made them cry. The Queen of Beacon Heights.'

'You really don't like that woman, do you?' said Joe.

'Don't tell me you've fallen in love with her?'

'No, but I haven't found out anything against her either.'

'Keep digging. I'm sure it's there. Take care, Sixsmith.'

Joe had been watching a shadow on the frosted door panel. As he replaced the phone it began to recede. He jumped up and hurried to open the door.

He'd been right. It was Beryl Boddington's sturdy/sexy back he saw receding towards the landing.

'Lost your nerve?' he called after her.

She turned and smiled and said, 'Hi, Joe. Just called to see you were OK. Mirabelle told me about the explosion up at Mr Woodbine's. 'Nother fine mess you got yourself into.'

Her attempt to be offhand didn't stop Joe feeling touched and flattered.

'Not my mess this time,' he said. 'Step inside and I'll tell you all about it.'

He made another pot of tea as he described the party. He kept the tone lightly comic but he didn't get many laughs.

Finally, exasperated, he said, 'You got that disapproving look. Why is that? I wasn't in any danger and none of this had anything to do with my job. I don't much like this disapproval game you and Aunt Mirabelle play, but at least you could stick to your own rules!'

With matching exasperation Beryl replied, 'Joe, you were at a party where your hostess *hey-boyed* you and your host *Uncle-Sammed* you, and an explosion blew a buffet lunch all over you, and why were you there? Was it because of your good looks and natural charm? Or because you can hit a right note three times in five? No, it was because you're a PI. You work in a sewer, you don't end up smelling of roses.'

'Yeah, but you always get a seat to yourself on the bus,' said Joe. 'And three out of five notes gets you a golden disc in hard rock. And finally, you are right, reason I was there had nothing to do with my looks or charm. It was entirely down to you.'

'How do you make that out?'

'You hadn't sent Butcher down to the station to bail me out that night, Willie would never have invited me. So just imagine how you'd feel if that oven had blown me up!'

Beryl appeared to be imagining this without too much distress and Joe felt quite relieved when there was a knock at the door. The relief faded when in reply to his, 'Come in!' the door opened to reveal Willie Woodbine.

'Just passing, Joe,' he said. 'Thought I'd look in and check you were OK. Oh, sorry. Didn't realize you were busy.'

'Just a social call,' said Beryl sweetly. 'Joe, I'll let you know how I imagine I'd have felt when I've had time to think about it, OK? Bye now.'

She was gone.

'Nice girl,' said Woodbine appreciatively.

'I think so,' said Joe. 'Like a cup of tea, er, Willie?' Might as well test whether they were on first name terms beyond the Sabbath.

'Greatly appreciated,' said Woodbine, sitting down. 'You had us worried yesterday, Joe, did you know that? Taking off without a word like that. When we started doing a head count and found we were short, well, you know how easy it is to think the worst.'

'Hey, I'm sorry, I didn't think, I mean, I thought someone would have seen . . .'

'No sweat, Joe. Someone had seen you going off with Dora Calverley. Soon as I heard that, I said, no blame for Joe!

Takes a stronger man than him to resist Dora when she gets a notion into her head.'

It occurred to Joe that as he and Woodbine had exchanged words in the ruined kitchen, all this about imagining the worst was a load of crap. So what was he really talking about?

Something to do with Dora Calverley, perhaps?

He said, 'Yeah, Mrs Calverley's a real toughie. Just who is she that everyone jumps?'

'It's mainly down to her, the kind of woman she is,' said Woodbine. 'But the name helps. The Calverleys used to be big. Fifty years ago they owned half the county. Lord lieutenants, that sort of thing. Dickie Calverley, Dora's husband, was just a distant cousin really, but when the mainstream of the family started drying up, they did a proper job. No money, no reputation, no kids. Dickie suddenly found himself heir to the only bit of the family estate which was entailed so that no one could touch it. He died out in Africa before he could enjoy it. It passed to Fred, his son, the last of the Calverleys, and he and his mother came back to live there a year ago. Word is that Dickie left nothing but a lot of debts back in Zimbabwe, so Dora's not exactly the rich widow.'

'Yeah, Hoot Hall looks pretty run down,' said Joe.

'You've been there?' said Woodbine sharply.

'Just for a sandwich,' said Joe. 'So if she's so poor and the family's skidded off the end of Skid Row, why's anyone pay any heed to the name?'

'Old habits die hard, Joe. There's plenty in Luton would still sacrifice a virgin on New Year's Eve if they could find one. And besides, as you so rightly observed, she's a toughie, she'd make people jump even if her name was Smith. But not even old Tin Can, who can get money out of a stone, has much hope of getting anything there, though he keeps on trying. Me, I'd be very chary about doing any work for her and not getting cash upfront. They've got a cavalier attitude to debt, the upper classes, 'specially to tradesmen.'

Joe thought uneasily of Mrs C.'s cheque for a hundred

pounds still nestling in his back pocket. She wouldn't dare bowl him a bouncer, would she?

'You're looking worried, Joe,' said Woodbine. 'Dora hasn't offered you a job, has she?'

His tone was vibrant with the warm sympathy of a concerned friend. But Joe knew as sure as taxes that this was what Willie Woodbine wanted to find out.

In the movies, your hard-boiled PI would have let him or herself be worked over with rubber truncheons before they broke client confidentiality. But Joe knew he bruised easily. And besides, Mrs C. hadn't exactly been reticent with Willie about her interest in the boy in the box.

Also, he couldn't get out of his mind the number scrawled on the boy's thumb. A real detective would want to test the cop's reaction.

Still, no harm in being diplomatic.

He said, 'Mrs C. thinks the Force may be too overstretched working on serious crime to have much time left over for unidentified dossers, so she's asked me to give a hand finding out who the kid at St Monkey's was.'

'I see,' said Woodbine, his expression neutral. 'And how do you propose doing that, Joe?'

'Don't know,' said Joe, playing helpless. 'Anyway, Willie, after what you said, don't think I'll be trying very hard till I see the colour of her money.'

'That's right, Joe,' said the policeman heartily. 'Don't move out of your class. Woman like Dora Calverley will have the shirt off your back without you feeling a draught.'

He finished the tea Joe had poured for him and stood up.

Joe said, 'Talking of shirts, I think I left my jacket in your garden.'

'Oh yes? Lot of stuff lying around. Always is when people get panicky. It'll all be stored safely. Just call round, Joe. My wife's taken the morning off school to supervise the workmen.'

This unsolicited opportunity of an encounter with Georgie Woodbine should have pleased Joe, but it didn't. Perhaps it showed, for Woodbine eyed him thoughtfully and said, 'I'll give her a ring, say you're coming, shall I?'

Does he want me round there? wondered Joe. If so, why?

He said, 'Thanks, er, Willie.'

'My pleasure, Joe. Private and public sectors should work hand in hand, isn't that what the chief said? Which reminds me, anything you turn up on this dead boy, you won't forget it's police business, Joe? Whether Dora coughs up cash or not, it's me you show it to first. You understand that?'

'I think I'm beginning to,' said Joe.

13

First things first.

Soon as Woodbine had left Joe headed round to the building society and went up to Gallie Hacker's window.

'You got something?' she asked hopefully.

It was early days to be telling her about Dunk Docherty, Joe decided.

'I'm working on it,' he said. 'Listen, Gallie, do me a favour. Cheque here I want to pay into my account but I'm not sure about it. Anyway, can you check it's kosher without it bouncing?'

'Hold on,' she said, noting the details. She vanished into a rear office and returned a few moments later smiling. 'Yes, that's fine,' she said.

'Good,' said Joe. 'I'll pay it in then. Hey, I enjoyed Saturday night. Sorry, I know it was work, what I mean is, I liked your mum and dad. And your granddad too. Nice people.'

Silly, he told himself as he left. Don't get too reassuring, Joe, not till you see how this thing's going to work out.

Slowly he drove up to Beacon Heights. Man whose life was full of problems didn't move too fast from one to another.

Being a top cop obviously got you service. All over Luton that morning there were probably householders scanning the empty streets anxiously for the sight of their promised glazier, painter, plasterer, joiner, or gas man. Vain were their hopes if the number of vans parked outside the Woodbine residence was anything to go on.

The front door was open and Joe followed a man with a large sheet of glass into the house. Here he found the craftsmen from the vans labouring like the slaves on Cheops pyramid under the pharaonic eye of Georgina Woodbine.

When she spotted Joe, the ill temper on her face heated up another ten degrees, then was almost instantaneously switched off.

'Mr Sixsmith,' she said. 'You've come for your jacket.'

'That's right,' said Joe. 'Did someone find it?'

'There was something, I think. It'll be in the utility room.'

She led him through the kitchen where activity increased a hundredfold on her appearance.

'Any structural damage?' enquired Joe.

'My father built to last,' she said as proudly as any stately home owner. 'You're in the Boyling Corner Choir, I believe?'

'That's right,' said Joe.

'A first-rate ensemble.'

The compliment was both marred and magnified by the faint note of surprise that underpinned it.

'You play in the Sinfonia, don't you?' said Joe. 'I'd not noticed . . . I mean, I don't pay much heed except to the conductor . . .'

'No need to apologize,' she said with a smile, as faint and as surprising as sunshine in a rainforest. 'I'm only a humble fiddler, easily missed.'

'I know what you mean, being in the chorus . . . but there'd not be a choir or an orchestra without us,' said Joe.

She didn't look too thrilled at this bit of unifying democracy. They had reached the unscathed utility room where a variety of articles were laid out across a dishwasher. Joe's jacket, folded so the lining showed, hit the gaze like a ripe tomato.

'There it is,' he said.

'And you really want it back?' she said.

'Yes, please.'

He picked it up and they retraced their steps. As they reached the entrance hall, Georgie Woodbine said, 'Would you care for a drink, Mr Sixsmith? Coffee is difficult till they sort out the kitchen but I can offer you a Scotch? Or a gin?'

'Thanks a lot, Scotch'ud be fine,' he said insincerely. He wasn't a spirits man, especially not at this time in the morning, but only a fool would miss a chance like this.

Or perhaps when it was so readily given, only a fool would accept it?

She led him into a spacious and elegantly furnished sitting room. As she poured the drinks she said, 'I do hope you and Dora got some lunch yesterday.'

'Oh yes,' he said. 'We went to Hoot Hall.'

'Hoot Hall. My my. It's years since I was there. I don't doubt one of Dora's kitchen staff managed to rustle you up something far superior to anything you'd have found in my little buffet.'

Like with the flowers yesterday, she was still playing her little games, thought Joe. She knew exactly the state of things up at Hoot Hall and was testing to see whether he'd contradict or go along with her.

'You haven't got some ginger ale I could put in this?' he said.

'Soda,' she said with distaste.

'That'll do,' he said. There was a delicate glass dish full of sugared almonds on the table in front of him. He slipped a couple into his mouth as she was squirting some soda into his whisky and was helping himself to another handful as she turned.

'I see you're not worried about heart attacks,' she observed.

Joe shrugged and said, 'Life's too short.'

She found this very funny, letting out a peal of spontaneous laughter, rising from some hitherto concealed warm centre which for the first time made Joe aware of her as a woman in the sexual as well as the social sense. She sat down on the sofa next to his armchair and curled her legs up under her.

Hello, thought Joe. It's buddy buddy time.

She said, 'Forgive my feminine curiosity, but I was wondering . . . no offence meant . . . what on earth it could be you and Dora Calverley had in common?'

Here we go again, thought Joe.

He said, 'I suppose it was music brought us together.'

'Really? I always thought she had a tin ear.'

This was how polite folk called you a liar.

Joe said, 'Maybe it was nostalgia then. All that time in Africa, maybe she just got homesick for a black face.'

Again the spontaneous laugh. Joe could feel himself being reassessed. Am I playing this wrong? he wondered. Often you got more out of folk when they rated you a dumbo.

Too late now. He said. 'When I was talking to, er, Edgar earlier, he was interested in me and Mrs C. too.'

'Really? Was he now?' she said thoughtfully. It came across as genuine, confirming what Joe had suspected. The Woodbines weren't working as a team. In fact, while he couldn't cite any objective evidence, it wouldn't surprise him if their marriage was a bit rocky.

So was she interested in his relations with Mrs C. on her own behalf or because Willie was interested?

As if reading his thoughts, she said, 'Forgive me, Mr Sixsmith. All these prying questions. I've been a schoolteacher too long.'

'Ready for a change then?'

'To what?'

'To grown-ups,' he suggested.

This set her laughing again. Thinks I'm a real comic turn, thought Joe. But at the same time he felt flattered at being able to provoke that rich deep laugh which registered on senses deeper than the ear . . .

Hey, watch it, man! This is Willie Woodbine's wife you're getting horny about, and could be she is a les anyway, so haul back!

She said, 'Yes, grown-ups would make a nice change, Mr Sixsmith. Perhaps you and I could be grown up together?'

The innuendo was unmistakable even if the tone was mocking. Any self-respecting hard-boiled gumshoe would have been on her like a flash, satisfying at a stroke his appetites and also his curiosity whether she was AC or DC.

Time to make an excuse and leave, thought Joe.

His mind seemed right out of excuses so he decided the simplest way was to be chucked out.

He said, 'Seems to me Mrs Calverley gets right up your nose. Like to tell me why?'

For a moment it looked like he'd succeeded. The body language changed, the back stiffened and the feet popped out from under the thighs and hit the carpeted floor with a thud.

Then she smiled and said, 'All right, Mr Sixsmith. We're both professional and maybe personal nosey parkers. Let's trade confidences. Deal?'

He said, 'Well, I'm not sure . . .'

'Don't play hard to get,' she said kindly. 'Not unless you don't want to be got. I'll start. Yes, you're quite right, I'm not overly fond of dear Dora, though it hasn't always been like that. Once we were very close. We were at school together, in fact. At Meegrims.'

Meegrims was Bedfordshire's poshest girls' boarding school, the kind of place that figured in the tabloids when minor league royalty went there, or pregnant pupils left.

Joe said, 'I'd have thought Mrs C. was a good bit older than you.'

She said, 'I see I'll need to watch you. In fact, there are only three years between us though since she let her skin dry up like an old Barbour, it looks more like ten.'

'But the age difference didn't stop you becoming friends?'

'Helped it, in a way. She was my House Fiend.'

'Sorry?'

'No, I'm sorry,' laughed the woman. 'Every new girl at Meegrims has an older girl appointed to look after her. She's called a House Friend.'

'Like what do you call it? Fagging?'

'In theory quite the reverse. The older girl is supposed to help the younger. But in practice, of course, it frequently descended to that level, which is why the "r" quickly disappeared.'

'And Mrs C. was fiendish, was she?'

'No,' admitted Georgie. 'Far from it. In fact, she helped me a great deal. I needed help too. I wasn't just a new girl, I was new money which made me particularly vulnerable.'

'Sorry,' said Joe. 'New money . . . ?'

She laughed again and said with an edge of malice, 'I'm glad to see that indifference to other people's problems isn't just the prerogative of the well to do. My grandfather established the family business and my father made it boom after the war. My brother and I were educated in the class to which the family could now afford to belong. Purchasing advantages, your red friends might call it. True, so long as you remember that advantages are often paid for with more than money. Parents dump a lot of lumber on their kids, don't they?'

Joe decided to ignore whatever 'ism' she'd committed by her crack about his friends' politics and said, 'You mean the kids who'd been rich longer got at you?'

'Certainly. You can't really blame them. Most of them were like me, away from home for the first time and scared to death, so naturally they looked around for someone to feel better off than. It gave them common ground with the others and provided a buffer between themselves and absolute misery.'

'You're very forgiving,' said Joe.

'I've paid in full for my advantages, haven't I?' she said, smiling wickedly. 'You don't think I'm going to undervalue them now?'

'And as a House Fiend, Mrs Calverley helped you out?'

'That's right. She saved me from a deal of grief.'

'I expect you were pretty grateful,' said Joe.

'I was madly in love with her,' said Georgie. 'Oh, don't look shocked. It doesn't do your PI image any good. You've heard of schoolgirl crushes, surely? Well, mine was the heaviest crush imaginable! I would have killed for her. And don't ask what I *did* do for her. Your dirty little male mind must devise its own fantasies. I'm not about to tell you.'

'I wasn't about to ask,' said Joe sturdily. 'In fact, I haven't asked you to tell me any of this, Mrs Woodbine.'

'You haven't?' She sounded genuinely surprised. 'No, I don't suppose you have, not in words, anyway. So why *am* I telling you? Oh, yes. So you will satisfy my idle curiosity about the nature of your business with Dora.'

She turned her wide-eyed mock innocent gaze upon him. Joe thought, idle curiosity my aunt!

He said, 'So how come you and Mrs C. stopped being such good chums?'

'What a nice old-fashioned word,' she said. 'But in fact we were never really *chums*. I was mad about her, true, but that's something different. Absolute passion either blows itself out, or is blown out by absolute betrayal. Such has been my experience anyway.'

Joe began to wonder if Willie had been putting it about. How come she'd ended up marrying Willie in the first place? How come, for that matter, with her well-off family and private education, she'd ended up as a teacher in a state comp?

And how come the most interesting questions were always those it was almost impossible to ask?

But you could get close. He said, 'This quarrel you had with her, what was that about then?'

She considered the question carefully, then shook her head.

'Perhaps you should ask Dora about that. Now it's your turn, Mr Sixsmith. What are you and she up to?'

He said, 'Sorry, can't say. But perhaps you should ask your husband. He knows all about it.'

He expected some kind of anger that he'd broken her one-sided deal, but she merely laughed her deep-draughted laugh and said, 'You detectives stick together, do you? I must remember that in future.'

She was definitely an odd one. But was it the kind of oddness that could lead to some kind of criminal interference with the kids in her care?

And what the shoot do I know about the way women work anyway? Joe asked himself as he made for the front door.

'It's been nice talking to you, Mr Sixsmith,' said Georgie. 'No doubt we shall meet again tomorrow evening.'

'What? Oh yes, right. Rehearsal. *The Creation*.'

'That's right. *The Creation*. Though if, as one imagines He must have done, the Almighty foresaw what we were going to do with it, can you suggest half a dozen good reasons why He bothered?'

The Glit . . . draught Guinness . . . Luton Town . . . breakfast fry-ups . . . Whitey . . . and . . . and . . . Beryl Boddington's body moving beneath her uniform.

'Beyond me, Mrs Woodbine,' said Joe Sixsmith.

14

Back in the car, Whitey let out a plaintive howl which reminded Joe they hadn't had a proper breakfast.

'I hear you,' said Joe.

It was lunchtime near enough, so he drove to the Glit. Merve Golightly was there drinking the Pepsi and lime which was his on-duty tipple, and eating a Glitterburger.

'Hey, Joe,' he called. 'What happened to you yesterday? When you didn't ring, I drove back to the pigs' party to pick you up anyway, and what do I find? Devastation, and you long gone. Now that's what I call suspicious.'

'I'm out on bail,' said Joe. 'How's the burger today?'

'Delicious. I think Dick's changed his kennels. Whitey, my man, how'd you like a piece of the enemy?'

He tossed the cat a morsel of burger. Whitey sniffed at it disdainfully, expressed his opinion by trying to cover it with floor tiles, then clawed at Joe's trousers till he got a packet of cheese and onion crisps and a saucer of lager.

'What about you, Joe?' asked Dick Hull.

'Well, I escaped with my life yesterday, so I'll ride my luck and have a double Sweenie and chips.'

The Sweenie Weenie was the Glit's famous savoury sausage.

'Ha, ha,' said Dick. 'Joe, my son, this *Creation* thing you're doing down St Monkey's, anything in that for our next Big Sho-Nite? Three or four of your mates from the chorus line came down and give us a couple of the snazziest numbers? There'd be a drink in it, and the publicity couldn't do your ticket sales any harm.'

'It's a kind thought, Dick,' said Joe gravely. 'I'll mention it at rehearsal tomorrow.'

Merv said, 'Don't be a prat, Dick. It's all hymns and such, ain't that right, Joe?'

'Nothing wrong with hymns,' said Hull. 'When old Stell Teacher from Gluck Street sings "Amazing Grace", there's not a dry eye in the house.'

'But lots of dry throats, you hope,' said Merv. 'Dick, while you're getting Joe's Sweenies, cut me a slice of rum 'n' plum gateau, will you?'

The manager moved away and Merv said, 'So what *did* happen up the Heights, Joe?'

Joe gave him the full story. Merv he counted as a sort of silent partner, though 'silent' wasn't a term many people would apply to the rangy taxi driver. But when it came to keeping his mouth shut about stuff Joe told him was confidential he could be quieter than a stopped clock.

When Mrs Calverley was mentioned he said, 'She the one lives out at Hoot Hall?'

'Yeah. You know her?'

'No, but I took the son home once, high as a house.'

'Fred? And you say he was drunk?'

'Well, he was high on something, though it could've been going up his nose as well as down his gullet, know what I mean? Talked a lot about mumsie and what she would say.'

'Scared of her, was he?'

'Wouldn't say that,' said Merv. 'I got the impression Fred knew she wouldn't be too pleased but was confident she wouldn't be able to resist his bonny blue eyes for long.'

This figured. Mrs C. might be tough with cops, vicars, PIs and houseboys, but when it came to sons, she folded like a pipe cleaner. And what had she given as her reason for wanting to identify the boy in the box? *Somehow he reminded me of my own boy* . . .

'Even a cop is somebody's son,' said Joe inconsequentially.

'Never believe it,' said Merv. 'Just a rumour the Pope's putting about. Word down the cabbies' shelter is, you do a job for Mrs C., get your money upfront.'

This echo of Woodbine's remark struck Joe.

He said, 'But the Calverley estate . . . ?'

'You been out there, you seen it,' said Merv. 'They were once rotten rich but the last lot knew how to spend it better than make it. Dickie Calverley, her husband, he wasn't mainstream family, but he had the knack, I gather. He had a job at the University, bit of a shafter by all accounts, lots of scandal brewing, then some ancient uncle pops his clogs and leaves him this farm out in the jungle . . . Rhodesia, I think it was . . .'

'Zimbabwe,' corrected Joe.

'Could have been,' agreed Merv. 'But the jungle anyway, so he ups and marries this Dora Strang and off they scoot to the mysterious Orient.'

'With geography like yours, how the shoot do you manage driving a cab?' wondered Joe.

'I charge extra for the scenic route,' said Merv. 'Anyway, all the Calverleys back here snuff it, and Dickie goes out in sympathy down there on the veldt, and young Fred cops everything that's left, which isn't much. Oh look. Here comes another hedgehog that didn't make it.'

Dick Hull had put his rum 'n' plum on the bar along with Joe's sausages.

They began to eat and into the silence necessitated by the superglue properties of the cream on the pudding and the Glittersauce on the Sweenies, Dick Hull said, 'She was in again last night, Joe, with her friends.'

'Who?' managed Joe.

'Galactic Galina, the Doll from Outer Space,' said Hull. 'Let's into the secret, Joe. You giving her one, or what?'

Before he could reply, the manager was summoned to the other end of the bar by a customer.

Merv said, 'Dirty-minded sod. But it's a good question.'

'You asking it?' said Joe.

'None of my damn business,' said Merv.

'In that case, I'll tell you,' said Joe.

Merv whistled when Joe finished.

'Sodding journalists,' he said indignantly. 'Always looking to dig dirt. But no problem now this Docherty's asked you to help him, is there?'

'How do you mean?'

'Easy. All you do is tell him he's barking up the wrong tree. Word of a pro sleuth. And if he doesn't buy that, then you fall back on little Gallie's scheme and give him a good kicking. You want some extra muscle, me and Percy are at your service.'

Joe smiled to himself. In a tight corner, Merv was no chicken, but he was better talking tough than acting it, relying on his own and Percy's great length to divert trouble to easier targets.

He said, 'Thanks, mate, but what Dunk Docherty thinks isn't really the point here.'

'Then what is?'

'What Gallie thinks. The poor kid needs to be really sure that her granddad's not a war criminal.'

Merv thought about this then said, 'But you said she got almost homicidal just because this newshound could even entertain the possibility . . .'

'Yeah. Think what that makes her feel about herself,' said Joe.

Merv shook his head.

'Joe, you sometimes worry me,' he said, 'this topsy-turvy way you see things. Why don't you just do what you get paid to do, always assuming you are getting paid. This girl wants you to find out who this guy is and what he's up to. You've done that. As a bonus you can maybe stop him doing it. Chances of her granddad being a war criminal are pretty slim. Chances of you proving it one way or another are non-existent. So forget what you imagine her feelings are. All that stuff was fifty years ago anyway. The old man will be dead in another ten, fifteen years, tops, maybe a lot earlier. When she's settled down with her own family, what's it going to matter to her what happened in some far-off foreign country a whole lifetime ago?'

'Like it or not, we're all what we come from, Merv,' said Joe.

'Well, shave my arse and call me Cheetah,' said Merv. 'The way you tell it, we're all born guilty, right?'

'That's what the Bible says,' said Joe. 'Least, that's what Aunt Mirabelle says the Bible says.'

'You tell Mirabelle she's way off beam,' said Merv. 'We're all born innocent. It's getting guilty that makes life worth bothering about. Hey, I gotta run. You take care, Joe. Don't get into any fights without me around.'

'It's all right, I'm going down Dextergate to wash my dirty linen in private,' said Joe.

'You mean, Long Liz at the Kwik Klene?' said Merv. 'Now that's a real woman. Forget your dolly birds. Long Liz'll tumbledry you so clean, you'll think you're a white man.'

'Does that mean I could join the golf club?'

'They'd be begging you.'

'Then I shan't bother,' said Joe.

15

Joe was very fond of the Kwik Klene launderette. If he was busy he just left his bundle in the care of the manageress, Mrs Elizabeth Pring, known to her friends as Long Liz, who for a consideration would sort it, wash it and have it all neatly parcelled for collection at the end of the day. But whenever possible Joe did his own. The launderette was to him like a church to a medieval felon. Here he could seek sanctuary and let his troubles drain away and feel his soul being cleansed with his socks.

Unfortunately, parking was bad in Dextergate which had more double yellows than a Bengal tiger. It was OK to leave the car for a quick dash in to dump your bundle, but anything longer would get you a twenty quid spot fine from one of Luton's incorruptible traffic wardens.

Happily, at the end of the eighties a hopeful developer had erected Wyatt House, a block of fairly swish apartments on some waste ground opposite the launderette, only to find when the property market went into a dive shortly afterwards, he was left with at least half the flats on his hands. This meant there was a surplus of parking spaces behind the block which, though technically private, were not guarded by any means as zealously as the Cloisters at St Monkey's.

After a quick check to make sure the Wyatt House janitor was nowhere in sight, Joe parked the Morris, then, with his bundle under one arm and Whitey under the other, he set off to the launderette.

As he walked along the narrow service road down the side of the apartment block, he thought he heard a footstep behind him. He turned just in time to see a figure step back into a doorway.

He called, 'Hey, don't I know you?'

After a moment, the figure reappeared and moved slowly towards him and he saw he'd been right.

He said, 'Mavis? It is Mavis, isn't it?'

He'd only seen the girl once and she had that sullen suspicious air which makes so many teenage kids look alike. But her long brown hair and also the Grandison comp uniform helped him identify her.

'Hello, Mr Sixsmith,' she said.

'Hi. What you doing round here? Long way from Grandison, isn't it?'

'I know,' she said.

He thought about this then said, 'I get it, you're bunking off from school so you want to be a long way away, right?'

He felt quite pleased with his deduction. She gave a half smile, perhaps in acknowledgement, and said, 'Yeah, I suppose so.'

Her eyes were fixed on Whitey. Joe said, 'You've not met my partner, have you? This is Whitey. Whitey, this is Mavis. Be nice to her. She's a client.'

The girl put out a tentative hand. Whitey eyed it, sniffed it, licked it, and closed his eyes.

'He likes you,' said Joe, meaning, he doesn't think you're edible.

'What are you doing here?' the girl suddenly demanded. 'Are you working?'

'No,' said Joe, surprised at the aggressive tone. Maybe she thinks I'm following her! 'I'm just on my way to do my laundry. Come and sit and talk a while, if you're in no hurry, that is.'

'Yeah, why not?' said Mavis.

Long Liz greeted Joe with a warm smile, until she realized Mavis was with him. A handsome if stately dame who admitted to forty-nine under subpoena, Liz felt pretty proprietorial about her unattached male customers. She hadn't been lucky with men, or they with her. At the moment she was between husbands, having just laid her fourth to rest in the boneyard.

Joe was on her shortlist. He naturally was blissfully ignorant of this, just as Liz was ignorant she didn't figure on any list of Aunt Mirabelle's. This wasn't because of either her age or track record. Truth was, a mature woman with plenty of experience of keeping men in order was just what the doctor ordered. But Mirabelle had a firm sense of proportion and no man should be expected to stand up before God's priest with a woman ten inches taller than he was!

'Can I hold the cat, Mr Sixsmith?' asked the girl as they sat down.

'You can try,' said Joe, placing Whitey on her knee.

He turned round twice to make himself comfortable then went back to sleep, while Long Liz, reassured by the formal address, retreated out of earshot.

'Hey, I met your dad yesterday,' he said, putting his clothes into a machine.

She didn't look overjoyed and he made a guess at the reason.

'No. I didn't mention you,' he said. 'It was just social.'

'You were at that cow's party, you mean?'

'That's right,' he said. She was looking at him with something like respect. Thinks I was there on her business, thought Joe. Well, so I was, in a manner of speaking.

'I met Sally Eaglesfield.'

'Yeah, she was off school this morning. Georgie too. Doesn't miss a chance to please herself.'

She spoke with great bitterness. Maybe she thinks Georgie and Sally are together, thought Joe.

'Mrs Woodbine did have her kitchen wrecked,' he pointed out. 'House is full of workmen. She certainly didn't look like she was enjoying herself when I was round there this morning.'

'You've seen her today?'

'Yes, this morning. And you'd have seen her this afternoon if you'd gone into school. She said she was going in.'

'You're sure she said that?'

'Yes, I'm sure,' said Joe, wondering if the girl feared Georgie's eagle eye would notice her absence. But surely someone would anyway?

'Thinks the place can't run without her,' sneered the girl, but without much force. 'This explosion, no one got hurt, then?'

'Didn't your dad tell you?'

'He just said something about an accident in the kitchen.'

Joe told her about the ruined buffet, keeping it light and comic. She laughed out loud, not so much at his comic style as in malicious pleasure at the thought of all Georgie's efforts going to waste. She and Butcher, they certainly both hated the woman, thought Joe.

He realized he'd never yet spoken directly to the girl about her allegations. It wasn't something he fancied doing, but it was always best to get things direct from the horse's mouth.

He said, 'Mavis, this thing that's bothering you, you are sure about it? I mean, OK, so you think something goes on at these out-of-school meetings. You ever actually been to one? What I'm saying is, you have any evidence from personal experience? Like, has Mrs Woodbine ever said anything to you or tried to touch you, anything like that . . . ?'

Like most of his forays into diplomacy, it failed miserably. The girl leapt to her feet, clutching Whitey to her breast.

'That's a filthy thing to say!' she screamed. 'Think I'd ever let that cow touch me? I'd rather roll in a cat tray!'

Whitey yelled in protest, both at the sudden movement and the implied insult. Long Liz and the other customers looked their way with lively interest.

'You must have a bigger cat than me,' said Joe, reaching out to stroke Whitey's head.

The fury vanished from the girl's face as quickly as it had come.

She said, 'I'm so sorry . . .'

She was speaking to the cat. Joe didn't mind. But he did mind having an audience.

He said, 'Look, let me give you a lift back home. School will be out soon.'

'What's the matter? Scared some randy bastard'll rape me round here?' she snapped.

'Not really,' said Joe truthfully. While a naked virgin with a bag of gold might have been ill advised to wander round

Dextergate after dark, it was a pretty respectable area during the day. 'Just think we should maybe sell tickets if we stay here.'

She took his point and said, 'OK. Thanks.'

He patted her avuncularly on the shoulder, then asked Long Liz to see his smalls through their final cycles. She agreed rather chillily. In her book, emotional girls needing comfort were definitely rivals.

On their way back to the car, Mavis kept looking nervously around her. Doesn't fancy being spotted by some friend of her parents wandering round with me during school hours, surmised Joe.

There was a large billboard on the side wall of Wyatt House advertising the alleged attractions of the flats. It had been there as long as Joe had been illegally parking there and he'd never paid it much heed before. But the name of the developers had never meant anything before.

'Hey, there's a thing,' he said.

'What?' said the girl.

'Oh, nothing. Just that they've knocked another two thou off the price. Keeps on like this, I'll be able to afford one early next century.'

For once, he'd thought before he spoke. What he thought was, it wouldn't contribute anything to the occasion to point out that Thomas Barnfather Estates Ltd was Georgina Woodbine's family firm.

In the car he asked, 'You rung Sally to see how she is?'

'I told you, we're not speaking.'

'If she'd been a bit nearer the kitchen when the oven blew, could be you'd never be speaking again,' said Joe.

She didn't respond. Joe tried to recall whether such a morbid appeal would have had any effect on him at her age, but he couldn't conjure up that distant country. Besides, he hadn't been a girl. This original thought made him smile. That stirred Mavis like his homespun philosophy hadn't been able to.

'What's so funny?' she demanded heatedly. 'I can't see anything to laugh at.'

'Shoot,' said Joe. 'When you're as antique as me,

117

sometimes you've just got to chuckle at having fooled the dear Lord into letting you live so long.'

'How old are you, anyway?' she asked.

'Let's just say I'm bumping up against the big four oh.'

'You're not forty yet?' she said in dismay. 'But my dad's in his thirties too . . .'

'I've been shut out of a lot of things in my time,' said Joe. 'Clubs, pubs, and even a taxi cab. But no one's ever tried to shut me out of a whole decade.'

She flushed and said, 'I'm sorry, I didn't mean to be rude.'

Joe said gently, 'I know you didn't, but sometimes we get things wrong without thinking. Maybe you've got it wrong about Mrs Woodbine . . .'

But immediately that stubborn unrelenting look was back on her face and she said, 'No! She's really evil. Someone's got to do something about her!'

Joe dropped her at the end of her street. No point in puzzling the neighbours. As she got out, she said, 'Maybe I will ring Sally.'

Joe said, 'Why not? If you only stay friends with folk who think exactly the same, you spend a lot of time sitting in front of the mirror.'

She nodded, placed Whitey carefully on the front seat, then strode away, tall and willowy, her long brown hair bouncing like on a shampoo ad.

As he drove away, Whitey gave a little derisive miaow which Joe had no difficulty in interpreting as, 'Ever think of writing mottoes for a calendar?'

'You so clever, how come you can't buy your own chips?' asked Joe.

Knowing his underwear was in good hands, he made for the office.

The phone rang as he entered. It was Dora Calverley.

'Just checking in to see if you've made any progress. Also, I've got an idea,' she said.

More than I have, thought Joe.

He said brightly, 'It's still early days, but I've got an associate working on it.'

Worldly wise ladies are not so easily fooled as teenage girls.

'An associate?' said Mrs Calverley incredulously. 'You mean, like that moggie you drag around with you?'

Joe looked at Whitey and hoped he hadn't overheard. He also thought that the cat and Dora Calverley had never met. She'd certainly checked him out pretty thoroughly.

He said as acidly as he could manage, 'No, I mean Mr Duncan Docherty of the *Bugle*. You may recall he did a piece a while back on homeless kids in Luton. He's got contacts it 'ud take me an age to make. And no need to worry about extra expense, he owes me a favour.'

That was a low shot, but she'd got to learn that the paddy fields stopped at Luton Airport.

She was a quick learner.

'Sorry,' she said. 'I didn't mean to be rude. That sounds good. This Mr Docherty, I know a couple of people on the *Bugle*, but I've not heard of him . . .'

No point in bulling her, thought Joe. She probably knew the editor!

He said, 'No, you won't have done. He's just a kid himself really, looking to make a name. That's what makes him ideal for this kind of job. He's the right age, knows all the moves, fits into the background.'

He didn't feel it necessary to add that Docherty's last attempt to fit into the background had cost him a busted nose.

'Well, that sounds excellent, Mr Sixsmith. Well done.'

'Thank you,' said Joe. 'You said something about having an idea yourself? I'm always open to suggestion.'

Having established his point, no reason not to be conciliatory. Also, it could be her idea might be more productive than the cocky but cack-handed Dunk Docherty.

'No, it was nothing really,' she said. 'I see you have things well in hand and don't need any interference from your client. Do keep in touch.'

The phone went dead. She took her bumps well, thought Joe. And there'd been just enough of a stress on *client* to put him in his undeniable place.

'Come on, Whitey. Let's go home and make us some tea,' said Joe.

He stopped by at the Kwik Klene. Long Liz had all his stuff ready

'Get your little friend home, did you?' she said, still frosty.

'What? Oh yeah. Is it my mistake or do kids today seem to have more troubles than we had?' said Joe.

'Maybe they don't have our kind of trouble so they've got to find their own,' said Liz. 'You got *real* trouble, you go looking for happiness.'

'Hey, I like that,' said Joe. Whitey was right. He did have a weakness for the greeting card school of philosophy.

He smiled at Long Liz. It was a frank open smile, marking a shared moment of mixed regret and relief that they were no longer kids. It hit the woman's chilly surface like a sun blast, melting her reservations and sending Joe soaring back up her list of possibles.

When he offered her the customary honorarium, she shook her head saying, 'That's OK, Joe. You can buy me a drink sometime.'

'My pleasure,' said Joe with instinctive courtesy, unaware that the gods sometimes use our pleasant virtues too for the manufacture of instruments to plague us.

'And mine, I'm sure,' smiled Long Liz.

16

That night Joe's sleep was troubled by dreams of Mavis Dalgety being chased by Georgie Woodbine round a large room at Hoot Hall where he was trying to sing a selection from the *Gary Glitter Song Book*, accompanied by Sally Eaglesfield on the clarinet while Mrs Calverley looked down from a minstrel's gallery and observed that this was not how they arranged things in Bulawayo.

He awoke feeling like a lost traveller who's not even sure he's looking at the right map.

Whitey, sensing his partner was out of sorts, watched hopefully as he prepared breakfast. But the fried bread, kidneys, tomato, sausage, scrambled egg and mushroom were divided seventy-thirty as usual and Joe's plate was wiped clean with a slice of Mother's Pride (thick cut). As Aunt Mirabelle had often reminded him in his young days, if you don't empty your plate for God, He'll surely empty it for you.

He decided to drop in at the Bullpat Square Law Centre. First thing in the morning you had a chance of beating the hordes of the distraught, the disadvantaged, and the dispossessed who put Butcher out of bounds during most of the working day.

Early as he was, the miasma of cheroot smoke hovering above her desk told him she'd been there a lot earlier.

'Sixsmith,' she said. 'Good to see you.'

'That's nice,' he said, flattered.

'Don't get carried away,' she said. 'I only mean it's good to see you because (a) you're not a customer and (b) I can tell you to sod off. As it happens, for once your incredible impatience can be rewarded. Piers happened to ring me yesterday. I put your point to him and he came back with an answer last night.'

'That's fast service,' said Joe. 'What you got on the guy? Headless photos?'

'Moral superiority,' said Butcher. 'Reason your Taras Kovalko appears in the frame is there was a Boris Kovalenko who got trained as an SS auxiliary, and ended up as a guard at Regensburg. Nothing further known.'

'And because Kovalenko's only a couple of letters more than Kovalko that was enough to set the dogs sniffing?' asked Joe incredulously.

'There's a bit more. If we're thinking fiddling identity cards, Boris isn't a million miles from Taras either. Also, they were both born in Vinnitsa. And Taras originally surfaced in a US Third Army field hospital when he got blown up in April 'forty-five as the Yanks advanced on, would you believe, Regensburg?'

'What happened then?'

'Displaced person camps, I suppose, till finally in 'forty-seven he got accepted to settle here.'

'There must have been some serious vetting done?' said Joe.

'What's serious when you're dealing with thousands?' said Butcher cynically. 'Taras's story was he'd been sent off to a forced labour camp by the Germans. Not much future in that, a hell of a lot of them died. But Taras was lucky. One of the German officers spotted he was a trainee chef and put him in the officers' kitchen, which explained why he was comparatively healthy when the Yanks found him, except for the shell splinters they'd pumped into him, of course.'

'Sounds reasonable,' said Joe. 'He's made his living as a chef since he came to England.'

'So? English cuisine back in the fifties, you didn't have to be Michelin guide standard to get by.'

'That so? I was still on Mammy's milk so I wouldn't know,' said Joe.

'Second time round, maybe,' said Butcher. 'To get back to your original question, back in the seventies when Wiesenthal's Nazi hunters were trawling their records to try to get a line on bastards like Ivan the Terrible, Boris Kovalenko's name came up. Nothing special against him, you understand, just the normal acts of brutality that went with the job of camp guard. It was circulated with a lot of others to all the countries he might have sought refuge in, including the UK.'

'And some bright civil servant thought Boris Kovalenko, Taras Kovalko, hello. Let's ruin someone's life.'

'Hey, it was across in Germany people's lives were ruined,' said Butcher. 'And it was probably a computer threw Taras up. You can see why. Name not dissimilar, picked up close to Regensburg, born in Vinnitsa . . .'

'This Vinnitsa place, it's what? Some kind of village? Pop. two hundred and fifty maybe?' said Joe.

'I think you know it's not, Joe,' said Butcher regarding him thoughtfully. 'You're not letting yourself get too involved here, are you? OK, so you'd prefer it if Taras gets a clean bill of health. But if he doesn't, it's not your problem.'

'I think maybe it is,' said Joe.

'You do? Well, so long as it doesn't cloud your judgement. OK, Vinnitsa has a population somewhere over a hundred thou, so it's not such a big coincidence. But worth a look, you must agree?'

'And they took a look and came up with nothing,' said Joe.

'You know about that? Then you'll understand how he came to be on List "C". It's like a query about your credit rating getting into the system. All a mistake but it's bloody hard to get out. How did you find out about the seventies check anyway?'

He told her about Dunk Docherty, just twisting things slightly to make it sound like he'd tracked the reporter down rather than just found him on his doorstep. Not that there was anything to be ashamed of in having a talent for finding things on your doorstep, but even from Butcher you got more credit for the conventional skills.

'You've done well,' she said, a faint surprise in her tone slightly compromising the compliment. 'So all you've got to do now is persuade him he's barking up the wrong tree.'

'That's right,' he said.

His tone must have lacked conviction for Butcher went on, 'Word of advice. When in doubt, follow the client's instructions to the letter.'

'Like a lawyer?' he said.

'That's right. Which reminds me, that's what I am and that's why I'm here at this ungodly hour. Good to see you, Sixsmith. Now sod off!'

'Wait,' said Joe. 'It wasn't Kovalko I came to see you about. It was Mavis Dalgety.'

He described his encounter in Dextergate.

Butcher frowned and said, 'You think she was following you or something?'

'She'd have had to run fast. I was in the car, remember? But it was an interesting coincidence. Look, I'm wondering if there's not something going on here I don't understand. I've met Georgie Woodbine now, and to be honest I just can't see her doing, well, whatever it is she's supposed to have done!'

'So Mavis is making the whole thing up because she's jealous?'

'Could be.'

'Yes. And it could be you're running scared because dear old Georgina is Willie Woodbine's wife!'

'No,' he said indignantly. 'It's like this Kovalenko business, it's easier to chuck mud than wipe it off.'

'It's completely different,' she said. 'All the big guns are on Georgie's side. She can take care of herself, you'd better believe it.'

She spoke with what seemed unwarranted force, or so it appeared to Joe.

He said, 'Why do I get the impression you know the lady personally?'

'Oh, we've met. A long time ago.'

Suddenly he grinned his sunrise grin.

'Hey, this fancy school you try to pretend you didn't go to, it wasn't Meegrims, was it?'

He saw he'd hit the mark.

'She's a lot older than you though,' he added diplomatically.

It occurred to him he'd had this kind of conversation with Georgie herself the previous morning.

'She was in the Fifth when I started,' said Butcher.

'So you'd not know her that well?'

'Well enough,' said Butcher rather grimly.

'She wasn't your House Fiend, was she?'

Suddenly Butcher was regarding him with deep suspicion.

'What the hell do you know about House Fiends?'

There was nothing to do but explain.

'Well, well. You do get into odd corners without trying, don't you?' murmured Butcher. 'So Dora Strang was Georgie's Fiend.'

'You know her too?'

'Just by reputation. She'd left before I started. Tough cookie by all accounts.'

'But a good House Fiend to Georgie, though this didn't have a knock-on effect, right?'

'What makes you say that?'

'Because I get a distinct impression you dislike her so much, you'd be willing to believe it if Maggie Thatcher bad-mouthed her!'

He couldn't hide his satisfaction at having got back at her so quick for the crack about letting himself be influenced by fear of Willie Woodbine.

She said, 'I don't deny that my experience of her when I was eleven and she was sixteen doesn't disincline me to believe Mavis Dalgety.'

This was real lawyer-speak. Time to cut the crap.

'So what happened?' demanded Joe. 'Look, we told all the dirty jokes and read all the dirty magazines at Robco Engineering. But I'm not sure this qualifies me for Girls' Own stuff.'

'Sorry, Joe. Nothing happened, or not much, not with me anyway. Nearest I can get personally is that once she offered me the choice of three across the knuckles with the edge of a ruler or one across my bare bum with the flat of her hand.'

'She could do that?' said Joe, appalled.

'Not officially. But like any closed institution, its own laws and conventions had developed over the years.'

'So what did you choose?'

Butcher made a face as if the question offended, then said, 'Naturally, I chose to tell her that if she touched me in any way, I would write to my MP. Also, I took the occasion to inform here I was opting out of the House Fiend system, and in future if she wanted her errands run, her toast buttered, or her knickers rinsed through, she could do it herself.'

'Butcher, you're something else,' said Joe shaking his head in wonderment. 'You were born knowing things I'll never find out!'

'We're all born knowing them,' she said quietly. 'It's finding out you know them that takes some folk a long time.'

'With luck maybe I'll miss out then,' he grinned. 'But all this must've been twenty years back. Bit early to get a lifetime judgement, wasn't it?'

'We've met since. When I was in the Sixth Form, she was at South Beds Uni. By this time I was pretty active in the local Party . . .'

'That'd be the Social Democrats?' said Joe, poker-faced.

'Wash your mouth out,' she said. 'Suddenly Georgie Barnfather was among us, claiming she'd seen the Socialist light on the road to Henley, and, like most new converts, she was extreme to her extremities. Everyone was delighted. Except me. I knew we had to recruit supporters through right reason, and whatever it was that was priming Georgie's pump, it wasn't reason. She kept it up for a good year, even got herself a nice working-class boyfriend. At least we all thought he was nice till someone discovered he was a trainee cop on day release to SBU for what was laughingly called civics.'

'Willie Woodbine.'

'That's right. Looking back, I sometimes wonder if she picked a cop deliberately so she'd have an excuse to quarrel with us.'

'That's a bit devious,' protested Joe.

'Par for the course with Georgie, as you may find out. The other thing about her is she never admitted a mistake. Her parents didn't reckon they'd put her through university to take up with a beat bobbie, so naturally she went the whole hog to disoblige them and married him. And when she realized just what a mistake that was, she didn't run home to mummy but set about prodding Willie up the ladder to the point where people would say, "Didn't she do well!" I speak from hearsay, of course, and may be doing her an injustice.'

She offered the disclaimer with little conviction.

Joe said, 'No, that's more or less what Mrs C. said . . .'

'Your friend Mrs Calverley?' Butcher laughed. 'Yes, must be a relief to her it all worked out.'

Joe considered this then said, 'Sorry?'

'Hey, Sixsmith, don't disappoint me. I've just got over being impressed how much you'd found out about Georgie and Mrs C. Don't say you've missed the big connection?'

Bluff it out? thought Joe. No. He didn't have the face for it.

He said, 'Worth missing just for the pleasure it gives my friends.'

'That's not bad,' she approved. 'I almost feel a rat. So here's the story. Hearsay again, of course, but good reliable ears. There was this guy worked in the Uni's Geography Department. Second rater academically – got the job through family influence, they reckon – but a real charmer, one of the old unreconstructed school of lecturers who believed academic freedom started at their students' pubes. Am I shocking you, Sixsmith?'

'Making me wish I'd worked at my "O" levels,' said Joe. 'So this guy was putting it around. Go on.'

'Lots of near scandals, and really his whole career was on the blink. What he needed was a good woman to make an honest man out of him, and he got Georgie Barnfather. She thought he was going to marry her. Maybe he was. But two things happened. First was he came into property, some kind of farm out in Zimbabwe. Second was, Georgie introduced him to her old House Fiend, Dora Strang. It didn't take long. Dickie Calverley – you'd guessed, of course – and Dora took off for Africa, getting married *en route*. Probably seemed a better bet to work the farm than sell it. When you're deep in crap, a wise man gets up and walks away!'

'Shoot! Poor old Georgie,' said Joe.

'You are the weirdest fellow, Sixsmith,' said Butcher in exasperation. 'Look, all that happened to her was she got rid of a lousy piece of goods, and she found her soul mate, PC Willie Woodbine, now Mr Big Tusk of the Gaberdine Swine.'

'She was hurt enough to join your Red Army on the rebound,' retorted Joe.

'True. Her big gesture of defiance against the upper classes!' sneered Butcher. 'Though naturally in her account of things, her conversion was a cause not an effect of her break up with Dickie Calverley. But why am I wasting my precious pre-work work hours educating you? Go, go, go!'

'Hey, you volunteered all this stuff,' protested Joe. 'What you haven't done is answer my question, what do I do about Mavis Dalgety?'

'What you do best, Joe. Forget the great detective stuff and follow your heart down the yellow brick road. You'll find it starts right outside my office.'

He turned at the door to shoot a parting arrow, but she was already reimmersed in a fog of cheroot smoke and a sea of other people's troubles.

One thing's for sure, he thought. We're neither of us in Kansas.

And he closed the door very softly.

17

Down at the office, nothing stirred.

It wasn't that he didn't have plenty of work on hand, just that he couldn't see how to proceed in any particular instance. Still, what was it Mirabelle said? No use fussing over what you can't fix.

Which, it occurred to him, was just another way of putting this negative 'ity' thing Rev. Pot said he had.

Pleased to feel his indolence confirmed by two such divine authorities, he made himself a cup of tea, gave Whitey a couple of his favourite anchovy olives and turned to his newspapers.

It was good to learn that peace and goodwill must have broken out all over the world. Why else would his tabloid's lead story be ENGLAND STAR SAYS SACKED MANAGER PUT PEPPER IN MY JOCK-STRAP. Pausing only to view with an astronomer's silent awe the mighty orbs floating across Page Three, he checked the sports pages for mention of Luton, then turned with a sigh of anticipatory pleasure to *The Times* crossword puzzle.

His technique here, Butcher had once suggested, had much in common with his detective method in that he wrote in his own solutions then made up clues to fit them.

He did well this morning, filling in two thirds of the grid before he joined Whitey in a purring sleep which would probably have borne them happily to lunchtime if the phone hadn't rung.

It was Dunk Docherty.

'Joe, hi. I think I may be on to something. I put the word out on the street I was interested in the boy in the box and

I've just had a call here at the office. No name, they're very cagey these kids, like wild animals, move too suddenly and they're off into the bushes.'

Could wild animals be cagey? wondered Joe.

'Just shows how lucky I am to know someone who knows how to treat them,' he said.

'That's right,' said Dunk complacently. 'This guy reckons he might know the guy who found the laddie in the box, I mean before you found him. He says if the price is right he could be willing to poke around and see if there was anything lifted from the kid's body.'

'And you believe him?'

'You don't get far in the news business disbelieving people,' said Dunk. 'Could even be this is the guy who robbed the body just being ultra careful, and of course upping the price.'

'More likely to be some chancer after an easy buck,' said Joe cynically. 'Talking of which, this price you keep mentioning . . .'

'Nothing's for nothing, Joe. These kids don't do social work, they've got social workers to do that. I mentioned a pony, he wants fifty, I said, hasn't he heard the Government's got inflation under control, he said those wankers at the Treasury should tell it to the dealers.'

'He sounds bright. Also a hop-head. He could be dangerous.'

'I can take care of myself,' said Docherty with more confidence than a man with a busted nose ought to have. 'But the money, Joe. Will your client cough up?'

'Yeah. Maybe. What did you tell him?'

'I told him to ring me back later and I'd see what I could do. If he's serious he'll come back, if not, no harm done. It never pays to be too eager with these guys.'

This was slightly more reassuring. Perhaps Docherty wasn't completely dumb.

Joe said, 'I'll check about the money. If he rings back tell him it's OK and set up a meet. Preferably somewhere full of light and people.'

'This isn't Chicago, or even Glasgow,' laughed Docherty.

'Assuming your client says go ahead, when can I meet you to pick up the cash?'

'Can't you manage fifty quid yourself?' said Joe.

'I'm not handing over my own hard-earned dosh then claiming a refund,' said Docherty firmly. 'Hell, this isn't even a story, just a private deal. Which reminds me, how's your side of things coming?'

Joe had to think hard to remind himself what he'd promised to do.

'It's coming along,' he said. 'I've made contact with the Hacker family, but getting their confidence will take time. Listen, tonight I'm tied up early part of the evening, but you can catch me in the Glit after say nine.'

'The Glit? That's where the weirdos go, isn't it? Never been there myself. First time for everything, eh? See you, Joe.'

Joe put down the phone, grinning. There was something about Docherty's brash self-confidence he couldn't help liking. Perhaps the fact that he hadn't yet got it quite right and the uncertain young lad, eager to make his way, kept on showing through. What was it he'd said? *You don't get far disbelieving people!* Well, he was going to find out the hard way, thought Joe rather guiltily.

He picked up the phone again and dialled Hoot Hall.

'Yes,' said a languid male voice.

'Hello,' said Joe. 'Is that Fred?'

'It could be. And is that Sheerluck Bones, the ethnic snoop?'

How come he recognizes me so easy? thought Joe. And do I have to take this sneery crap from a racist kid?

'Is your mother in?' he started to ask, but before he got the words completely out, there was a sound on the line, then Mrs Calverley's voice saying, 'Mr Sixsmith? Sorry about that. How can I help you?'

He told her about Docherty's lead.

'Yes, of course, pay the man. As long as he produces something for the money. Can you take it out of the advance I gave you and I'll settle up when we meet?'

I'd rather have the extra fifty in my hand, thought Joe. But he didn't know how to say it.

'Sure,' he said. 'I'll let you know how we go on.'

'Soon as you can, Mr Sixsmith,' she said imperiously.

The only other thing to disturb this nice quiet day was a call from Aunt Mirabelle to remind Joe of that night's choir practice and to say she wouldn't need the lift which Joe hadn't offered to give, because she was going straight to St Monkey's from visiting a friend in town.

'And Joseph, don't you come rushing in late with your mouth still greasy from all them chips you eat. Can't expect to sing properly unless you're rested and digested. Lots of folk saying, what's Boyling Corner doing with St Monkey's Chorale when the Anglicans got so many other choirs of their own? We got to show them we're there because we're the best. Only one more rehearsal after this, and that's the dress rehearsal. Which reminds me, what you going to wear?'

'My suit of course, Auntie,' said Joe.

'Suit? Not *that* suit? I need to talk to you about this. I'll see you tonight!'

The phone went dead.

'Shoot, Whitey,' said Joe. 'I'm not going to shell out for new clothes when I got a lot of work to do on the Morris!'

'Easy to be brave by yourself,' yawned the cat. 'I'll wait till tonight!'

Whitey was right, of course. At least he'd start on the right foot by following Mirabelle's other advice, thought Joe. He played his tape of *The Creation* and sang a few of the trickier choral sections. He skipped lunch altogether, much to Whitey's disgust, and he went home early, had a slice of ham and some salad, got his head down for an hour, rose and showered, and set off to St Monkey's feeling ready to deal with anything Haydn or Mr Perfect could throw at him.

Naturally, because God loves a joke, the rehearsal came close to disaster.

At first it was the instrumentalists who were in trouble. They couldn't get the orchestral intro to anywhere near Godfrey Parfitt's satisfaction. He was not nicknamed Mr Perfect for nothing, and as he had quite a nice line in abuse, to start with the singers were happy enough to relax and enjoy the not unpleasant spectacle of someone else getting a bollocking.

'This music is meant to depict chaos,' Mr Perfect cried. 'But that is not the same as sounding chaotic. While I am not so sanguine as to expect you to adhere slavishly to the precise notes that Herr Haydn inscribed on the staves, I would be grateful if you could at least keep your variations within the same key!'

This was good stuff, but eventually the choristers grew bored, with the inevitable result that when their turn to perform arrived, their turn to be abused was not far behind.

'Haydn wrote this music for angels,' declared the conductor. 'He left the howling of cats to Mr Lloyd Webber. For *heaven*'s sake, even if you find it hard to rise above your human condition, at least try to avoid sinking beneath it!'

After an hour he declared a break. Musicians and singers mingled, united by a common resentment. Joe spotted Sally Eaglesfield and made his way to her side.

'Hi,' he said. 'How're you feeling?'

She looked at him, puzzled for a second, then recognition dawned.

'Oh hello, it was you at Georgie's – Mrs Woodbine's – wasn't it? I never got to thank you.'

'That's OK. I'm just glad you weren't damaged.'

'I was a bit shook up,' she admitted. 'I've not been back to school yet, but I didn't want to miss the rehearsal.'

'Maybe you wish you had now,' grinned Joe.

The girl smiled back and said, 'Mr Parfitt isn't in a very good mood, is he? But he's got cause. We were playing awful. At least I know I was.'

'And we haven't been singing so hot either,' said Joe, impressed by her honesty.

'Can anyone join this mutual denigration society?' said Georgina Woodbine. 'Sally, my dear, how are you? You look very pale. I really think you might have been wise to miss the rehearsal as well as school.'

To Joe it sounded like genuine if rather schoolma'amish concern, but Sally took it very differently.

'Why? You going to report me then?' she said sharply, almost insolently.

The woman looked disconcerted and glanced at Joe as if to ask him what he had been saying. Joe gave a little shrug.

'Don't be silly, my dear,' said Georgina, trying for a lightness. 'That explosion was a shock to all of us. I took a morning off myself . . .'

'A whole morning?' mocked the girl. 'I bet things fell apart.'

Before the woman could respond, Mr Perfect rattled his baton on his music stand and called, 'Places, please!'

Musing on this interesting exchange, Joe was heading back to the baritones when Beryl's voice said, 'Cutting me dead, Joe?'

He realized he'd walked right by her.

'Sorry,' he said. 'I was thinking about something. The music.'

'Oh yes. The music,' she said, smiling her disbelief. 'And here's me thinking you must be solving the Bermuda Triangle mystery at the very least.'

'Working on it,' he said. 'You on duty tonight?'

She wasn't wearing her uniform.

'Time off for good behaviour,' she said.

'Fancy a drink down the Glit?' he asked.

'Don't know if that would count as good behaviour,' she said. 'Better get back to our places before Mr Perfect sends out the dogs.'

She headed back to the sopranos, leaving Joe unsure whether he'd got a yes or a no.

Things went slightly better for a while and they got through the creation of fish, fowl and the animal kingdom with no more than a few volcanic rumblings. But when they reached the third and final part of the oratorio, where Adam and Eve and the chorus express their joy and gratitude for the gift of life, Mr Perfect's discontent finally exploded.

'No, no, no, no!' he cried. 'This is Eden before the Fall, not the North Stand after a Luton goal! This is a world in which everything is fresh and new, where hope is unnecessary because you have certainty, where even the beasts of the jungle are vegetarian and Adam and Eve don't have belly buttons because they were created, not born. I want you to take your voices and your instruments and scrub out of them everything you know, and everything you are, and everything you've ever done; then sing and play with what remains. Go back to childhood first, but even that's not far enough for the kind of innocence we are dealing with here. Our parents have stamped their sins upon us and the very first breath we breathe is of polluted air. Go further till you glimpse that immortal sea which brought us here, then cross it till you hear its mighty waters rolling on the further shore. Can you do that for me? Will you do that for me? I believe you can. I beg you to try!'

He raised his baton. They started to sing. Something happened, Joe wasn't sure what. But there were moments during the next half hour when he felt he was as close to getting back into the lost Garden as he was ever likely to be.

Mr Perfect thought so too. He put his baton down, smiled gently and said, 'Thank you, ladies and gentlemen. Thank you very much.'

It was a subdued breaking up with little of the usual post-rehearsal hustle and bustle. Even Mirabelle's grip upon Joe's arm was more salad tongs than nutcracker.

'Going to give your old aunt a lift home?' she said.

'Car's parked at the Glit, Auntie,' said Joe. 'Thought I might call in for a little refreshment.'

'You visiting that hellhole after making music like we made tonight?' she demanded indignantly.

'Ready to buy me that drink now, Joe?' said Beryl with the perfect timing of the eavesdropper.

Mirabelle looked from one to the other, clearly torn between moral objections and matchmaking objectives. It was no contest.

'You two children enjoy yourselves,' she said. 'Rev. Pot will take me home on his pillion.'

And she hadn't even mentioned the suit, thought Joe as he and Beryl hurried out of the church.

Just ahead of them Georgina Woodbine was walking alongside Sally Eaglesfield, holding her arm and talking earnestly into her ear. The girl suddenly pulled away, shouted, 'No! I don't believe you any more. Keep away from me!' and ran away down the side of the church where Joe had found the boy in the box. Georgie stared after her, then, as if feeling Joe's gaze, she slowly turned her head to look at him. It was not a friendly look. Then she strode away, presumably to the Cloisters car park.

'Don't think you've much chance of playing an air on her G-string,' said Beryl judiciously. 'Mrs Woodbine, isn't it?'

'That's right. And I hope you ain't thinking of bringing your nurses' home humour into the Glit.'

'Too subtle, huh? So what've you been doing to rattle the lady's cage?'

'Don't know,' said Joe.

'Maybe she thinks you blew up her kitchen,' said Beryl.

'No. We got on OK when I called for my jacket. I mean, at least she was polite. It was only after she saw me talking to Sally . . .'

'That the girl with the clarinet? Tell you what, Joe. If I were a detective, and I could prove that child had been anywhere near Mrs Woodbine's kitchen before the bang, I'd have her straight in the padded room for questioning.'

Joe said, 'But she was . . . I mean, why should she . . . ?'

Beryl laughed and said, 'Don't take me so seriously, Joe. And try to remember, we're both off duty, right? So let's get down to the hellhole and start enjoying ourselves!'

18

The Glit was pretty full for a Tuesday and they stood at the bar while they looked around for a seat.

'There you are, Joe,' said Dick Hull, pushing a pint of Guinness at him. 'Saw you come in. Thirsty work this singing, eh? You in the choir too, miss?'

'Yes,' said Beryl. 'And it's thirsty work for us sopranos too. I'll have a lager till my friend comes out of his trance.'

'Sorry,' said Joe. 'I was just going to ask. Hello, Gallie.'

It had been the sight of the girl's approach which distracted him. She was wearing an outsize Save the Whale T-shirt, with a dog chain round the waist to make it a mini. Her legs were pale and skinny and slightly knock-kneed and her make-up would probably have won prizes in a geisha house. But to Joe, his mind still echoing with Haydn's joyous rhythms, her outrageousness was only the shocking freshness of Spring.

'Can I have a quick word?' she said.

Joe glanced uneasily at Beryl, who gave him an old-fashioned look.

'Back in a mo,' he said.

Galina led him to a corner where her gang had kept the usual pair of seats. Locking one of his legs firmly between her bony knees, she leaned forward and said, 'Grandda says he's resigning from the club.'

'What? Why? Is this because of the other night?'

'He won't say. I'm so worried about him, Mr Sixsmith. If I could lay my hands on the bastard who started all this, I'd tear his balls off!'

Her vehemence didn't fool Joe. This was a bright kid and

if Joe, on the strength of one encounter, had got a sense that old Taras wasn't acting like an innocent man, how much more strongly must she have felt the same thing?

He said, 'Look, try not to worry. I think I'm getting somewhere and I think we can make this whole thing go away. Old folk don't like upsets, that's all it is. Couple of weeks and things could be back to normal.'

His concern for Galina had made him offer more reassurance than was his to give. It was a trap his concern to ease pain often laid for him and he'd trained himself to be nimble enough to steer clear of it. But with her eyes desperately seeking succour at a range of less than six inches, it was hard to count consequences.

He sat up straight and pushed his chair back a foot.

'I know you're doing your best,' she said without conviction. 'I think someone wants you at the bar.'

Beryl, he thought guiltily. But when he turned he saw that she was deep in conversation with Dick Hull. His gaze moved along the bar, and suddenly he found himself looking at the smiling face of Dunk Docherty. What the hell had he been thinking of, saying he could be contacted here? Worse, as he watched, the young reporter slid off his stool and started moving towards them. He thought of bluffing it out. But if his abacus mind could add up Dunk's job, description, and swollen nose to make the mysterious investigator, the girl's hi-tech calculus would have no problem getting there.

He turned back to her and said urgently, 'Gallie, I've found out who it is asking all these questions. He's a reporter on the *Bugle*, and I think we can control him, but the thing is, this is him approaching, so please, stay cool, play him along, OK? If you make a fuss it'll only make things worse. *OK*?'

There was no time to get the reassurance he'd have liked. Docherty was at his side, smiling broadly and saying, 'Hi, Joe. Now I see what brings you here. All this lovely talent. I must get in more often.'

He was wearing stonewashed jeans and a sandwashed silk shirt in a repulsive shade of puce. He looked like a teenage kid up from the country determined to show he knew his way around. Gallie's friends were viewing him with the jaw-dropping horror of the first guy to see the vampire in an old Dracula movie while the girl herself looked ready to sink her teeth in his jugular.

Joe said heartily, 'Dunk, nice to see you. Gallie, meet an old friend of mine. This is Dunk Docherty, ace reporter on the *Bugle*. Dunk, this is Gallie *Hacker*.'

'Hacker?' repeated Dunk, puzzled. Then light dawned and he said, 'Oh, *Hacker*.'

He didn't quite give Joe a thumbs-up, but his *nice-one* smile was like a neon ad. He perched on the edge of the table, causing the gang to grab their drinks with exaggerated concern.

'Hey, sorry, fellas. It's a wee bittie crowded here,' said Docherty flashing an all-boys-together smile which provoked them to an unprecedented articulacy.

'What's he on about?'

'Want a wee, piss off to the bog.'

'You a foreigner or wha'?'

'No, he's a doughnut. Dunk the doughnut!'

This pinnacle of wit left them all dizzy with laughter.

Joe stood up, seized the young reporter by the arm, said, 'Need a word. See you later, Gallie,' and led him forcibly to the bar.

'What the shoot do you want?' he demanded.

'You said I could contact you here about the dosh,' protested Dunk. 'Also, I've had another tickle.'

'You what?'

'Someone else rang, said they'd heard I was asking about the boy in the box and she had info.'

'She?'

'Yeah, you know. A girl. A wee hairie. I've fixed up for you to meet her.'

'Me? Why can't you meet her yourself?'

'Because the first guy rang back and I'd fixed up a meet with him already. It's OK about the dosh, is it?'

He counted fifty into Dunk's hand. All around him, eyes looked the other way. Think I'm making a score, groaned Joe inwardly. Bang goes my reputation.

'And here's something for you,' said Docherty.

It was a photocopy of a photo of the boy in the box's face. Joe supposed some attempt had been made to liven it up, but the *Bugle*'s editor had been right. No way this face was anything but dead.

'I've been passing a few of these around the drop-outs,' said Dunk. 'The girl saw one, says she recognized him.'

'From where? When?' asked Joe.

'That's what she'll tell you when you show up tonight.'

'*If* I show up,' said Joe grimly. 'You could have arranged to meet her some other time, couldn't you?'

'Yeah, I know,' said Docherty a trifle shamefaced. 'Sorry.'

Joe was on to him. He said, 'You thought, why should I be doing all the work when there's no guarantee this guy's going to come through for me? Right?'

'Joe, if I'd known what a fast mover you were . . . how'd you get a line so quick on the Hacker chick anyway?'

'Trade secret,' said Joe curtly. 'So when are these meets?'

'Half an hour. But you'll need to start moving soon. Yours is down the Scratchings . . .'

'The Scratchings?' said Joe aghast. 'You've fixed for me to go wandering round the Scratchings at dead of night?'

'I thought you PIs were indomitable.'

'I'm domited, you'd better believe it,' said Joe grimly. 'And where's your meet?'

'St Monkey's boneyard, which ain't no picnic either,' protested Dunk.

'It's a garden party by comparison,' said Joe.

'Yeah. Look I'm sorry, Joe. If you don't want to go, then just scrub it. This chick who phoned, to tell the truth she sounded a bit Waldorf, know what I mean?'

'Waldorf?' said Joe.

'Off the wall,' said Dunk. 'Probably just desperate to score and got the notion this was an easy way of making a buck. So forget it. If she rings again, I'll go.'

Joe considered then said, 'No, I'll go. You've been to so much trouble to fix for me to meet with a possibly desperate druggie in the Scratchings after dark, it'd be a professional discourtesy not to turn up. How'll I know her?'

'I described you and that old banger of yours, so she'll find

140

you,' assured Dunk. 'I'll just get myself another beer before I hit the road. Contact you later at home to cross check?'

'I'll give you my number.'

'Don't worry, I got it,' grinned the youngster. 'The *Bugle* knows everything.'

'You mean I'm on file?'

'Yeah, it's a big blueish one. It's called the phone book. See you, Joe.'

He turned to the bar and Joe went to rejoin Beryl.

'Hi, Joe,' she said. 'You still here? Dick was just telling me about this idea you and him have cooked up for some of us to come down from the choir one night, do a trailer for *The Creation*. Why've I not heard about it? Not trying to cut me out, are you?'

'No, of course not. I mean, it's just an idea, I mean it's not even an idea, it's one of Dick's crazy notions . . .'

'Joe thinks you're too good for us,' said Dick Hull.

'Joe, is that right? That sounds downright elitist to me. But he's right in one way, Dick. We *are* good, we've won prizes, you know about that?'

'That's what I need,' assured Hull. 'A class act for a class venue.'

'You say so? Well, as you'll know with your showbiz experience, Dick, you've got to pay for class. So what kind of fee had you and Joe come up with?'

'Now hold on,' said Dick anxiously.

Joe, who knew from experience that Beryl was capable of keeping him and Dick and another two or three fellows besides spinning in the air till they didn't know their asses from their elbows, cut in quick, 'Beryl, I've got to go now. Business. Sorry.'

'That's OK. Business has got to come first. What business in particular tonight, Joe? Saving whales, is it? No, sorry. I see the safety of whales is in someone else's hands.'

Joe followed her gaze. To his horror he saw that Galina had joined Dunk Docherty at the bar.

'Oh shoot!' he said.

'Don't take it to heart, Joe,' said Beryl kindly. 'Whatever goes around comes around, and I'm sure your friend goes around quite a lot. Now, Dick, we were talking money. Here's the way I see it . . .'

When the whole world turns against you, anywhere dark and lonely can seem like a refuge. Even the Luton Scratchings.

With a deep sigh, and unnoticed by more than half a dozen pairs of eyes, Joe turned and left.

19

The *Lost Traveller's Guide*'s sole reference to the Scratchings is sinisterly brief.

> *If, having strayed into Luton, your efforts to regain the right road lead you into an area of dust, decay and derelict brick kilns called the Scratchings, then you are lost indeed.*

It might be assumed that the name derives from the excavation of the local plum-red clay from the many uncapped pits which add to the area's perils. But in a paper read to the Luton Archaeological Society by Rev. Pot who was an amateur of such matters, it had been pointed out that the first recorded form of the name, in agricultural records long preceding the brick industry's workings, was *Scratches Ings*. Scratch, or more commonly Old Scratch, being a popular agnomen for the devil, and this area being damp, low lying, and frequently aswirl with sinister and misleading mists, Rev. Pot theorized it was more than likely that the superstitious locals should have named it the Devil's Meadows.

Joe had been present at the meeting, hijacked there by the irresistible will of Aunt Mirabelle as part of a Boyling Corner Chapel claque. He had found Rev. Pot's paper even more boring than his sermons, but that had been in the fusty lecture hall of the old library where the Archy. Soc. held their meetings. Now, as he turned off the narrow metalled road and began to creep down the even narrower rutted and pot-holed track which led to the old workings, boredom was not a factor. Alongside the superstitious fear roused by memory of the pastor's paper there was the plain physical fear caused by his awareness that when the drop-out elements in Luton society could drop no further, the Scratchings was where they usually ended up.

The track levelled off and widened. In the headlights he could see the tumbledown buildings wreathed with mist like mistletoe on dead oak trees. He stopped the car, but kept the headlights on and the engine running and he made sure the doors were locked. The place looked completely deserted but he knew better. Places like this were never unoccupied. Forget Rev. Pot's devil, forget the casualties of the way we lived now. Any place where people had once worked, day in, day out, for enough years to leave a mark on their individual lives had something stamped in it which not even the reclamative powers of nature could totally erase. He felt it most strongly, of course, whenever he went near the empty buildings which had once housed Robco Engineering. There his own personal memories were the key. Here it was the memories of all those long gone under, who had once centred their often short lives and certainly little hopes on this place, that trailed around his mind like the mist around the buildings, seeking a purchase and a shape. He felt this deeply. Blood sympathy, Butcher had once called it, meaning he didn't know exactly what, except that maybe it was having it that kept him sure he was in the right business even when everything – and everyone – else said different.

There was a tapping at the window. He jumped so violently that had he been any bigger he'd have bumped his head on the roof. 'Shoot!' he said, angry that his preoccupation with the dead had made him forget the living. He was lucky it was only a knuckle that was coming in contact with the misting glass, not a coal hammer.

He wiped away the condensation of his breath and saw a woman's face, so emaciated it looked like the flesh had been painted on the skull with a watercolourist's brush. She could have been anything from sixteen to sixty.

He wound down the window a space too small to permit even the skinniest finger to get a purchase.

'You the one wants to know about the dead kid?' she asked.

144

'Yeah. You knew him?'

'No.'

'Know his name?'

'Maybe.'

You don't know much then,' he said.

'More than you, dickhead,' she snarled. 'So what're you paying?'

Joe considered. It was the denial of personal acquaintance that made up his mind. If she'd got nothing to sell, she could have made up a whole genealogy to con him.

He said, 'Ten, if it's any good.'

'Sod off. I need twenty, I've gotta have twenty.'

No difficulty in guessing what she needed it for. The need meant he shouldn't have much problem haggling her down to ten or even less. But that was like those bastards who got themselves laid for a packet of fags after the war, any war.

He said, 'OK, twenty.'

He opened his wallet, took out a note and slipped it through the crack in the window.

'This is only ten!'

'You get the other ten when you tell,' he said, showing her a second note.

'How do I know you'll give it me?'

There was something so childishly plaintive in her question that the upper parameter of her age plummeted.

'How old are you, dear?' he said gently.

'What's it to you?' she snarled.

Fourteen, fifteen, he guessed. Perhaps, God help us, younger. He wanted to tell her to get in the car, he'd take her home or if she didn't want to go home, he'd take her somewhere they'd look after her. But he knew that if he wanted to make her run, the biggest threat was kindness.

But he couldn't stop himself asking, 'Why do you do this stuff, dear? It's screwing up your life. Why do you do it?'

It was a really pathetic question, pointless to ask, impossible perhaps to answer. But surprisingly she gave him one.

'Because it makes me feel like you bastards say I ought to feel!' she screamed. 'Now do I get that other ten or what?'

'You got something to tell me, you'll get it,' he said, pushing a corner of the note through the crack. 'So talk.'

'I only saw him once but I recognized his face from the photo.'

'Where'd you see him?'

'Down the Uni.'

'The University? What were you doing there?'

'What's up? Think I'm not fucking bright enough?'

'Not old enough, maybe.'

'I'm as good as any of them wankers!' she yelled.

'I'm sure you are,' Joe assured her. 'So what were you doing there?'

'There's a lot of stuff gets moved down there, know what I mean? And them stupid gits sometimes leave it lying around if you can get into their rooms.'

Shoot, thought Joe. The weak preying on the weak, the lost on the lost.

'Was he a student then, this boy?'

'Naw. He wasn't one of them. More like me, just hanging around. I asked him if he'd had any luck.'

'What did he say?'

'Said he had some speed, nothing else. He gave me a tablet. Didn't help much but it was better than nothing.'

'Did he tell you his name?'

'Said to call him Rob or Robbie, didn't matter which.'

'And was he there like you, trying to score?'

'No, he was after something else. He went in asking questions but no one paid any heed and they just told him to leave.'

'What kind of questions?'

'I don't know. Something about his parents. He said they were students here. Or his father was. Or his mother. I don't know. Parents are stupid. Who gives a fuck about parents? Can I have the money?'

'In a moment,' said Joe. 'What else did he say? Where else did you go?'

'Nowhere. We went nowhere. He said nothing. I mean, look, you're not the filth are you?'

'Do I look like the filth?' asked Joe.

146

'You tell me, they all look alike,' she said illogically. 'Listen, he broke in. Not me. Him. I told him it was stupid.'

'That was very moral of you,' said Joe.

'Moral shite. I told him if he was going to break in, hit the student rooms or the med. centre. But he went into the offices. Jesus, I thought at least he might get his hands on some money or something we could flog. But when he came out . . .'

'You waited?' said Joe.

'He asked me to keep watch, said he'd help me out. All he had was some stupid telephone number scribbled on his hand. That was all. And me he gave another lousy tab of speed. I asked him what the fuck use that was and he told me it was all he had but he was expecting some cash soon . . .'

'Where from?' asked Joe.

'I don't know. From his parents, I think.'

'But you said he was trying to trace his parents, didn't you?'

'Did I? I don't know. I don't know anything. Let me have the other ten, fuck you, fuck you, fuck you, let me have it, you black bastard!'

She was pulling desperately at the corner of the note with her fingernails but all she managed to do was tear a small corner off.

Equally desperately, Joe was seeking for all the questions he was going to regret not asking later.

'Where was he going next? Where did you leave him? Did he tell you where he came from? What did he sound like?'

But she was almost hysterical now, beating at the window with her small fists.

'Please, please, please, I gotta have it . . . He spoke sort of funny . . . he asked about the Heights . . . Please, I've got to have it, I gotta go, you gotta go, *please*!'

It was past bearing. He pushed the note through. She grabbed it, pulled it from his fingers, turned and ran.

And at the very same moment, the passenger window

exploded behind him, showering his head with flying glass.

He twisted round, then jerked his head backwards to avoid the iron bar being driven at his face. The man holding it had bright mad eyes above a black beard through whose tangles jagged teeth glinted as he grinned in delight at the terror he was causing. Another man had his hand in the car feeling for the door lock. Behind them, Joe could see a couple more.

Consciously or unconsciously the girl had done a great job of holding his attention while this lot crept up, he thought bitterly.

Fortunately, the two prongs of the attack were getting in each other's way, with the man trying to open the door interfering with the man wanting to put a hole in his head with the iron bar, and vice versa.

Fortunately also, as often happened, Joe's limbs were way ahead of his mind. His hand had crashed the gear lever home and his foot was standing on the accelerator leaving the would-be door opener sprawling on the ground. But the guy with the bar had flung himself forward through the smashed window. Joe took his left hand off the wheel and grabbed at the bar as it came swinging at his head. His mind, which was so much better at problem stating than problem solving, was pointing out that if he wanted to survive he had to (a) get this car turned round and heading the other way, and (b) stop this bastard from smashing his head in. Trouble was, both problems required two hands and his full attention to solve.

He was among the derelict buildings now, on the road to nowhere except a water-filled clay pit. For some reason his left hand had released the iron bar and gone to the control panel. He hoped it knew what it was doing. The sudden removal of resistance had the temporary good effect of sending the bar swinging over his head to crash against the roof. But this left the back of his head vulnerable to the return swing. And about sixty yards ahead, in the beam of the headlights he could see the sharp curve of darkness which marked the edge of the pit.

Old Scratch was waiting down there, indifferent to whether he got the good, the bad or the undecided, so long as he got someone. Time to forget the man with the beard and concentrate on driving the car. Time to show all those exhibitionist kids on the no-go estates that he'd learnt about handbrake turns while they were still hijacking each other's perambulators.

He grabbed the brake and spun the wheel. The car began to whip round, only this was no hard metalled road but rough clayey ground, greasy with the mists of autumn. He felt the beginnings of a skid which could only have one end, unless the Almighty lent a helping hand.

The iron bar crashed into the back of his head. For a second the night sky lit up with jags of lightning, then all was dark again. There was pain, but it was bearable. Perhaps the man with the beard had suddenly reasoned that in a situation like this, the last thing you wanted was an unconscious driver. Whatever the reason, the blow had reminded his left hand that it had another job to do besides hauling on the handbrake. It let go. The car was now sliding sideways towards the brim of the pit. The left hand meanwhile was grabbing the cigar lighter which a moment earlier it had pressed in. Now it pulled it out and thrust the glowing element against the bearded man's long pointed nose. He screamed and jerked back with the lighter still wedged there. At the same moment the car side-swiped a low protective fence placed around the pit by the Council or by God. The wire screamed against the door panel. The posts bent and cracked. But finally, miraculously, the car shivered to a halt.

The man didn't. Out he popped into the darkness of the night, his scream fading away till it terminated in a loud splash and a tiny sizzle.

Joe hoped he could swim or that despite his many obvious unattractive traits he'd made some friends, though he doubted if many of the dark shapes running down the track towards him purposed to plunge in and haul their fellow attacker out.

The engine had stalled. Joe couldn't blame it. Instead, he sent out little waves of confident affection and turned the key. It coughed, groaned, and caught. With a silent prayer of thanks to God and Lord Nuffield, Joe swung the wheel over and sent the marvellous old machine roaring up the track towards the golden glow which marked the civilized world of Luton. Right and left the figures scattered. Left and right fists and voices were raised in angry threat. But Joe was up the track and away.

20

When he got into his flat the phone was ringing but it stopped as he closed the door. He was glad of that. He didn't feel that the link between his tongue and his mind was quite in working order at the moment.

He had left the Morris with the keys in by the pavement far below. He hadn't been able to look at the damage inflicted down at the Scratchings. Perhaps by morning someone would have stolen the car. All he wanted to do now was collapse into bed and sleep for a year.

Pausing only to unplug the telephone and drag his outermost garments off, he fell on to the bed, disturbing Whitey who was in there already.

'Move over,' groaned Joe. And closed his eyes.

When he opened them again it was daylight. He didn't feel any better. He tried to sit up but his head felt it weighed a ton.

It was only when he put his hand up to it that he realized where the extra weight came from. The pillow had somehow got stuck to the back of his skull. He prised it loose, very painfully. It was brown with congealed blood.

The doorbell was ringing. He answered it still clutching the pillow.

It was Dunk Docherty.

'What happened to the car?' he said. 'Oh holy Jesus, what happened to you?'

Joe didn't want to go to hospital but he found he had neither the strength to resist nor the voice to protest and with commendable alacrity, Dunk had him in his tiny Fiat and down at Casualty where the mere sight of Joe's ghastly appearance got him to the head of the queue.

Half an hour later, he found himself cleaned, injected, bandaged and back in bed again, this time in hospital.

'But I'm fine,' he claimed in his returning voice.

'You've lost a great deal of blood, your head was full of glass splinters, and you may have a fractured skull,' retorted the sister. 'At the very least, you have a severe concussion. Now would you kindly leave?'

This last was to Dunk Docherty who had been hovering anxiously during all these ministrations.

'Aye, now I see he's in such good hands,' said the reporter with a charming smile which clearly warmed the nurse all the way through. 'Joe, I'll be back. I've got to do a wedding, would you believe? But great news about last night. I think you'll be pleased.'

'What? What?' asked Joe.

'Out, out!' insisted the nurse, driving Dunk before her.

Joe didn't mind too much. He wasn't feeling well enough yet to give even good news the attention it deserved, a condition he confirmed by being sick when they told him his skull wasn't fractured. But by early afternoon he felt able to give brief audience to a steady stream of would-be visitors.

Beryl Boddington possibly initiated the recovery when she gave him a kiss which had his body sending faint signals that there might be life in the old dog yet. She neither questioned nor reproved him but went off willingly to feed Whitey. Then Mirabelle came and compensated for the lack of reproof and questions from Beryl. Then Gallie Hacker appeared in her building society mode.

'How did you know I was in here?' asked Joe.

'That reporter told me.'

'Dunk? Gallie, you didn't say anything to him . . . ?'

'About Grandda? No, of course not. But he tried chatting me up last night so I thought I'd go along with it, and we went off in his car round to St Monkey's of all places. He was very mysterious so I pretended to be impressed. And then we went down to Headbutts and discoed for a while . . . He's dead full of himself, isn't he? And he rang me today to try to make a date and he told me about you being in here, so I asked if I could come round in my tea break. Are you all right?'

'Fine,' said Joe. 'Now you head back and look after my money, will you?'

Next came Willie Woodbine.

'Joe, just heard the news. Anything we should know about?'

'No,' said Joe with the utmost sincerity. 'Just a bit of a shunt in the car. No other vehicle involved.'

'And you didn't want to hang around in case one of our bright young things made you blow in a bag, is that it?'

Maybe you hope that's it, thought Joe.

'Yes, that's it,' he said. 'Mrs Woodbine OK?'

'Fine,' said Woodbine. 'She'll be sorry to hear about you, Joe.'

I doubt it, thought Joe.

In between visits Joe had a lot of time to think. Interestingly, his concussed brain, in its efforts to get things back in their proper order, still kept on slipping up, except that sometimes the new disorder, with B coming after C instead of before it, seemed to make more sense.

When Merv Golightly came visiting late afternoon, Joe brushed aside his expressions of concern.

'You want to help me, there's something you can do,' he said. 'You know Wyatt House?'

'Aye, Dextergate? Fancy flats, lousy tippers. Yeah, I know it.'

'Then here's what I want.' He handed Merv a piece of paper. 'Find out if there's anyone got a flat there of that description. That's the name but he may not be using it. And be subtle, Merv. Tell the janitor you've been called out, or maybe this guy left something in your cab. Don't just ask!'

'Hey, I've watched all the movies,' said Merv, who not too secretly reckoned he'd make a much better Eye than Joe. 'So shut your face, Merv's on the case!'

Perhaps this hadn't been such a good idea, thought Joe as he watched the long taxi driver stride purposefully away.

Then Merv was erased from his mind by the return of Dunk Docherty.

'Joe, you look so much better,' he said. 'I thought this morning, the poor wee soul looks set to cash his coupons.'

'Less of the poor wee soul,' said Joe. 'You said you got something last night.'

'Aye, did I,' said Dunk, his face aglow with delight. 'Jackpot. Your troubles are over. I tried to ring you last night but I got no answer. Then I had to see that wee lassie home.'

'Via Headbutts, I gather,' said Joe sourly. 'What the shoot you playing at, Dunk? No, never mind. Let me see what you got.'

With an air of triumph too childlike to be offensive, Docherty reached into his inner pocket and with a flourish pulled out three objects which he placed on the counterpane in front of Joe.

'One wallet, empty,' he said. 'One letter, full. And, best of all, one passport, Australian. You owe me twenty, by the way. Passport cost me the fifty. But when he mentioned the letter and the wallet, I thought I should have them too. Good value, I think you'll agree.'

'I'll be the judge of that,' said Joe.

But one look at the passport told him Dunk hadn't been ripped off. Travel, and growing up, and hardship, and a habit, and of course death had taken the boy in the box a long way from this fresh-faced youngster smiling out of the passport picture, but it was clearly the same kid.

He was, had been, Robert Vicary, of Melbourne, Australia, brown eyes, fair hair, no distinguishing marks, and he had died two days before his twentieth birthday.

Immigration stamps showed he'd come to England the slow way: Thailand, India, Turkey, Italy, France, Holland, docking at Harwich last month.

The letter was addressed to Robbie Vicary, c/o the D.U. Club, Earls Court Terrace, London SW5. It was from his mother, writing from the same Melbourne address that figured on the passport.

Dear Robbie,

*Here's the money you asked for. Hope it's enough, and there'll
be some more coming on your birthday. But I hope you'll ring
again before then and for God's sake, don't let yourself be cut off
this time. Transfer the charge. No problem about getting
Malcolm, he's in the States for a couple of months. It's a good
breathing space for us both. There was so much anger flying
around when it all came out, and I know that to you it all seems
black and white, a divorce would solve most things, but life's not
so simple and Malcolm's got rights too. Also there's something else
I should have told you. I would have done on the phone, only
we got cut off. Please ring so we can talk things through. Better
still come home so we can talk face to face. It's really important.
I know I've managed to get everything wrong. You do what you
think best then later it all falls in on you. I don't want this to
happen to you too, so please ring. Please.
With all my love to you.*

Mum.

He put the letter down and examined the wallet. It was
soft expensive leather with the initials R.V. gold-stamped in
one corner. It was empty as Joe's mind.

'So what do you think, Joe?' said Dunk, eager as a puppy
for praise.

'You've done well,' said Joe. 'You'll get the extra twenty.'

'No sweat. Tomorrow will do,' grinned the boy. 'Now I've
got to scoot. I've got a date.'

'Not with Gallie Hacker?'

'Yeah, that's right. How'd you guess?'

'But why?' pleaded Joe.

'Beneath all that warpaint, she's a sweet kid, Joe,' said
Dunk reprovingly. 'I like her fine.'

'And that makes it OK? You're trying to prove her grandfather's a Nazi war criminal, remember?'

'Yeah,' said the youth, a look of concern momentarily
clouding his face. Then it cleared and he smiled and said,
'But not tonight I'm not! See you, Joe!'

Joe watched him go then returned his attention to the

letter, passport and wallet. They required an effort of concentration which in his present condition was beyond him. Better to sleep on it – in fact, on them. He pushed the items under his pillow but before he could compose himself to slumber, Dora Calverley came hurrying down the ward, her face and voice filled with concern. 'Mr Sixsmith, I tried to get in touch with you to find out how things were working out with this possible contact, then I heard you were in here. How are you? I hope to heaven this had nothing to do with our business? If so, I want you to forget all about it. It's certainly not worth running physical risks for.'

'No, it was just a stupid car accident,' he heard himself lying.

In fact, her concern touched him deeply and he almost reached under the pillow for Dunk's trophies. But if he did that, besides confirming that she was indirectly responsible for his damage, her next reaction would probably be to wave the passport triumphantly in Willie Woodbine's face. Joe was uncertain of many things but one thing he knew beyond doubt. No way did he want the Woodbines brought into this till his suspicions, not to mention his legs, felt a lot stronger! At the moment he had nothing but a phone number he wasn't sure of and which had probably been washed off the boy's hand by now anyway, plus the ramblings of a junkie.

Though there was something else. His mind which was once more shuffling images like a kaleidoscope had superimposed Georgie Woodbine's kitchen calendar on top of the girl in the Scratchings. *Said to call him Robbie or Rob*, the girl was crying. While behind her on the calendar there glowed the mysterious entry which he'd read as *Rob Vicar*.

'Are you all right, Mr Sixsmith?' said Mrs C. anxiously. 'Shall I call a nurse?'

'No, I'm fine,' he said, closing his eyes. 'Just a bit tired.'

'Then I'll leave you. Take care.'

He was a better actor than he thought. When he opened his eyes again to check that she'd gone, he saw from the clock on the ward wall that nearly two hours had passed.

It came to him that he felt much better and that all that

156

was wanted to complete his recovery was a good night's sleep in his own bed followed by the full English.

He swung his legs out of bed and put his feet on the floor. For a second everything swam round, then as quickly settled back into place. He tried a couple of experimental steps.

'Mr Sixsmith, what on earth are you doing?'

It was Sister, looking very stern.

'Going home,' he said. 'Can I have my clothes, please?'

'Don't be silly. We're keeping you in overnight.'

'Look,' said Joe reasonably. 'I haven't broken anything, right? And Town have a home match tonight. So come closing time, win or lose, Casualty will be crowded and they'll be ringing up here, begging for beds. Here's mine. You don't even have to pay me for it.'

'But you can't just go. How will you get home? There's no ambulance available . . .'

Over her shoulder Joe saw Merv Golightly come into the ward.

'It's OK, Sister,' he said. 'I got a taxi waiting.'

21

Despite its proximity, Joe tried to avoid London. Even a small fish could swim around Luton and never be far from other small fish he recognized, but stepping off the train at St Pancras was like falling off an ocean liner.

His flat, which someone (Beryl? Mirabelle?) had thoroughly cleaned, had performed the anticipated therapy. Whitey had acted a bit pissed off, though it was clear he'd been very well fed. And his own bed had wrapped itself around him like a mother's embrace.

Not that he'd been permitted to sleep without hearing Merv's news.

'Joe, you were spot on. Guy fitting that description to a "t" got a first-floor flat on the front. Calls himself Alan Douglas, claims he's a writer who needs somewhere he can come and work away from the kids from time to time. Turns up two, three times a week maybe. Sometimes spends the night, but not often. Oh, and here's a nice bit, janitor reckons he got a good deal on the rent 'cos he did the deal through the boss's sister!'

'That's great, Merv,' said Joe. 'You remember you were saying how much you admire Long Liz? How'd you like to spend some time in her flat?'

That had all been arranged satisfactorily. And by ten o'clock Joe was submerged in a sleep deep and dark as a barrel of Guinness from which he didn't surface till eight the following morning.

The full English completed the cure and by nine Joe was driving to the station.

He'd winced when he saw the Morris. Merv had had the

broken window replaced but the damaged bodywork was going to need major surgery.

He'd left a thoroughly disgruntled Whitey on guard in the flat and a note on the door saying he was fine and had gone out on business. It would not keep the female flak from flying but at least it might stop them from calling out the police search squads.

Not that a police search squad wouldn't have been useful in London. Even with his old *A to Z* he managed to get lost twice before he finally found Earls Court Terrace.

The D.U. Club's portals looked sinister enough to be the entrance to the UK centre of the White Slave trade, which ought to have been reassuring but wasn't. D.U., as he'd guessed, stood for Down Under, though a team of graffiti artists had other ideas, the least offensive of which was Diggers' Urinal.

He pushed open the flaking door and found himself in a dim vestibule smelling of joss sticks. A young man was sitting behind a reception desk.

'Help you, mate?' he said.

'It's about some mail,' said Joe.

'Name?'

'Vicary. Robert Vicary.'

The young man turned to a bank of pigeon holes behind him and after sorting through a bunch of envelopes extracted one fairly large one.

'Not resident, are you?'

'No.'

'Got ID?'

'Sort of,' said Joe, producing the passport.

The man looked at the picture and said mildly, 'Been lying in the sun, have you?'

'It's not me,' said Joe.

'You're shitting me,' said the man in mock amazement.

'I'm a private investigator,' said Joe.

'Don't entitle you to someone else's mail,' said the man.

'Robert Vicary's dead,' said Joe. 'There was a letter from his mother in his things, addressed c/o here. I've just been hired to tidy things up around him and I thought I'd better check if there was anything else. No need for me to take it though. I'll notify the police and they'll make it official.'

It was, like most of his lies, as near the truth as he could keep without actually telling it.

As he'd hoped, mention of the police did the trick. Young folk today regarded the cops like old folk regarded doctors. Once you started messing with those jokers, they hated to let you go without sticking something on you.

'You might as well take it, but you'll have to sign.'

He produced a dog-eared ledger in which he wrote the date and *one letter addressed Rob Vicary, received by* . . .

He looked at Joe queryingly.

'Sixsmith. Joe Sixsmith.'

J. Sixsmith, he wrote. 'Sign here.'

Joe turned the ledger round. The page was crowded with dates and signatures.

'You get a lot of mail,' he said.

'Yeah. Folk come from Oz not knowing where they'll be staying, they say, write care of the D.U. Got to be so many, we had to have a system to stop people just walking in and helping themselves.'

'So what exactly is this place?'

'Started as a water hole in the basement, then sort of expanded upwards to take in a few rooms to let.'

'So people live here permanently?'

'You gotta be joking,' laughed the man. 'It's a stop over till you find somewhere better which, to tell the truth, isn't all that difficult. Why? You're not looking for somewhere for the night?'

'No thanks,' said Joe. What he was doing was passing the time while he ran his eye back over the name column. There it was, *Rob Vicary* again, presumably the letter from his mother . . . except the date . . .

'That'll be one pound,' said the man.

'Eh?'

'We have to make a charge,' said the young man defensively. 'Cover our overheads. You OK?'

'Yes, I'm fine,' said Joe, still staring fixedly at the ledger. He handed over the money and took the envelope.

'Hey, this is sealed up with Sellotape,' he said suspiciously.

'Some folk believe in belt and braces,' said the man. 'Or maybe Customs had a little poke around to check no one back home was sending a few grams of happy dust. It happens. Are you sure you're OK?'

'No,' said Joe returning his attention to the ledger. 'I think I'm having delusions. There's another letter for Robert Vicary recorded as being collected back here.'

He pointed.

'Yeah. So what? You said you got on to us 'cos his mother wrote him here. That must have been her letter.'

'I don't think so,' said Joe. 'Or at least I hope not. You see, this one was collected four days after the poor sod died.'

A little later he sat in a pub and sought clarification in a pint of stout. It wasn't Guinness but another brew which the barman assured him was very popular, presumably with people who liked their stout to taste like Guinness diluted with ten per cent ditchwater. It certainly muddied his mind considerably.

The receptionist at the D.U. had been unable to help him much. If someone came in with some form of ID which stood a cursory examination, chances were they'd get the mail. He'd checked back till he found Vicary's signature acknowledging receipt of presumably his mother's letter. The forged scrawl wasn't a million miles away.

So what did it all mean? Joe shrugged. No use drowning in what you couldn't fathom. Time for that thing Rev. Pot had gone on about. Negative capability. Perhaps the envelope would contain a clue. He took his penknife out and carefully sliced through the Sellotape.

What it contained was a letter with a fancy heading declaring it was from the Melbourne law firm of Greenhill, Travers & Pearce. It was dated three weeks after the letter from the boy's mother.

Dear Mr Vicary,
I hope that before you get this, you may have tried to contact home and so received the tragic news I have to impart in a less

161

impersonal manner. In a letter, there is no kinder way than the most direct. I regret to tell you that your mother has died in hospital during the course of major surgery for cancer. It is not clear to me how much she had confided to you about her condition, but I gather from her physicians that the critical point was accelerated by the emotional distress she suffered as a result of yet another piece of tragic news. Your stepfather was involved in a car accident on his way to San Francisco airport and died a week later of his injuries. Your mother insisted on travelling to be by his bedside and she returned from the trip in such a weakened condition that her doctors advised that immediate surgery was necessary.

I deeply regret having been the bearer of such unhappy news. I am sending copies of this letter to all points at which there is a chance you may pick it up. On receipt please either contact me at the above number or take this letter along to your nearest Australian Embassy where I will make arrangements for money to be made available to fly you home. This is not the place to go into business details, but you should be aware that on your stepfather's death, the great proportion of his considerable estate passed to your mother and thence to you, so there is no reason to let any financial consideration delay your return by even an hour.

With deepest regrets.

Yours sincerely,
Jeremy Greenhill.

When he'd finished reading, Joe sat for a long while just staring into his glass. Sometimes the world seemed such a randomly shitty place, you didn't know why you bothered. Where was the point in getting your mind all snarled up over one lost life, when with a weary indifference God could kick any number of others into touch on a mere whim?

Maybe the way to look at it, God's the enemy and I'm a member of the Resistance, thought Joe.

Keep on fighting. Good old Winnie's across the Channel and he'll never give in!

Two Australians were talking at the next table. Joe leaned over and said, 'What's the time in Melbourne?'

They exchanged glances then one said, 'You taking the piss, mate?'

'No. Just drinking it.'

'In that case, it's about ten or eleven at night.'

There was a Greenhill faraway who might be able to throw some final light on this thing, but not till he got to his office.

'Thanks,' said Joe, rising.

There were other things he might as well do while he was here. He got a tube to Tottenham Court Road and went into a big bookshop he remembered. It was as easy to get lost inside as out. He looked for an assistant to ask directions. Assistants were easy to recognize. They were the ones wandering around like displaced persons, speaking to each other in broken English. He found himself by accident in the Travel section and he checked out hotels in Vinnitsa and Kiev. Mrs Vansovich and her friends had been right. No Hotel Pripyat in Vinnitsa but there was one in Kiev and had been since the early years of the century. The confirmation was no pleasure.

Next he drifted with no conscious effort into History of War. What he wanted was something on the concentration camps. He knew about them, of course. He'd passed through the English school system and World War Two had figured large on the History curriculum. But like most human minds, his was only capable of keeping on the front burner the knowledge immediately necessary to his work, his well-being and his survival. The rest, like, for instance, algebra, or *David Copperfield*, or concentration camps, it consigned to the storage cellar in no particular order of importance.

His mind knew what it was about, he decided five minutes later as he leafed through a dozen pages of pictures at the centre of a scholarly tome. After a while he had to sit down. When he felt able to get up again, he took the book to one of the displaced persons and persuaded her to take his money. Then he continued up Tottenham Court Road and along Euston Road till the sanctuary of St Pancras came into view.

Half an hour later he was breathing the clean invigorating air of Luton.

He drove straight round to Bullpat Square. Butcher was just ushering a client out of her office.

'Sixsmith,' she said. 'I heard you were in Intensive Care.'

'More like intensive farming in there,' he said. 'Butcher, I need help from your computer.'

She said, 'I know you're a marvel with a lathe or a motor engine, but I'm not letting you get those oily fingers on my nice shiny computer.'

'You'll have to do it anyway,' he said. 'I don't know the University entry codes.'

She dragged him into her office and shut the door.

'What the hell are you doing, Sixsmith?' she hissed. 'Trying to get me jailed?'

'Then I'm right?' he said. 'I just asked myself, who do I know who'll be able to hack into every file in town?'

'Sixsmith, be careful,' she warned. 'OK, I may occasionally need to dip into the odd set of records when Social Security, say, or the credit agencies are playing silly buggers with one of my clients, but that doesn't mean I'm in the private data selling business. I leave that to the seedy end of your profession where I'm disappointed to find you.'

'That's where I may end up if you don't help,' he said. 'Listen, all I want is to access their old records twenty years back. Nothing current, nothing personal. I just want to check whether there was an Australian student name of Vicary there at the time.'

'That all?' she said.

'Brownie's honour,' he said.

She turned to her computer. A minute or so later she said, 'There were two Vicarys, a married couple, Pamela and Malcolm. There for a year.'

'Great. And was . . . ?'

'Hang about, Sixsmith,' she cried. 'You said you had just the one query.'

'Of the computer,' he said. 'You can probably answer this one yourself. Was this the same year Willie Woodbine was doing his police civic course at the Uni?'

She thought and said, 'Yes, it would be. Sixsmith, what the hell . . . ?'

But Joe was on his way out.

His mind was getting weighed down with knowledge. Time to share the load. He got in his battered car and headed for Hoot Hall.

22

His first impression of Hoot Hall as run down and depressing was confirmed, but Dora Calverley did her best to compensate by welcoming him warmly and sitting him down with an excellent cup of tea. This, plus her air of calm authority, reassured Joe he'd come to the right place to shift at least one of his troubles.

She examined the passport and the letters carefully.

'So he never got this from the lawyers?' she said. 'Poor boy. Though it does mean he was spared this terrible news. Is that a compensation, do you think, Mr Sixsmith?'

'Wondered that myself,' said Joe.

'Yes. I suspect you are a great deal more sensitive than is usual in a man of your profession,' she said thoughtfully. 'I don't mean that as a criticism. On the contrary. And you have done marvellously well here. When you pass all this on to the police I hope they are suitably abashed.'

'That's what you want I should do?' he asked.

'The whole purpose of the exercise was to try to put a name to this poor child. Now I think the official process needs to take over. In fact, I suspect that to withhold this information might in itself be a breach of the law. But I'll bow to your expert knowledge there.'

Joe made a mental note to apprise Butcher he was being deferred to as a legal expert, then scratched it, envisaging her scornful laughter.

'Is there a problem?' asked Mrs Calverley shrewdly when he didn't reply straightaway.

'Maybe,' he said. 'I think there could be a connection between this boy, Robbie Vicary, and the Woodbines.'

'What on earth do you mean?'

He explained. It didn't sound much as he set it out step by small step, but she listened with so little sign of scepticism that he felt able to take her to the mistiest limits of his speculation.

'Then there's the verger,' he said. 'He's firm there wasn't any box lying around the churchyard at five-thirty when he arrived. When we found him at half-nine he was cold and pretty stiff. I'm no expert, but I'd guess he'd been dead several hours.'

'So he died at six-thirty,' she said reasonably.

'Which means that during the hour from half-five to half-six, while it was still dusk, he turned up at St Monkey's with a huge cardboard box, climbed into it and died.'

'If he came in from the back way, there wouldn't be much chance of being spotted,' said the woman. 'As for the box, doesn't the lane behind St Monica's run into the service road up to the Buymore Supermarket?'

She'd been using her head too. Joe liked that.

'True,' he said. 'But they don't sell, and they don't use, Alfredo Freezers. Georgina Woodbine's got one, though.'

Now for the first time Mrs Calverley's tone of voice shifted towards incredulity.

'You're not suggesting that Georgie Woodbine dumped the box and the boy at the church?'

'She drives a Volvo Estate which could manage both quite easily. And it was parked round the back in the Cloisters that night.'

'While she was in the church, singing.'

'She'd have needed an accomplice to get the box and the boy out and lug them round the other side. A strong man could do it.'

'Edgar Woodbine, you mean? Mr Sixsmith, for heaven's sake, think of what you're saying!'

'I'm just playing possibilities, Mrs C.,' he said. 'Pam Vicary and Willie Woodbine were at SBU at the same time. Suppose they had a thing. Suppose Robbie's been told by his mum that she reckons Woodbine is his real father. Suppose Robbie turns up at the Heights and starts shouting "Daddy!" And suppose while he's there he shoots up and overdoes it, and dies. In those circs, I can see how Willie and Georgie might not be too keen to have him found on the premises.'

'So you're not saying they were actually responsible for his death?' she probed.

'I'd like to think not,' said Joe. 'Except in that case I can't see Willie Woodbine pulling a crazy stroke like this. He'd simply tough it out.'

'Perhaps it was Georgie's idea. She's a strong-willed lady.'

'True. But why'd she be so desperate to get the body off the premises?'

'Pride? Embarrassment? Or perhaps some other reason which I don't know and you probably would not understand.'

'Eh?' said Joe.

Mrs Calverley smiled and said, 'A woman's secrets and a man's secrets are very different things. What one will bury beneath the sea, the other won't give a toss about! So what do we do now? It will take a brave man to reveal these suspicions to the police.'

'That's why I think we should hang on to the passport and letters till we've had a chance to talk to this lawyer fellow, Greenhill, in Melbourne.'

'And if he tells you that the boy's real father was a young policeman called Woodbine . . . ?'

'I might ask him how I can emigrate to Australia myself,' said Joe.

Mrs Calverley laughed and said, 'So let's ring him. Now, I suspect it's some ungodly hour down under . . .'

'They're about ten hours ahead of us,' said Joe authoritatively.

'Then we'd better leave it till midnight. Why don't we do this together? Can you come back out here? No reason for you to catch the cost of the phone call.'

'Sure,' said Joe.

'And don't worry, Mr Sixsmith. Whatever happens, we'll get it sorted out. But I should keep your suspicions to yourself till we know one way or another.'

'Don't worry, Mrs C. If I'm wrong, fewer people who know the better! Bye now.'

She patted him on the shoulder as he left. There were times, he thought, when a bit of colonial self-assurance must come in very useful.

As he drove carefully towards the creaking cattle grid beneath the collapsing arch, he saw the Range Rover hurtling down the approach lane with the certainty of passage of a Governor's carriage through kraal or kasbah. He just had time to pull into the side before it thundered through the gateway with no diminution of speed. Fred Calverley was driving. He didn't even glance in Joe's direction.

And there were times, Joe resumed his thought, when colonial self-assurance got right up your nose!

When he got home he found Dunk Docherty was standing on his doorstep.

'Where've you been?' he said accusingly. 'I called at the hospital, they said you'd discharged yourself last night. I tried your office. Nothing. So I came round here.'

'You'd better come in,' he said.

First things first. Whitey had probably been sleeping all day but he was clearly ready to complain to the RSPCA of neglect till Joe started defrosting a chicken tikka. That done, he took a can of Guinness from the fridge, offered one to Docherty who shook his head, then he held it to his mouth till the London muck was washed out of his throat.

'So how'd your date go last night?' he said.

'Fine. Well, mostly fine. We ended up having a bit of a row.'

Joe examined the youngster's face for a sign of new damage. There was none.

'So what did you do?'

'Went to the Thunderdome. Bowled, roller skated. Sat on a bench with a couple of cokes and a burger . . .'

'I see. Softening her up before you started the hard probing.'

'No!' he said indignantly. 'Why do you want to make it sound so nasty?'

'Why don't you tell me what you want to see me about, Dunk,' said Joe.

The young man had sat on the sofa where he was quickly joined by Whitey, hopeful as always that there were goodies to be charmed out of the newcomer's pockets or purse. Joe noticed how Dunk's hands stroked the cat's fur as though in search of comfort.

'Just wondered, well, you know, you got on to Gallie so quick, I wondered if you'd had a chance to, you know, sort of suss out anything about her granddad. I mean, have you met him? How does he seem to you . . . ?'

'What you mean,' said Joe, 'is do I think he's the kind of guy who could have been mixed up with this kind of stuff?'

He took the book he'd bought in London out of its bag, opened it at the photograph pages and placed it in the young man's hands.

'Oh shit,' said Dunk Docherty after a few moments' turning pages.

'That's what we're talking about, Dunk,' said Joe. 'Not some civil servant who may have been taking backhanders, or some bankrupt director who's got half a mill stashed away in the Caymans. That's what you'll be telling Galina Hacker you think her grandfather is mixed up with.'

Dunk snapped the book shut with a bang which sent Whitey leaping from his lap.

'Now hold on, Joe. Don't go loading that on me! We don't invent the news, you know . . .'

'. . . you just distort it,' completed Joe.

'Ha ha. Look, it's not me whose nose you should be rubbing in these pics, it's Taras Kovalko's, see what they do to *his* stomach.'

'Yes, maybe,' said Joe.

Dunk was eyeing him keenly.

'You have met him, haven't you? And you're not sure, right?'

Maybe the boy would make a good reporter after all.

'No, I'm not sure,' said Joe. It wasn't the whole truth, but it would do for now.

'Me neither,' said Dunk. 'Can I be frank with you, Joe?'

Joe almost laughed aloud at the idea that the youngster could be anything else. He had a face built for frankness. That open eager expression would probably take him through doors slammed shut in Tony Sloppe's foxy face. The moment of truth would come when Docherty started realizing its potential.

'Who else?' said Joe.

'Like I said, Gallie and me had a great time after a bit of a sticky start. It was just meant to be the afternoon, but spilled over so far into the evening, it seemed daft not to have a meal together. Maybe that was a mistake, too much first time out, I don't know . . . We had a couple of wee drinks, not too much, you know, but enough to really loosen us up. And I got to talking about what I wanted to do, public interest stuff, Watergate, Woodward and Bernstein, that sort of thing. And she said, yeah, but how was it in the public interest for papers to be sticking their nebs into people's private lives just for a juicy headline? And before I knew where we were, there was a full-scale row going on. End of a lovely night.'

'I should tell you, you've come to the wrong shop for lonely hearts advice,' said Joe, feeling himself being drawn ever deeper into something he'd rather keep out of.

Dunk ignored him.

'And I've been thinking about it all night. I mean, what is the public interest here, Joe?'

Joe picked up the discarded book and let it fall open at the photos.

'How about this?' he said, wondering why the shoot he wasn't taking advantage of this young-love wavering to get the boy to back right off his investigation. Of course, he knew full well why. The selfish reason was, it was the young reporter who was ultimately responsible for getting him mixed up in this mess, so why should he walk away from it now? The unselfish was, no way the boy could walk and keep his interest in Gallie going. He might think there was now, but there wasn't.

'I've thought about that, of course I have,' said Dunk angrily. 'The way I'm looking at it is, the old man will die pretty soon and that'll be that. If he was mixed up in this stuff, he's obviously got his head around it after all these years. Not much chance of making him feel guilty, and not much point in locking him up for what's left of his life. All we'd be doing is laying the guilt on the family and sentencing them to suffer for it all the rest of their lives.'

Emotion made him quite eloquent.

Joe said, 'Not knowing can be as bad as knowing sometimes.'

Dunk said, 'But Gallie wouldn't know she didn't know, if you see what I mean.'

For a moment Joe was tempted to come clean, but he couldn't do it. This side of legality, the client had to call the shots.

He said, 'You never know what's going on in people's heads, Dunk. And deciding not to know is no decision.'

'What the hell does that mean?'

'Not really sure,' admitted Joe. 'I think it means, you've got to get the truth of a thing before you decide what to do with it.'

'And just how do you plan to get the truth about what Taras Kovalko really did in the war?' demanded Dunk Docherty. 'Just come right out and ask him?'

'Hey, you've guessed,' said Joe. 'But to do that I'll need to get him by himself. Look, why don't you give Gallie a ring, ask her out again. Lay it on thick, tell her you're sorry, you really enjoyed the evening and would like to try again. Think you could do that, Dunk?'

'Well, aye, I think I could,' said the boy hopefully. 'But I'm not sure if she . . .'

'No harm in trying, and it's in a good cause.'

'Right, I'll do it. Can I use your phone?'

'Sorry, I'm expecting an important call,' said Joe. 'But you've got plenty of time. Off you go now.'

As soon as the youth was out of the door, Joe picked up the phone and dialled the L and B Building Society.

'Hello, Gallie,' he said. 'Enjoy the Thunderdome last night? Pity about the row.'

'How'd you know about that?' demanded the girl. 'You've been talking to him! What did he say?'

'I think he's in love,' said Joe.

'Don't be stupid!' cried the girl, then in a less strident tone, 'Why'd you say a soft thing like that?'

'Because he's stopped being the great boy reporter and started worrying about setting you up. Makes you laugh, doesn't it? Still, it solves the main problem. Just you keep stringing him along, and he'll soon keep out of your grand-dad's hair.'

'What do you mean, stringing him along?'

'You know, fooling him like he thought he was fooling you. Listen, he's going to ring in a minute to ask you out again tonight. Say yes. It's a good ploy. Just keep jerking him around till when you finally dump him, he'd rather write about the Council flower fête than your family. Your mum and dad at home tonight?'

'No, it's their indoor bowling. What do you want to see them for?'

'Don't,' said Joe. 'But I thought I might drop by and have a word with your grandda.'

'What about?' she demanded suspiciously. 'Something to do with this . . .'

'Just a social call,' said Joe. 'You just keep the boy wonder out of my hair. Don't stint yourself. Like my Aunt Mirabelle says, true love's got a deep pocket. Bye.'

He put the phone down. *True love's got a deep pocket*! Well, it was the kind of thing Mirabelle liked to say! He realized he was grinning broadly. Maybe that old aunt of his wasn't so foolish after all, trying to play Cupid all the time. It certainly made you feel good!

Whitey let out a noise which said it only made him feel *sick*.

'Tough tittie,' said Joe, dialling again.

'Customs and Excise Service. Can I help you?'

'Hope so,' said Joe. 'If you decide to take a look inside an envelope, what's it look like when you've finished?'

After a little demur, they told him. He replaced the receiver and dialled the Bullpat Square Law Centre. Butcher herself answered.

173

'Oh God, if I'd known it was you again, I'd have let it ring,' she said.

'Something I need to know,' said Joe. 'Someone dies, there's no will. Who inherits?'

'Depends,' said Butcher. 'Is there a spouse? That's husband or wife.'

'I know what a spouse is,' said Joe. 'First thing they taught us at Oxford. And there isn't one.'

'OK. Kids?'

'I doubt it.'

'Then it's Boxing Day for the rest of the family. Parents first. Then brothers and sisters, then half brothers and . . .'

'Whoa,' said Joe. 'Far enough. You know anything about establishing parentage, Butcher?'

'I chase the State. I let the State chase fathers,' said Butcher. 'I gather it's pretty easy these days with DNA testing and stuff like that. But if you want scientific detail, I'm still at the blue eyes, brown eyes level.'

'What's that?'

'I thought it came in Chapter One of the Janet and John All-About-Detection series. How's it go? Brown is dominant, blue is recessive. That means if one parent has brown eyes, all the kids will. Ergo, only two blue-eyed parents can have blue-eyed kids. Very useful if you're recruiting for the National Socialists. In your case, Joe, your eyes could be red, white and blue and I still don't think you'd get in.'

'My eyes *are* red, white and blue,' said Joe. 'One thing more. That school of yours you're so ashamed of, you still got contacts?'

'I may have. Why?'

'It's something Georgie Woodbine told me about Mrs C. I'd like to check it out.'

Butcher listened and said, 'For heaven's sake, Joe! Have you been reading those Sherlock Holmes stories again? How on earth can I check a thing like that? And why on earth do you want to know?'

'Idle curiosity. Can you find out or not?'

'I suppose I can try, but why I should . . . How are you getting on with this Georgie Porgie thing anyway?'

'Should have something for you soon,' said Joe ambiguously.

'Should I hold my breath?' said Butcher. 'OK, don't answer that. Right, Joe, you've sweet talked me into it. I'll see what I can do, on one condition. Triumph or cock-up you give me the full story. No hiding your crap under a bushel. Right?'

'Deal,' said Joe. 'I'll be here till I hear from you.'

'What? You didn't say it was that urgent.'

'Matter of life and death,' said Joe.

He put the phone down and looked at his watch. Early hours of the morning in Oz. Maybe all the answers were there. Or maybe none. How did Sherlock Holmes manage without the phone? Or had it been invented then? He'd have to read the stories sometime. Might pick up a few tips.

At seven-thirty the phone rang.

Butcher said, 'Chalk one up for Georgie Woodbine. She was telling the truth.'

'First time for everything,' said Joe. 'Thanks, Butcher.'

He didn't put the phone down but merely depressed the rest then dialled a number. If he gave himself time to think he wouldn't do it. Being a PI was one thing. Sticking your nose into your friends' business was quite another.

'Trades and Labour Club.'

'Hello,' said Joe. 'Stan Bewley there?'

It would be a wonder if he wasn't. Stan had been Joe's union shop steward at Robco Engineering for twenty years and was renowned for not having missed more than a dozen nights down at the Labour Club in all that time.

'Bewley,' said the familiar gruff voice.

'Stan, it's Joe Sixsmith.'

'Hell's bells! How're you doing, Joe? Spent all your redundancy yet?'

'Long gone,' said Joe honestly. 'Stan, something I'd like to know, from way back. Twenty years, about. How's your memory?'

'Selective,' said Bewley. 'What do you want to know?'

'It's about when a student called Georgina Barnfather joined the local Party. Remember her?'

'The one who married the cop? I remember.'

'Well, before she married the cop, did she get mixed up with anyone in the group? I mean seriously mixed up?'

There was a long silence. Then Bewley said in a voice noticeably less friendly than before, 'You're a private tec now, I hear. Can be a dirty business, that. Can make you forget your friends.'

'Not me, Stan. If you're talking about the same person I'm thinking about, this is in her own interest, believe me.'

'I'll believe you, Joe. You weren't very big on carrying the banner, but the lads all had you down for dead straight. This is the way I remember it.'

Joe listened, made a note.

'Thanks, Stan. I owe you a pint.'

'Not for that, you don't,' said Bewley sternly. 'I'm not your snout! But you can buy me a couple any time you like for beating my brains out to keep you lot in work long as I did!'

Joe put the phone down. It rang almost immediately.

It was Merv Golightly.

'Joe, I'm at Long Liz's. He's just turned up.'

'Great. You're sure it's him?'

'Yeah. I got a lovely view right into the apartment. Doesn't seem bothered about drawing the curtains either. No sign of the cop's wife yet though.'

'She'll come,' said Joe confidently. 'Can you hang around?'

'How long?'

'As long as it takes.'

Merv lowered his voice.

'Might be a bit difficult. Room with the best view is Liz's bedroom.'

'I'm sure you'll work something out,' said Joe.

Joe put the phone down. It was getting on for eight. Time to move. He picked up the book he'd bought in London and put it in a Tesco carrier. Whitey, who associated plastic carriers with food, sat up and took notice.

'Sorry,' said Joe, full of guilt. 'I know you've been stuck

in here for ages, but it's better than waiting in the car on a cold night, isn't it?'

He went to the door. The cat, realizing he was being abandoned again, let out his I-may-not-be-here-when-you-get-back howl.

'Make sure you send me a postcard,' said Joe Sixsmith.

23

The Hackers lived in a 1930's semi on a neat little estate in the southern suburbs of Luton.

Joe walked up the concrete path alongside a tidy square of lawn flanked with Michaelmas daisies. At the door he pressed the bell lightly once and stood back. Something told him it would be enough.

It was, but it wasn't fast. First there was a movement of curtain at the front bay. Next came a light in the hallway twinkling through the peephole in the door till it was darkened by the pressure of an eye. Then came the sound of bolts being drawn, and the door opened on a chain, and the eye became visible. After a long scrutiny, the door was closed again. For a moment, it felt final. But at last he heard the sound of the chain being removed.

'Come inside, Mr Sixsmith,' said Taras Kovalko.

He led the way into a cosy parlour containing a three-piece suite a little too large for it, a coffee table bearing a shot-glass half filled with a colourless liquid, and a television with the sound switched off showing three men chasing a fourth across a gloomy marshy landscape. The emulsioned walls were hung with paintings, mostly classic reproductions, but interspersed with watercolour landscapes in whose bottom right-hand corner appeared the initials T.K.

'These yours?' asked Joe.

The old man nodded.

'Not so good,' he said. 'But my daughter is proud of what her old father can do, and she had them framed. It is good for children to be proud of their parents, isn't it?'

'I've always thought so,' said Joe. 'They don't look like round here.'

'No. They are from home, from the Ukraine. Painted from memory, of course. Best way to paint landscape, I think. You do not have to sit outside on a little stool in the wind and rain.'

He shivered at the thought. There was a fire crackling in the grate though the night was not too cold.

'Old blood runs thin,' said Taras, as if catching Joe's thought. 'I find a little vodka helps thicken it. You will take some?'

'No thanks,' said Joe, feeling that already the setting was far too cosy for his mission. 'Mr Kovalko, there's something I want to talk to you about. First, I think that recently you've been bothered by a young man who's been asking questions about you, particularly about what you did and where you were during the war.'

'Ah. A historian, perhaps?' said Kovalko, faintly mocking.

'No, he's a journalist, and he's interested in whether or not you worked for the Germans.'

The old man bowed his head, as if to hide an emotion. Then he said, 'Is that all? One way or another every one of my countrymen worked for the Germans. If anybody tells you different, they are lying. To themselves, at least.'

'Come off it!' protested Joe. 'A lot of them must have fought in the Red Army.'

'To defeat the Germans, you mean? Same thing. Look at Europe now. That too was working for the Germans.'

He's diverting me, thought Joe. This is a cunning old sod. But keep plugging away, you'll get through.

'You don't seem all that surprised to see me here,' he said.

'What's to surprise? You are a detective, everyone knows that. The other night at the club I saw you talking a long time with old Vansovich. No one talks long with that one without a purpose. Later she said what a nice young man you were, so interested in the old days. You should try to be more subtle if you want to surprise people, Mr Sixsmith.'

'I'll work on it,' said Joe. 'Mrs Vansovich thinks it's a pity you remember so little about the old days, 'specially coming

179

from the same town. No street scenes from Vinnitsa in your paintings, I see. Memory not so hot on bricks and mortar?'

'That's right. Trees and skies and water I recall, but buildings will not come.'

'Not even the Hotel Pripyat?'

There! First penetration! Kovalko reached for the vodka bottle and refilled his glass, taking his time.

Joe said encouragingly, 'That's right. Have another drink. Seems to help the memory. You'd had a few the other night when you mentioned the hotel. It was where you trained as a chef, you said.'

'Is that so? A name, nothing more. A piece of debris from the past. No picture with it.'

'Understandable,' said Joe sympathetically. 'Even Mrs Vansovich couldn't remember it. Not even the name. Not in Vinnitsa. Though there was Hotel Pripyat in Kiev. Still is.'

'A man is not tied to the town he is born in,' said Kovalko, back in control.

'No? So it was in Kiev you worked as a cook?'

'Who knows?' said the old man. 'I wish I could remember.'

'Well, it would help if you could,' said Joe. 'It would help shut up all these nosey people who can't get it out of their minds that you might really be some other guy. Someone called Boris Kovalenko, maybe. He worked for the Germans too. Not like you though. You worked in the kitchens, didn't you?'

'Yes. In a forced labour camp.'

'They'd want trained chefs there, of course,' said Joe. 'Somewhere near Regensburg, wasn't it?'

'I don't know. It was just a place in Germany they sent us to.'

'But it wasn't too far from Regensburg you were picked up,' said Joe. 'There was a camp, another kind of camp, at Regensburg. That's where this guy with the name like yours worked. Boris Kovalenko. Change a couple of letters, scratch out a couple more, and it would be exactly the same, wouldn't it?'

The old man picked up a remote control unit from the floor and pointed it at the television set. The three pursuers had caught up with their quarry and were systematically beating him up.

'They chase, they catch, they beat. Without the sound, who is the good, who the bad, can you tell me that, Mr Sixsmith?' He pressed the zapper and the picture vanished. 'None of this you say to me is new. Do you think they have not investigated this possibility before, the man Wiesenthal and his helpers, back in the seventies?'

'I know,' said Joe.

'Then you will know they had descriptions of this man Kovalenko. He was tall, I am short. He had black hair, mine used to be brown. He had dark eyes, almost black, mine are blue. I do not understand why, when the professionals have proved me innocent once, the amateurs should start asking the same stupid questions again.'

'That's a good point,' agreed Joe. 'Here's another. Why, when like you say, the pros have found you innocent, should you be so worried about an amateur asking questions?'

Taras Kovalko held his drink out to the fire, warming the glass and his hands.

'I am now much older and less able to bear pain,' he said. 'I know what trouble the press can cause even by just hinting at guilt, even when they have no evidence.'

'But you didn't know it was the press asking questions, not till I told you,' said Joe. 'And when you heard, you were relieved, weren't you? Why was that? Because it wasn't the pros back again, the pros who might have the tools to really dig, especially since the Iron Curtain went up?'

Kovalko smiled, apparently genuinely and said, 'Mr Sixsmith, I did not take you for a fantasist. What is your part in this anyway? Think how desperate a newspaper man must be to hire a private detective to do his dirty work!'

'Well, that's where you're wrong,' said Joe. 'It's not the journalist who's hired me. It's Gallie, your granddaughter.'

That really was a body blow. The old man's pale face turned grey. Joe watched uneasily.

'Gallie . . . but why?'

'To protect you, of course. When she heard about this reporter and saw the way it was bothering you, she wanted to get it stopped. But she's a bright lass. She got really indignant when she realized what it was all about, but like me she started to wonder about the way you were reacting to it. Me too. And this business about you not being able to remember anything about Vinnitsa. That seemed a lot too convenient.'

'But I told you . . . they have a description of this man . . . it is not me . . .'

He was completely on the defensive now, ageing ten years in the last couple of minutes.

Joe said, 'Shoot, anyone with half a mind has to know you're definitely not this guy Kovalenko. I mean, there's no doubt he *was* born in Vinnitsa, so if you were him, you'd know all about the place. No, the only reason for you to fake amnesia is that you've never been near the place!'

The old man was clearly only half following him. Joe felt a bit of natural disappointment. It was a fair bit of deduction that he'd made, and it would have been nice to get an appreciative nod. On the other hand, the poor old devil was obviously in a hell of a state from hearing that Gallie was mixed up in all this. Time to get to the truth and hope it did as much good as the trick cyclists and Aunt Mirabelle liked to claim.

He said, 'Here's what I think, for what it's worth. You're not Boris Kovalenko, but you're not Taras Kovalko either. And you're hiding something you did during the war that you're frightened might still be used against you after all these years, so it has to be something pretty big.'

The old man said desperately, 'So you admit I am not this man? Tell this to the journalist so he will stop persecuting me . . .'

'The journalist's no problem,' said Joe gently. 'It's Gallie. And me telling her anything isn't going to be enough. Doesn't matter how much you love someone, an idea gets in your head, it's like a worm in an apple. Nibble nibble. Doesn't matter even if the person you love dies. The worm's there in the memory, nibbling forever . . .'

He was getting quite poetic. But he wasn't sure if he was

182

getting anywhere else. He picked up his carrier bag and took out the book he'd bought in London.

He said, 'Taras, or whatever your name is, I don't know what it is you're hiding, but take a look at these pictures. This is what your granddaughter is starting to worry about.'

He opened the book at the photographs and thrust it into the old man's trembling hands.

'Look at it,' he urged. 'Ask yourself if any truth you have to tell can be worse than her suspecting you were mixed up with *this*!'

He stood up and turned away. He didn't want to watch the old man suffering. Also, he thought there'd been a noise outside. He opened the door into the small entrance hall. The front door was opening and he heard a voice. Gallie's. He stepped into the hallway and closed the door behind him as the young woman came over the threshold followed by Dunk Docherty.

'It's no use,' she said when she saw Joe. 'We couldn't keep it up. Neither of us.'

Dunk said, 'You fooled me, Joe. Nice one.'

Joe said aggressively, 'You here as a journalist or a friend of the family?'

'It's OK, Mr Sixsmith,' said Gallie soothingly. 'We got things sorted. After I told him I'd kill him if he ever wrote anything about Grandda. Where is he?'

'He's in there, but don't go in just now, not till I've . . .'

She was a strong-willed woman in the making, and in her own home she wasn't going to have anyone telling her what to do. More in irritation than anger, she pushed by Joe and entered the sitting room.

'Grandda!' she cried. 'What the hell has he been doing to you?'

The old man was sitting with his head bowed over the open book, with tears streaming down his face and dripping into the shiny pages. She ran to him and knelt by his side, embracing him with fierce love. The old man stroked her hair with his gnarled fingers and his gaze met Joe's over her head.

'You are right, Mr Sixsmith,' he said. 'I do not know what I have been thinking of. It is time for the truth.'

24

Midnight. And a black one with a light drizzle falling. The headlights of the Morris opened up the dark like a surgeon's knife. Behind, the wound closed without trace of a scar.

Joe was in a hurry. He had spent longer at the Hackers' house than he intended, but with some things you couldn't force the pace.

The old man's story had been dramatic and moving, holding them riveted from the moment he said, 'My name is Victor Maksimov. That is the first time I have spoken it or heard it spoken since 1945.'

He'd been nineteen, commis chef at the Hotel Pripyat, when the Germans took Kiev in 1941. Much of the city had been stomped flat by shells and bombs but miraculously the Pripyat had survived with the loss only of its windows and a few tiles. An intelligence colonel and his staff had quickly grabbed this prize.

'When the SS started rounding up all the able-bodied men, Colonel Pacher said, "The cook stays." He was slightly mad and most people were afraid of him, even the SS. It helped that I was ethnic German from my great grandfather. Colonel Pacher called me Maxim and told people that the Paris restaurant was named after me. When I saw what the other choice was – forced labour camps or fighting with the Germans against the Reds, I was glad to stay. So anyone who says I collaborated with the Germans is telling the truth.'

He looked around defiantly. No one spoke. He went on with his story.

During the next three years he'd accompanied Pacher all over the place. He didn't pay much attention where they went. All he knew was that as long as he stuck close to the colonel, he was safe. Early in 'forty-five they were stationed in Regensburg.

'Everyone knew the war was lost but no one dared say so. It was a hard time for civilians. American bombers came over night after night, everything was in short supply. Only the military had any guarantee of food or cigarettes. I did OK. Pacher used to say "Grow fat, Maxim. No one trusts a skinny cook!" There were many women who were willing to give favours for food. There was one I knew who seemed different. I thought she liked me for my own sake. I thought I was in love with her. So because I wanted to look after her, I asked her to marry me.'

'Was that possible?' asked Joe. 'A German woman to marry a prisoner? I mean, that's what you still were, right?'

'A prisoner? Hardly. I am telling the truth here. For a long time I had enough freedom to run away any time I liked. But where would I run to? No, I had as much freedom as any other man on Pacher's staff. But you are right. For a German woman to marry someone in my position was impossible in normal times. But times were far from normal. We found a priest who was only too pleased to save at least one of his flock from prostitution. Under Nazi civil law, perhaps we were not married. In the Church's eye, we certainly were.'

A small furry creature scuttled out of the hedgerow and halted petrified in the car lights. Joe slammed the brake on and skidded to a halt. The animal fled into the darkness. It had done him a favour, he realized. The final turn off to Hoot Hall lay just ahead and he might have overrun it in these conditions.

He negotiated the turn carefully then began to build up speed again on the long straight lane.

Victor Maksimov's happiness, if happiness there had been, didn't last long. The man had been blunt.

'I was a fool not to guess that I was not the only man she had used for essential supplies. Though I was certainly the only one who offered marriage. Obviously she could not come to live with me in my official quarters, so I still used to visit her in her room in the town. I called it our home! Was there a moment when she believed it too? I do not know. All I do know is that getting away from my duties unexpectedly early one day, I went round to this *home* of ours and found her in bed with another man.'

'Kovalenko,' said Joe, who could spot a rat when it sat in his headlights.

'Yes, I did not know him but as soon as he spoke to me in my own language, I guessed that he must be a guard from the camp. No other way for a Ukrainian to be at liberty in this city.' He laughed bitterly and added, 'Unless, of course, he was a German officer's cook.'

'Did you know what was going on in the camp?' asked Joe.

'I knew nothing except that this terrible world was so full of people ten thousand times worse off than me that I was terrified to do anything that might send me plunging to join them.'

He regarded them defiantly. Don't press it, thought Joe. He said, 'But you risked getting married?'

'In terror and alone, love is the only medicine to give you sweet dreams,' said Victor. 'And now I saw this man lying with my wife. Worse, when he saw me, he showed no fear, but spoke to me in my own language, pulling the blanket off them to reveal her nakedness, and saying, "Don't look so shocked, my friend. Come in and join us. There is plenty here for two." She turned her face to the pillow and tried to pull the blanket back. But he would not let her.'

He fell silent. Galina and Dunk were sitting side by side, their young faces showing how far beyond their experience this story took them. Joe noticed that Galina's hands had grasped the reporter's arm and she was hanging on to it like a lifebelt.

'So what did you do?' asked Joe.

'I killed him,' said Victor Maksimov, very cold, very precise. 'With my bare hands. She was screaming so I hit her in the face and she fell to the floor and lay quiet. Then I went through his pockets and found his identity card. Boris Kovalenko. It was a good card, giving even more freedom of movement than mine. It had been folded so the middle letters were almost rubbed off in the crease. I scraped them off entirely and with a pen turned it into Kovalko. Then I altered Boris to Taras. It was the best I could do. To be found without a card meant certain arrest, if not instant death. The authorities would be looking for Victor Maksimov, not Taras Kovalko. My wife was recovering. I knew beyond doubt that if she started to talk to me I would kill her too. So I left. I headed west, towards the light of the setting sun. I had no plan, no hope. Perhaps because I didn't act like a fugitive nobody troubled me. Two days later, I walked through a company of fleeing *Wehrmacht* soldiers till a shell blew me off my feet and out of my sense. I awoke days later in a US Field Hospital. I said nothing, I could remember nothing. I was Taras Kovalko, born in Vinnitsa. I am not sure to this day how much I was faking. My personal pain meant more to me than all this terrible war, all these horrors the allied forces were finding.'

'But when you got better, why not tell the truth?' urged Joe.

'That I was Colonel Pacher's personal cook? That I had married a German woman and murdered her lover? Where do you think that would have got me? No. Better to be Taras Kovalko. Finally, I came to England. I found work. I met an English girl and courted her. Victor Maksimov, the murderer with a wife in Germany, could not do this, but Taras Kovalko could. I put Maksimov right out of my mind and he did not return till they came to me in the seventies to check if I could be Kovalenko, the camp guard. That frightened me, but I thought, at least if they were still looking for Kovalenko that meant his killing was not on record. Perhaps I was not officially a murderer after all! That was a small comfort. But not much. In my heart I knew what I was. So when they went away, I was glad to return to being Kovalko again. At last I felt safe forever.'

He turned his head to look at Docherty for the first time.

'Then just when it seemed it was all between me and God, you came along, young man. Who you were, I did not know. All I knew was that here, at the end of my life, my beloved

daughter and her family would perhaps find out that her
father was a murderer, her mother was a dupe, and she
herself was a bastard.'

'I'm sorry,' stuttered Dunk. 'I didn't realize . . . I mean . . .'

'No!' cried Gallie. 'There's no need for you to be sorry. It
wasn't your fault. It wasn't a fault at all. Grandda, can't you
see all this is nothing now? It's dead, it's in the past. All that
matters is that you had nothing to do with any of this!'

She pointed at the book which had slipped to the floor,
still open at the photographs.

'That is what your friend here says,' said the old man. 'I
am so very very sorry . . .'

He was close to breaking point and the girl knelt before
him and put her arms around him. Joe motioned to Docherty
to follow him out of the room. He intended to escape and
leave the Hacker family to their own soul searching, but as
he stepped into the entrance hall the front door opened and
George and Galina Hacker came in.

So everything had to be gone through again. The elder
Galina was splendidly matter of fact.

'Crime of passion,' she said dismissively. 'You get probation
nowadays. And probably your wife divorced you straight off.
Or maybe you weren't properly married in the first place.
You ever think to ask her if she didn't perhaps have a husband in the army somewhere? At the most, it just means
I'm a bastard and I've been called worse things. Dad, I see
you've been at the firewater of yours; George, dig out that
bottle of Scotch. I think we all need a decent drink!'

What was it Dora Calverley had said? 'A woman's secrets
and a man's secrets are very different things. What one will
bury beneath the sea, the other won't give a toss about!'

When he'd finally left, he'd stood in the front doorway
with Dunk Docherty and said, 'You won't be writing about
any of this, I take it?'

'No!' the young man had exclaimed with indignant
emphasis. Then he had grinned his charm-the-birds-from-
the-trees grin and added, 'Of course, I may have to be persuaded.'

'Dunk! Got a moment?'

Gallie had followed them to the door.

Joe said, 'Good night. See you over the counter, eh?'

The girl ran forward, put her arms round his neck and gave him a long, hot kiss.

'Thanks a million, Mr Sixsmith,' she said.

'Won't cost you as much as that,' said Joe.

'I'm going to pay you,' she said. 'I mean it. I earn good money, better than you from the look of your account!'

'Hey, I wasn't hinting,' protested Joe. 'But you can start by making sure when the next phone bill comes, you pay your dad for those calls I made tonight. Long distance costs a fortune.'

'It's worth a fortune, the way you've put things right,' said the girl, embracing him again.

'Yeah,' said Dunk, clearly eager to interpose his own body. 'I second that. Next time Tony Sloppe puts you down, I'll tell the old sod!'

'Well, thanks for that,' said Joe. 'Good night.'

He left them in the doorway together and walked away, full of both pity and envy.

They would learn that putting everything right was beyond the scope of anyone, let alone a balding, middle-aged redundant lathe operator.

But as their arms went round each other and they drew each other close, oh, how very very right everything must seem!

Meanwhile, good old put-it-right Joe Sixsmith was firmly back in the old creaking upright world with miles to go before he'd get to sleep.

The miles, he realized, were passing at a rate considerably over one a minute.

He recalled the perilous archway with the creaking cattle grid that lay ahead. Familiarity may have bred contempt in the Calverleys so that they could send their Range Rover hurtling through it without troubling the brake. Ordinary folk like the Sixsmiths were a bit short on contempt. He began to slow down.

Even so, when suddenly it was before him in the headlights, he was still going a lot faster than he cared to be.

He hit the brake hard, got a little skid going, corrected it, dabbed the brake a couple of times more, and was down to under ten m.p.h. when the Morris's nose bisected the arch.

That deceleration probably saved his life, though it didn't feel like it at the time. What it felt like was the driveway ahead of him suddenly flipped up like the handle of a stepped-on rake and hit him smack in the bonnet. He was flung forward against the steering wheel but saved from fatal collision by his seat belt, which likewise felt more like being lassoed from behind by a mad cowboy than salvation.

At the same time the thin drizzle turned to huge hailstones which battered against the roof of the car.

Wrong! cried the part of his mind which was still desperate to see facts as facts, before all the facts stopped together.

What had happened was the old cattle grid had given way, plunging him into the pit with such force that the decaying stonework of the arch had finally collapsed too and was now avalanching over the Morris. Two things crossed his mind. First was relief that he'd not had time to get the damage caused by his trip to the Scratchings repaired. The second was renewed gratitude to Lord Nuffield that he'd made the shells of these old buses so strong.

He tried to open the door but found it was wedged tight. Same on the passenger side. Nothing for it, he was going to have to break glass to get out of this one. He could smell petrol and the resemblance between cattle grid and a barbecue pit was strong in his mind.

He twisted round with his feet against the dash to look up at the rear window which was almost over his head. This was the only glass which hadn't crazed. Through the spatter of rain and dust he could see the blackness of the sky. The window wouldn't be easy to smash, he realized, and cast around for something to use. Then suddenly there was something between him and the blackness – a head, then a face pressing close against the glass. He cried in terror for in that brief glimpse it seemed to him that the boy in the box was peering into his eyes.

Then the face withdrew and next moment the window exploded in, peppering him with tiny shards. Joe shook his head and blinked. His face felt like it had suffered a massive course of acupuncture, but his eyes were OK. He pushed his head through the gap. The figure was still there, hovering over him, and to his great relief he realized it wasn't the boy in the box but young Fred Calverley. In his hands was the large stone from the fallen arch which he'd used to break the window. He raised it again.

'It's OK,' gasped Joe. 'I think I can get through now.'

But the young man didn't seem to hear and for a terrible moment Joe thought the stone was going to come crashing on his head.

Then a beam of light hit Fred full in the face and Dora Calverley's voice said, 'It's all right, darling. I think help's on its way.'

Something was on its way, certainly.

The distant headlights of a car had appeared moving fast down the long straight lane.

Then behind them, another set. Then a third. And as they watched, a blue light began to pulsate on the roof of the leading vehicle.

Joe pulled himself from the wrecked Morris. His legs felt like somebody else's. He touched his face and when he looked at his hand the whorls of his fingers were contoured in blood.

He said to the boy who was still standing with the stone raised high, 'You can put it down now.'

And to Mrs Calverley, he said, 'I invited Willie to the party. I honestly thought there was a real chance he'd come by himself, but he's brought his friends and that's bad news for you, Mrs C.'

She smiled at him and said, 'No need to apologize, Mr Sixsmith. I'm very good at coping with unexpected guests. No, it's I who should apologize to you. I should have had this grid repaired ages ago. Poverty's my only excuse. We all try to make do and mend, don't we? Till finally something gives. Edgar, thank God you've come. There's been a dreadful accident. Perhaps some of your men could assist poor Mr Sixsmith up to the house. As a matter of interest, what brings you out here so opportunely? Not poachers again, I hope?'

Willie Woodbine, who had got out of the first car, looked across at Joe with puzzlement and interrogation in his eyes. Like the good book says, there's a time to every purpose under heaven. This seemed a very good time to faint.

Joe fainted.

25

'Let's get this straight,' said Willie Woodbine incredulously. 'You told Mrs Calverley you reckoned I might have murdered that boy in the box?'

'Yes,' said Joe.

He was sitting on the edge of one of the ancient sofas in Hoot Hall drinking a mug of very sweet tea. Over Woodbine's shoulder he could see the portrait of Dickie Calverley, in every sense the father of his woes, regarding him with a knowing, amused, now-get-out-of-this expression.

It hadn't been so bad when he came round. A pretty little WPC had been leaning over him to pick bits of glass out of his face.

'Looks a lot worse than it is,' she said cheerfully. 'Can't find much else wrong apart from a bit of bruising, but they'll check you out properly at the hospital.'

'Hospital?' he'd said, struggling upright. 'I've done hospital. I ain't doing it again.'

'Now listen here, sweetie,' she said, very serious. 'The ambulance is on its way and that means coming across two fields because of the mess you made of that gateway. I reckon if you tell them you don't need to go back with them, they'll soon put you in a state where you do!'

Then Woodbine had come in bearing the mug of tea.

'Off you go and join the others,' he told the WPC. 'I'll take care of the invalid now.'

But when he started asking questions he didn't look much like a carer to Joe.

'Now why would you tell her a thing like that?' he now pressed.

'To make her think I didn't suspect her,' said Joe.

'But why should she think you suspected anyone of anything?'

'No reason. But I wanted her to think I did,' said Joe.

Woodbine covered his face with his hands. When he removed them he looked disappointed to see that Joe was still there. Joe, on the other hand, felt merely relieved to have confirmed once more that the policeman's eyes were bright blue. Like Pam Vicary's. Jeremy Greenhill, the Australian lawyer, had been very helpful for a man dragged from a breakfast meeting by Joe's call from the Hackers'. Unfortunately, Pam had never told him the name of Rob's putative father. If only Joe had been able to remember the colour of Willie Woodbine's eyes, he might have saved himself a lot of hassle!

The policeman was now asking with the reluctance of a man unsure whether he really wanted to know, 'Why should you want her to think that?'

'So that if she was up to something, she'd get worried that when I found out whose son the boy really was, I'd get on to her,' said Joe. 'You see, how it worked was this. I spelled it all out, what I thought might have happened. How the boy came over here looking for his real father. How his real father, who I said was you, didn't fancy having an Australian bastard dumped in his lap, so when the boy died, he decided to get rid of him by letting him be found dead in a cardboard box, like he was some common or garden drop-out who'd taken some bad stuff. So he, that is, you, put him in the back of his wife's – *your* wife's – estate car and dumped him round the back of St Monkey's while the choir was rehearsing. Only all the time, of course, it was her and Fred who did it, using the Range Rover which they parked in the Cloisters. You see, Mrs Calverley said she'd been listening to the music, but your wife, who, incidentally, gave Robbie Mrs C.'s address when he rang her, said she, that's Mrs C., had a tin ear. And I got Butcher – you know Ms Butcher – to check it out. She was at Meegrims too, you see. And it did check out. So she certainly wasn't there for the music. So there you are.'

Woodbine was looking shell shocked. Great, thought Joe.

He didn't mind the cop thinking he was two rhymes short of a limerick so long as he didn't get within smelling distance of how very real Joe's suspicions of him had been!

Joe had rung him from the Hackers' too, offering the same theory as he'd outlined to Mrs Calverley, only with her name headlined instead of Woodbine's. He'd finished by saying he was heading out to Hoot Hall now and put the phone down before there could be any questions. Guilty, Joe reckoned Willie would come out by himself in an effort to put a gag on him. What he hadn't reckoned on was how far the Calverleys might go in their efforts to keep him quiet. It was a large failing in a PI, not being able to grasp just how wicked folk could be!

'So what else did this Ozzie brief tell you, Joe?' asked Woodbine.

'Just confirmed what I knew or had guessed,' he said immodestly. 'Pam and Vicary got married when they both got postgrad scholarships to come to SBU for a year. No need to. They could have just come and shacked up together, but Australians were still pretty conventional back in the seventies. Things were a lot looser over here and Pam found herself having an affair. From what she told the lawyer, she thought it was the real thing and was willing to throw Vicary over and go the whole hog, but the guy had different ideas and dumped her. So she stuck with what she'd got, and when she realized she was pregnant, pretended it was her husband's.'

'But it was Dick Calverley's, that what you're saying?'

'Had to be,' said Joe with the firm confidence of a man who hadn't been sure of anything till half an hour ago. 'Seems that Robbie and his assumed dad never really hit it off and ever since he reached adolescence, they'd been in a state of open war. Pam finally broke and thought she might defuse the situation by confessing that Robbie wasn't Vicary's child. Robbie took off.'

'And Vicary?'

'He wasn't happy. But they'd been married a long time. Also, he found out what Pam had just had confirmed, that it wasn't just the hassle of family trouble that was making her feel so lousy, it was cancer.'

'Then he gets himself killed, and she dies, and the kid . . . Life can be a shit,' said Woodbine.

'You're not wrong,' said Joe, relieved to find that even a cop could forget his personal niggles in face of other folks' larger grief.

But not for long, it seemed!

'Still don't see how Georgie got into this in the first place,' said Woodbine.

Time for the famous soft shoe shuffle!

'I think Mrs Woodbine – Miss Barnfather she'd be then – was a student of Dickie Calverley's, and somehow Pam Vicary got the idea that she, your wife, was the reason Calverley had dumped her. So all Pam'd be able to tell Robbie about his real dad was that he'd been a lecturer at SBU and had possibly been involved with, maybe even married, another student called Georgina Barnfather. Robbie broke into the admin records office, couldn't find anything about his father, but in the old student files, he tracked down your wife with her family address and phone number.'

Woodbine was regarding him like he was trying to sell him a VCR in a pub.

Why the shoot am I so worried about his feelings? thought Joe, suddenly fed up of it all.

'Listen, Robbie had your number scribbled on his thumb. OK, so it may have got rubbed off during the PM, but it was there, and he rang your good lady 'cos Hoot Hall is ex-directory and there aren't any Calverleys in the book, and she gave him Mrs C.'s address. And if you don't believe me, ring her now and ask her.'

'She's up in town tonight, staying with a friend,' said Woodbine.

'In town. Oh yes,' said Joe noncommittally, except he wasn't very good at noncommittal, and Woodbine's face darkened with new suspicion.

Time to attack.

'Listen, Willie,' he said. 'Any way we can speed this up? I mean, my lovely old car's been wrecked, I'm battered and bruised, and I've got enough broken glass about my person to build a greenhouse, so can't you just take Mrs C. down

197

to the cells and bang her up till she coughs everything?'

'I'd like nothing better,' said Woodbine. 'Except we got rules now, and one of them says you've got to have reasonable grounds for holding a suspect. Where's the grounds, Joe?'

'I've told you . . .'

'You tell me you had pancakes for breakfast, that's not evidence,' interrupted Woodbine. 'In fact, there's plenty in this town would reckon that most likely you had porridge and just can't tell the sodding difference!'

Joe took a deep breath and said, 'I know I've not come to you with a barrow full of proof . . .'

He paused to let the policeman get a cynical snort out of his system, then went on, '. . . but what I think she's done is too disgusting not to turn over every stone looking for ways to prove it. This ain't no middle-class tax fraud. She murdered her own husband's son!'

'So you say,' said Woodbine. 'But how are you going to get a court to believe it?'

'No chance without I get you to believe it,' said Joe. 'Look, Willie, just imagine it. This poor kid suddenly has his life stood on its head. He hates the guy he's grown up thinking is his dad. That's enough to turn anyone's skull inside out. Then suddenly he's told this guy isn't his dad after all, so he needn't have felt all that hate and guilt anyway. Then he comes here, looking for his real father. All he wants at Hoot Hall is to find out anything he can about Dickie Calverley. But what does Mrs C. see?'

'You tell me,' said Woodbine.

'She sees danger. She sees some cheeky chancer who's come to take away from her own boy the only bit of inheritance he'd picked up from his useless father. Robbie was the elder son. If Robbie could prove his parentage, this place and the estate would go to him.'

'You sure of that?' said Woodbine.

'Pretty sure. And that's all that Mrs C. would need to be to make her decide the simplest thing was to get rid of him. Perhaps he was in a bad way. He'd clearly picked up a habit

198

on his travels. Perhaps it was easy to give him a nudge in the right direction . . .'

'Perhaps he just keeled over and died,' suggested Woodbine. 'They might have just shifted him to save the embarrassment.'

'Maybe,' said Joe. 'Except you don't try to kill someone to avoid embarrassment, do you? And I reckon they tried to kill me. I hope you're taking a long careful look at that cattle grid.'

'Believe me, I've got men going over every inch of this heap,' said Woodbine. 'All on your say so. And if they don't come up with something, and she starts complaining to the chief, you may find out just how far a reasonable man will go because he's been embarrassed! You know what she's going to say, don't you? If I was so worried by the possibility that this boy might be my husband's child that I killed him to conceal the fact, why then did I hire a private detective to establish his identity?'

Joe began to laugh.

'I'm sorry,' he said. 'There's so much to explain, I'd forgotten I'd not got on to that.'

'Oh God. There's more. Fact, or just another flight of fancy?'

'You decide,' said Joe. 'The kid dies, no matter how. They dump him at St Monkey's, problem solved. Then something comes up which changes everything. Here's the way I see it. Fred, who's got an expensive little habit himself, spots that Pam Vicary has promised to try to send her boy some more cash for his birthday. So along he goes to the Down Under Club with Robbie's passport and instead of money from Oz, he gets the lawyer's letter. This he shows to his mum who I bet does a bit of discreet checking. You know what she finds? What I found out from Greenhill on the phone tonight.'

'Tell me,' said Woodbine, with an unconvincing air of resignation.

'That Malcolm Vicary was worth a couple of million quid. That it all went to his widow, and when she died, it all went to Robbie, her son. And when *he* died, without making a will of course, you know who's first in line to cop the lot?

His half brother, Fred Calverley! But only if it can be proved they *are* half brothers. So suddenly Mrs C.'s problem is not to hide the connection but find a way to bring it out with minimum suspicion.'

'So she hires a PI she reckons wouldn't notice a clue unless it jumped up and hit him, then she fixes for a few to be thrown in his face?' mused Woodbine. 'You know, Joe, for the first time you're beginning to convince me.'

Joe felt this was a bit gratuitous, but he had to admit it made unflattering sense. Dunk Docherty had come along as a bonus to the woman, meaning that Fred could hand over the passport and letter without risk of recognition.

'But the lawyer's letter?' objected Woodbine suddenly. 'You say that Fred picked it up from the D.U. Club. But it was still there when you went.'

'Simple. His mum made him go back to town one morning, hang around till the postman delivered the club's mail, then pushed the letter through the flap to land with the others. I wondered why it was sealed with Sellotape. I checked with Customs and they said, yes, they sometimes opened letters and packets, but they always resealed them with their own special tape and it was marked on the envelope that Customs had opened it.'

'Proof, proof, proof!' demanded Woodbine.

'Someone picked up some of Robbie's mail after he was dead, it's in the club's record book,' said Joe. 'And it could be worth fingerprinting the lawyer's letter and envelope in case Fred left his dabs.'

That was the best he could do. He felt very, very tired. Time to get out of here.

The door opened and Dora Calverley came in. She didn't look like a woman under suspicion of murder.

'Edgar,' she said, 'I don't know what it is your men are looking for, but I must admire the energy they're expending looking for it. The poor dears will be quite exhausted when they've finished so I've made a pile of sandwiches in the kitchen. Do feel free to help yourself. And Mr Sixsmith, how are you feeling? The ambulance is just coming across the field. It should be here any moment, then you can get those cuts and bruises seen to properly, can't you?'

Before Joe could think of a reply, a pair of paramedics came into the room with a stretcher.

'Right, sir,' one of them said to Joe. 'You look like the one. Let's have a look at you.'

Joe said, 'I'm OK. But I'll come to Casualty with you. Anything to get out of here.'

As he made for the door, aided by the paramedics, he heard the woman say to Woodbine, 'Poor chap. This is the second car accident in a couple of days. Perhaps he got up too soon after the first. I should have guessed he was still in a bad way, the things he was saying about you and that poor child in the box.'

Joe halted in the doorway and turned round.

'Give it a rest, Mrs C.,' he said wearily. 'You know, and I know, and soon the whole world will know, that that poor child in the box was your husband's kid, and you and his precious half brother conspired to get rid of him.'

He didn't anticipate she was going to collapse in a paroxysm of guilt. He half expected she would throw an indignant rage and suggest his destination should be the psycho unit, not Casualty.

Instead she regarded him dumbstruck for a moment, then said, 'Is that what this is all about? Dickie's son? But that's imposs . . . Dickie's son? Oh God, Mr Sixsmith, that would explain it, this obsession of mine! Didn't I say that to you, Mr Sixsmith? I had this sense of empathy amounting almost to recognition . . . as if somehow I knew . . . Oh God. Isn't that what I said to you, Mr Sixsmith?'

I'm being rehearsed as a defence witness! thought Joe.

And recognizing that there are traps deeper even than a cattle grid that a clever woman can set for a foolish fellow, Joe said, 'Take me out of here!'

26

At Casualty they patched him up and talked about keeping him in but he said he had a nervous friend who needed him at home.

The nervous friend clearly couldn't believe his eyes that Joe was coming home in this state again. But next morning when Joe, feeling he'd been beaten by experts, set about dispensing an extra large dose of his favourite medicine, the English breakfast, the nervous friend nobly gave his forgiveness and took his own medicine like a cat.

Feeling a little better, Joe decided he would be safer at the office. He didn't spell out to himself what he'd be safer from. Trouble was, he recalled with a pang, he had no transport and he certainly didn't feel fit enough to fight his way on to a bus.

He rang the firm who had Merv on their books.

'Hi, Joe, sorry, Merv's not available, hasn't been since last evening, thought he was doing some job for you.'

'That's right, I forgot,' said Joe. 'He's probably grabbing a bit of sleep. Just send someone who can stay at twenty and likes to keep at least three wheels on the deck, OK?'

At the office he ignored protests from Whitey who didn't like the lift but did like company up the stairs, and got in the narrow tin box. As usual it took for ever, but that's what he felt like he had this morning.

The office smelt damp and cold. He switched the electric fire on with a kick of his foot and collapsed into his chair. Professionally, there was no reason to be here. He'd had three clients. Gallie Hacker was happy, if knowing your granddad was a killer and a bigamist was happiness. Dora

Calverley was (he hoped) under arrest. And Mavis Dalgety. He could foresee little comfort there, but there was nothing he could do about it just now. Time, in fact, for a bit of the negative whatsit. Let the rest of the world do the worrying.

The only other thing of immediate concern was *The Creation*. Just two more rehearsals then the big night. He drew in a deep breath of anticipation and felt pain flicker across his bruised ribs.

'Oh shoot, Whitey,' he said in alarm. 'Suppose I can't sing?'

The cat, somnolent after his share of the full English, yawned his opinion that this would be no great loss to the world of music, sacred or profane.

'Thank you, Pavarotti,' said Joe.

Only one way to find out. He went to his tape recorder. *The Creation* was still in. He pressed the start key. It came on at Part Three, Scene Three, during the recitative introducing Adam and Eve's final duet. He listened for a while, then as the duet itself commenced took a deep breath and joined in, easy at first then increasing the volume.

> *Graceful consort! At thy side*
> *softly fly the golden hours.*
> *Every moment brings new rapture:*
> *every care is put to rest.*

Not bad, not bad, he thought as he listened to Eve's response.

> *Spouse adored! At thy side*
> *purest joy o'erflow the heart.*
> *Life and all I am is thine:*
> *my reward thy love shall be.*

It wasn't till the third line that he realized another voice had joined the soloist's. He turned to see Beryl Boddington standing in the doorway.

'Hi,' he said.

'Hi,' she said. 'Heard you'd been in Casualty so thought I'd check. How're you feeling?'

'Fair,' he said. 'How'm I sounding?'

'Fair,' she said with a smile. 'Shall we?'

The solo exchange had finished. Now Adam and Eve's voices were joined in sweet unison.

'Why not?' said Joe. 'Only chance we'll get to star.'

Together, eye beams twisted, they began to sing.

> *But without thee, what is to me*
> *the morning dew,*
> *the breath of ev'n,*
> *the savoury fruit,*
> *the fragrant bloom?*
> *With thee is every joy enhanced,*
> *with thee delight is ever new,*
> *with thee is life incessant bliss;*
> *thine, thine it whole shall be.*

Joe pressed the stop key.

'That was good,' he said. He didn't just mean the singing.

'Yeah,' said Beryl. 'Incessant bliss aside, Joe, what have you been up to?'

He listened carefully for the exasperated hectoring note Mirabelle would have injected into the question. Not finding it, he said, 'Had a bit of a do with the Morris. Cattle grid collapsed. Reckon I've totalled it.'

'Oh Joe, I'm so sorry.'

Her sincerity of feeling touched Joe more than any concern for himself would have done. She knew how he loved that car. Letting what matters to someone else matter to you is a large step . . . to what?

With thee is every joy enhanced

Whoops. Careful, boy, he admonished himself. And then got angry with himself for being so mean spirited.

He said, 'Fancy some tea?'

'I'll make it,' she said.

She went into the tiny washroom to fill the kettle. With perfect timing, Willie Woodbine came through the door.

'No half measures with you, Joe,' he said almost admiringly. 'Guessed if you weren't in hospital, you'd be here.'

'Good news or bad?' asked Joe.

'Mixed. Bad is we can't find anything to show Robbie

204

Vicary was ever at Hoot Hall. No evidence either that anyone tampered with the cattle grid. Could have been natural decay.'

'And John Lennon could've died of heartburn,' said Joe. 'You said the news was mixed. Anything better?'

'Well, I've spoken to my wife.'

Chance for a real PI wise-crack here.

'She's home then,' said Joe neutrally.

It still got him the suspicious glare.

'Yes, she's home. And she says there was a call, someone asking about Dickie Calverley. Could have been an Australian accent. And she did put him on to Hoot Hall.'

'Well, that's something,' said Joe.

'From a prosecution point of view it's nothing. Pointless even trying to work it in. Just imagine what a defence brief would do with it!'

Joe imagined. *Senior policeman's wife backs hubby and tries to fit up old friend.*

'I'm sorry,' he said.

'Sorry gets you no baked beans,' said Woodbine. Joe didn't know the phrase but recognized it meant Woodbine had his own Aunt Mirabelle. Perhaps everyone did.

He said, 'We've had the bad and the not-so-bad. You promised mixed. So what's the good?'

'You were right about Fred Calverley being a user. We found a nice little stash at the Hall. I wanted to bring him in for questioning but Dora insisted on ringing the family lawyer first. And in the meantime, young Fred did a bunk.'

'You don't sound too worried.'

Woodbine smiled.

'You don't get far questioning a junkie with a smart brief and a doting mother on the spot,' he said.

Joe was with him. Cut off from his stash, Fred would have to surface again soon. Get him before he scored and he'd be a soft target for some hard questions before his lawyer and mother could put in an appearance. Might not be admissible, of course, but knowing what it is you want to know is half the policeman's game.

Joe didn't approve, but so what? Tell the Pope you didn't

like poverty and he'd say it was better than damnation.

He said, 'Take it easy. He's only a kid, and from what I hear, he's had a hard time.'

'With a mummy who thinks the sun shines out of his arse? You're joking,' said Woodbine incredulously.

'There's all kinds of hard times,' said Joe.

'I never had you down for a bleeding heart,' said Woodbine.

'You neither,' said Joe. 'So what brings you here apart from giving me an update?'

Woodbine said, 'I need some names. Who was it told you about Vicary asking questions up at the University? Who was it who picked up the wallet and passport?'

Joe hesitated and Woodbine snarled, 'Come on! If this thing's going to go anywhere, I need to talk to all these people myself.'

Joe felt some sympathy for him. The guy was in a fix, he could see that. Mrs Calverley couldn't be a comfortable person to investigate. Too many old boy strings for her to pull, so Willie would need to be a lot surer of himself than he was before pushing forward. Equally, he had to be sure that there was nothing going to jump up and kick him in the butt if he decided to drop the whole thing.

But feeding him that poor kid from the Scratchings and Dunk Docherty needed some thought. Could be argued the girl could only benefit from being put under the spotlight. Find out who her folks were, get her some medical help. But Dunk was another matter. Pressurize him and all the Taras Kovalko stuff could come spilling out, either to Woodbine, which was bad, or to his editor, which was worse.

He said, 'I'd need to think about that.'

Woodbine shook his head in mock amazement.

'What's this I'm hearing? Request from the police for assistance and you need to think about it? Oh Joe, Joe. This isn't grouchy old Sergeant Chivers you're jerking around. This is me, your friend in need. And be assured you'll need a friend if you start pulling my plonker!'

His voice had harshened to a threat and he took a couple of steps towards Joe as if he were minded to grab him.

There was a gentle cough from the washroom door. Beryl stood there holding the kettle.

'Hello. Mr Woodbine, I'm just making a pot of tea. Would you fancy some?'

Woodbine turned and stared at her for a long moment.

His mind's ticking up everything he's said, thought Joe.

It didn't come to enough to cause concern, but enough to call a truce.

'No thanks, Miss Boddington,' he said. 'Things to do. Joe, keep in touch, eh?'

He left.

Beryl said, 'He remembered my name.'

'That's the first thing they teach them at police college,' said Joe. 'Never hit anyone whose name you don't know. I could murder that tea.'

When it was brewed and they were sitting drinking it, Beryl said, 'You like to tell me what precisely you've been up to? Or shall I just make up my own story round what I overheard?'

Did client confidentiality still apply when you were trying to put your client in jail? Joe decided not. It was the thin end of a wedge, however, and when Dunk Docherty's role came up, he found himself telling Beryl about the Kovalko affair too. Of course, there was a hidden agenda here, he recognized. It meant he could clear up any residual misunderstanding about his relationship with Galina. Though why he should want to do that, he wasn't ready to be clear about.

The only thing he didn't mention, because there was no need to, was his other interest in Georgie Woodbine.

When he had finished, Beryl sat in silence for a while then said, 'So you're not going to tell me about Mrs Woodbine?'

'I'm sorry?'

'There's something else there. I saw you talking to her at the rehearsal the other night. There was definitely something.'

'Yeah, well, I've explained all that, about Robbie Vicary having her number and me getting this idea that maybe Willie was up to something . . .'

'No,' she said with an emphatic shake of the head. 'It was later that night that you went down to the Scratchings . . . You dumped me, remember? And you didn't get the wallet from Docherty till the next morning. So give!'

Joe hesitated. God decided. The door burst open and Merv Golightly exploded in.

'Joe, my man! And the beautiful Ms Bodytone. Are you both glad to see me!'

'What gives you that stupid idea, Merv?' asked Joe.

'Well, Ms B. certainly is, because with good-looking girls, it's a condition of service to be glad to see old Merv. Talking of which, that Long Liz runs a mean laundry. She certainly knows how to spin a man dry, don't she? You could do a lot worse for yourself, Joe, present company excepted!'

'Merv,' said Joe warningly. 'We were having a private conversation . . .'

'Say no more,' said Merv with a huge wink. 'But cast an eye on these, then carry on with your private conversation, feeling real mean and ungrateful!'

He pulled a large brown envelope out of his donkey jacket and spilled its contents on to the desk.

Joe looked at them aghast.

From the doorway Merv said, 'No need for apologies and thank you's straight away, Joe. I'll be down the Glit at opening time with all orifices open! Bye, Ms Bodytone!'

He left explosively as he'd arrived.

Joe said, 'Sorry about that . . .'

Beryl said, 'No need to apologize for your friend, Joe. All this concern for mixed-up kids and trying to straighten them out had got me thinking that maybe I was being a bit hard on you doing your PI thing. But now I see what really makes up your bread and butter stuff. You telling me that this kind of shit's better than drawing the dole? Time to look at your priorities, Joe boy.'

She was making for the door.

Joe said, 'Beryl, it's not like it seems, I can explain . . .'

But she was gone, leaving him staring down at the scattered photographs.

Merv had done well for an amateur. Joe laid out the photos

in sequence. The man alone in the Wyatt House apartment. The woman coming in. The two meeting in a passionate embrace. Clothing falling to the floor, the couple too absorbed to care about the light or the curtains. Then, half naked and still locked together, the half naked pair sinking out of sight. The last print showed an apparently empty room.

No problem with identification. The woman was clearly Georgina Woodbine, the man Andrew Dalgety.

Joe shuffled the photos together, put them back in the envelope, reached over to the tape deck and pressed the start key.

The angel Uriel's fine tenor rang out.

> *O happy pair, and always happy yet,*
> *if not, misled by false conceit,*
> *ye strive at more than granted is,*
> *and more to know than know ye should!*

'You got it, Uri,' said Joe Sixsmith.

27

This all finished when Joe Sixsmith came sneaking out of the small side door at St Monkey's.

He'd taken the photos to Butcher and spread them out in front of her.

'What's this crap, Sixsmith?' she said. 'I don't do divorce.'

'You can see what it is. The woman's your old schoolmate and temporary fellow traveller, Georgie Woodbine, who, when she was dropped by Dickie Calverley, didn't just join the local Red Brigade because she'd been politicized, but because she wanted to show the world pretty quick she didn't give a toss. There was this good-looking Party worker, Harry Hopegill, who set the girls swooning. Georgie got her teeth into him and when she'd got him good and hot, dumped him to show she was her own woman. She probably didn't notice that there was this little teenager madly in love with Harry. Other people noticed though.'

The cheroot miasma was impenetrable.

'Is this going to take forever, Sixsmith?'

'Not long. The man is Andrew Dalgety. His daughter thinks he's Superdad, so when she finds out he's having it off with Georgie, she reckons the woman's all to blame and looks for a way of getting her out of the picture with maximum pain. What better than a corrupting-the-kids scandal? Maybe she got the idea when she told her best friend that Georgie was making it with her dad, and Sally told her she was making it all up because she was a jealous cow and Georgie was the best thing since Madonna in any form. I don't know.'

'What the hell is it you imagine you do know, Sixsmith?' said a voice from the smoke.

'I imagine Sally was so obsessed with Georgie she didn't want to believe she could be involved with anything so sordid as sex with a man – husbands not counting, of course. But she's a bright kid and she kept her eyes open. And when she caught Dalgety with his hand up Georgie's skirt at the party, she had to recognize it was true. Her guru and goddess was banging away like an old bucket with her best friend's father!'

'This going to get any coarser?' asked Butcher.

'No, I'm nearly done. Sally gets so angry she decides to wreck the party by turning on all the gas taps. Result is a bit more spectacular and a lot more dangerous than she anticipates. So now we've got two mixed-up kids, as well as two mixed-up adults. Or do I mean three?'

'That some kind of accusation?'

'Just an observation. It's OK letting your emotions get in the way of judgement when you're in your teens. Us mature adults ought to look a lot closer at things before we go along with them, that's all.'

'So where do you go from here?'

'Me? Nowhere. I'm out. End of case, report to client, collect fee. Only this time there's no fee to collect and I'm letting you have the pleasure of reporting to the client. Maybe you can talk to her like you should have talked in the first place. The kid needs help, not encouragement!'

'You can be really self-righteous when you try, did you know that, Sixsmith?'

'No good, Butcher. You know you got it wrong. That kid's hurting. Try to sort it. I'll see you.'

He'd left. When he got back to the office, he said, 'This self-righteous stuff ain't so bad once in a while, Whitey. Gives you a kind of glow.'

Next night he'd gone to the dress rehearsal. There'd been some talk of black jackets and bow ties but Boyling Corner democratic principles had prevailed. 'Like always, you'll wear your best suits,' Rev. Pot had commanded. But when he saw Joe in The Suit, his eyes rolled and he said, 'When I say *like always*, no need to take me so literal, Joe.'

'I got a new white shirt for tomorrow night,' said Joe.

'Great. Well, keep all three buttons fastened and don't draw attention to yourself.'

Keeping even one button fastened wasn't in Joe's game plan. His ribs still ached and he needed all the freedom of chest expansion he could get to sing without groaning.

'Don't you worry about me, Rev.,' he said. 'Excuse me now.'

He'd just seen Sally Eaglesfield come in. He went towards her, smiled broadly and said, 'Hi.'

'Oh hello,' she said unenthusiastically.

Strictly speaking she was none of his business. What the shoot did he know about the pains and problems of growing up in the nineties?

More than I did a couple of weeks ago, he told himself. And isn't growing up what I'm still doing?

'How are you keeping?'

'Fine,' she said.

If he could have believed her, he'd have been pleased to leave it there. But she still looked so pale and drawn he couldn't walk away.

He said, 'You talking to your friend, Mavis, again?'

'We've spoken, yes. Why do you ask?' she said suspiciously.

'She needs a friend to talk to. Really talk to. She's got *real* troubles.'

This was the Aunt Mirabelle school of psychology. 'You got the toothache? Find someone been run over by a bus, that'll stop you moaning.'

'What's it got to do with you?' the girl was demanding.

Do I tell her I know she turned the gas on in Georgie's kitchen? wondered Joe. Do I rely on honesty, truth, confession, getting in touch with your feelings, all that stuff?

No, the answer came. What a kid this age really needs is magic.

He said, 'Hey, I'm sorry. Just that in this place, all the atmosphere, you know, I sometimes hear these voices, not so much voices, more a message in my head. And tonight it said to me, that girl Sally is going to be all right, she's going

212

to come up smelling of roses, and I thought I should let you know.'

She was looking at him as if he was mad. He couldn't blame her. What did a middle-aged balding PI have to do with magic?

Over her shoulder he saw Georgie Woodbine approaching.

He said, 'Shoot. Here comes that mouldy old schoolma'am of yours. Always makes me feel like I ain't done my homework. I'm on my way.'

And his reward for this entirely selfish and spontaneous remark was to see a sudden smile light up the girl's pale face, giving it the life and colour it so required.

Thinking about it as he moved away, it came to him that maybe a balding middle-aged PI didn't rate very high as social counsellor or even magician. But when the same balding middle-aged PI saw the object of your desire and jealous rage as a mouldy old schoolma'am, it could produce a very helpful shift in perspective.

A hand grasped his arm. He recognized the touch without needing to see the grasper.

'You still chasing this young stuff, Joseph? And in God's house. You ought to be ashamed of yourself!'

'Auntie, I'm not chasing anyone,' he protested.

'No? Well, I believe you, Joseph,' said Mirabelle. 'But only because you don't have the talent for it. These girls grow up too fast nowadays. They know how to take advantage of a simple soul who knows nothing of the world. Not like when I was a child. Then you stayed a child till you stopped being a child. Nowadays I swear some of them are born guilty!'

'Thought we all were, Auntie,' said Joe. 'Isn't that what it says in the Good Book?'

'Don't you start telling me what it says in the Good Book,' she said fiercely. 'All I want to hear from you is what you been doing to Beryl.'

'Why? What's she been saying?'

'Nothing, that's what. Mention your name and she says nothing. So what is it you've been up to?'

Joe gently removed her hand from his arm and said, 'Auntie, it ever occur to you that maybe sometimes Beryl could get things wrong? Or *you* could get things wrong? Or anyone else in the world but *me* could get things wrong? There's Mr Perfect wanting us in our places. I'll see you later.'

He left her looking as close to dumbstruck as she'd ever come. As he joined the baritones, he passed Beryl looking very fetching in her white blouse and black skirt. She gave him a cool nod but didn't offer to speak.

Women! thought Joe. Don't know whether they're born guilty; they're certainly born knowing more than they should!

The baton rapped commandingly, the orchestra poised itself for Chaos, and Joe surreptitiously undid the three buttons on his jacket.

The rehearsal went well. They went through the oratorio with scarcely an interruption and at the end Mr Perfect said, 'Thank you, ladies and gentlemen. Give me that on the night plus an extra ten per cent for the paying customers, and we will truly have given Luton a rare taste of heaven!'

Joe suddenly realized he didn't want to speak to anyone, not Aunt Mirabelle, not Beryl, not Sally Eaglesfield, not Georgie Woodbine, and certainly not Rev. Pot who was glowering accusingly at his flapping jacket.

And his feet, without waiting for conscious command from his brain, took him into the side aisle, through the little chantry and out of the side door.

It wasn't till he was outside in the dank autumn night that the sense of having done this before hit him. Sensible thing to do would have been to go right back inside or at least turn towards the front of the church. But those bossy feet were taking him deeper into the darkness which lay in the other direction. He was hit by the certainty that once more he was going to find a large cardboard box by the wall with a figure stooping over it, so this minimalized the shock when that was precisely what he saw.

Only it wasn't exactly the same as before. This time the stooping figure belonged to Dora Calverley.

She too showed little surprise as she straightened up at his approach.

'You worked it out too,' she said. 'You've been a great

disappointment to me, Mr Sixsmith. People should live down to their reputations.'

Joe didn't need to ask what it was he was supposed to have worked out.

'Is he in there?' he said fearfully.

'No, but he has been. One thing he inherited from me was an overactive sense of irony.'

Now Joe felt able to look in the box.

It was empty except for a few old newspapers.

'How can you be sure it's him?'

'You recognize the scent of your own child, Mr Sixsmith,' she said. 'I must confess that, like yourself, I had a moment's fear that history was repeating itself.'

'Not quite,' he said. 'I didn't think you'd dragged him round here from the Cloisters.'

She gave him her old cold stare.

'You're still persisting with that calumny?'

'I'm not wired up if that's what's bothering you,' said Joe.

Her face relaxed and she gave a faint smile.

'No, I don't imagine that you are. Not your style. So I'll tell you the truth. Robbie Vicary died naturally, Mr Sixsmith. If you can call pumping that stuff into yourself natural. I couldn't let him be found at the Hall, of course. The police might have got nosey about Fred's problem. Also, if the business of his parentage came up, that might have caused speculation. Fred was very upset, I think he quite liked the notion of a half brother. As always, I had to be the practical one and finally I persuaded him that dumping him here was for the best.'

'Then Fred picked up the letter and suddenly you realized there might be money in this for you,' said Joe.

'For Fred,' she corrected him. 'I can't benefit from the death of my dead husband's bastard.'

'So you hired me to trip over the truth which you personally laid out in front of me. Only when you realized I'd managed to go a lot further than you wanted, you got panicky and decided to dump me.'

'It was pure accident, believe me. That grid has needed fixing for years. Why should either Fred or I wish to kill you?

215

To stop you accusing me of not reporting Robbie's death? Come now, Mr Sixsmith, that's hardly reason for murder, is it?'

'Not by itself, no,' agreed Joe. 'Which is my point exactly. There has to be something else. But none of it matters any more, does it? All's well that ends badly, and even if you walk away from a murder charge, you're not going to make a profit, are you?'

'I really don't understand what you're talking about,' she said helplessly. 'What profit could there be in that unfortunate boy's death?'

'Robbie Vicary died a rich man,' said Joe. 'And the money's got to go somewhere.'

'So I gather. And if indeed it can be proved that he was Dickie's son and the laws of inheritance say that his half brother is the legal heir, then naturally Fred will claim his inheritance.'

'Nice one, Mrs C.,' said Joe with a smile. 'Except there's one little problem. Don't see how you're going to prove Robbie was Dickie's son without drawing attention to the fact that Fred isn't! Which means that not only does he miss out on the Vicary loot, he's not even legally entitled to be playing the Squire up at Hoot Hall!'

'What do you mean?' she said softly.

'It's all down to dominant genes and recessive genes,' he said with the confidence of one who'd popped into the library and checked out Butcher's information in the *Children's Medical Encyclopaedia*. 'You see, you got blue eyes and Fred's got blue eyes, and Pam Vicary had blue eyes. But Dickie had brown eyes, at least he's got them in that painting hanging up in your house. Now this would explain why Robbie's eyes were brown. But no way can Dickie be the father of blue-eyed Fred.'

In fact, there *were* ways which the encyclopaedia had spelt out, with the odds against them. But they weren't into odds here. All he wanted was to test his notion that Dora Calverley hadn't hesitated to play around when she found that dear old Dickie wasn't the catch she'd hoped for.

One look at her face told him he'd hit the nail on the head.

A second look suggested that maybe it hadn't been one of his better ideas. Not at this particular time, in this dark coign of St Monkey's, with the rising mist forming a barrier in the mind which lent assurance to the delusion that whatever happened here at this place in this time had nothing to do with the world of light and life and people only a few dozen yards away.

She took a step towards him. He could see something in her eyes which an animal psychologist might have interpreted as the maternal instinct to defend her young but which looked like plain murder to Joe. He opened his mouth to speak, perhaps to remonstrate, perhaps to yell for help, but something – the mist, or pure terror, or maybe (worst of all!) simple embarrassment – clutched at his throat and reduced his words to one of Whitey's silent miaows.

And then it was too late. She brought the heavy rubber-bound torch up into his crotch. He doubled forward in agony and she smashed the torch into his face. The glass broke. He staggered back, something caught at his legs and he fell over backwards into the graveolent depths of the cardboard box.

So this was what it was like, to drop through the holes in society and have nothing left to catch you but the discarded container of someone else's consumer durables. Could be OK if the alternative was having your head beat in by a mad woman. Maybe that's what they thought when it all started back in the eighties. And maybe they found, like he was finding, that not even a cardboard box could hide you from the mad woman's revenges.

The torch bulb was shattered but he could see the club-like shape silhouetted against the light grey mist as Dora Calverley raised it to finish him off. No point in her stopping now. All the rest she might brazen her way out of, but she knew Fred's future was finished if she left him alive. Not that any such logical thought was troubling her mind. Could be it would be a conscience-saving rationalization later, but at the moment sheer blood lust was enough.

The torch came swinging down.

I ain't no lady killer, thought Joe Sixsmith, but at least they'll have to admit I was killed by a lady.

He closed his eyes.

After a while he opened them again.

There were two figures above him now. The second one had grabbed the torch with one hand and was pulling Mrs Calverley back with the other. A voice was shouting, 'Is it true, Mother? Is what he said true? Why did you never tell me? Why? Why?'

It occurred to Joe that Dora Calverley was now discovering what Pam Vicary had discovered – that being a mother meant you were always in the wrong. Maybe you had to somehow be born without parents to start free and clear. Like Adam and Eve at the Creation. *And God saw everything that he had made; and behold it was very good* ... Wonder if the old boy felt quite so self-satisfied now? Wonder if maybe I should start shouting for help in case these two decide to postpone their row long enough to finish me off?

But it soon appeared it wasn't necessary. The illusion of isolation created by the mist couldn't survive the kind of noise Fred Calverley was making. A gruff voice – the verger's? – was shouting, 'What's going on there?' Then there were other voices, and finally figures leaning over the box, till suddenly they were swept aside and Aunt Mirabelle said, 'What you doing in that box, Joseph?'

Then she too was moved aside and someone else stooped low over him and Beryl's voice at once concerned and crisply professional said, 'He's been hurt. Don't try to move him till I've taken a closer look.'

'Close as you like,' said Joe. 'Close as you like.'

28

The Creation was a sell out. Everyone who was anyone in Luton turned up, and lots who weren't anyone in particular. The Hacker family were there, all three generations, with Gallie, very demure in a little black dress and next to no make-up, sitting alongside Dunk Docherty who had misjudged the occasion and looked very uncomfortable in a Luton Town tracksuit. Willie Woodbine was there, flying the flag for his wife, and in the row behind sat the Dalgetys and a couple of rows further back, Butcher. Even Dick Hull from the Glit was there, come to suss out the opposition.

Joe was present too, despite all medical advice. His face had more stitches than a Welsh sampler and he walked with the slow dignity of a Great War veteran. But he wore a splendid new suit. Rev. Pot had taken one look at him after his return from hospital and said, 'Joe, you look like you've been put together by the same guy who made your suit. Mirabelle, burn that abomination and drag him to a tailor, naked if necessary.'

The new jacket was much easier on the chest. Not that this mattered much as every time he tried to let himself into a note, it felt like his face was cracking. So after the opening chorus, he simply mimed the words, but presumably God heard them anyway.

Not that Joe was sure he believed in God. Or rather, he was pretty sure the God he believed in wasn't the same as the one he'd been brought up to serenade at the Boyling Corner Chapel. His God was an absent-minded old boy who liked Gary Glitter as much as Haydn and who lived in an old wooden house overrun by cats. Sometimes he overslept for days, or weeks, or even years, and when He woke up and saw how the scales of justice had got out of kilter due to His neglect, He felt real guilty and scattered a bit of divine revelation on the Good scale to try to re-establish the balance. For some reason Joe didn't understand (but he didn't kid himself it was part of any masterplan!) he seemed to get in the way of more than his fair share of this haphazard scatter. Or maybe he'd just found himself a job where it paid to take heed of it, especially when the alternative was applying the power of inductive reasoning, of which he'd got less than his fair share.

One thing for sure about this odd God of his, He didn't offload His own guilt on to kids. That was human business. Which meant trying to put it right was human business too, and that was work a man could be proud of.

He reckoned he'd not done too badly recently. Galina Hacker was a definite success. He'd restored to her a grandfather whose human frailties her love could transcend. The things she now knew he had done were hardly even a test of her love, whereas the things she'd started to fear he might have done would have destroyed it.

As for Mavis Dalgety, when Butcher came to see him after the attack, he asked her what she'd done about the pics.

She said, 'I went straight round to see Georgie at school, scattered them on her desk and said they'd be pinned up on the main school notice board and on the "Wanted" board outside the police station if she didn't dump Andrew Dalgety. The headmaster stuck his head through the door while I was there and Georgie almost fell across the desk. I knew we'd got a deal then.'

'Why go for her and not Dalgety?' asked Joe, curious.

'Men can get macho, decide to make the grand gesture, all that crap. Women are much more sensible.' She hesitated, smiled and added, 'Besides, you were right about me hating that cow, Joe. I really enjoyed it. Now we're even.'

She'd also had a word with Mavis. 'Girls' talk,' she told Joe mockingly. Whatever had been said it seemed to have worked, thought Joe, looking at Mavis sitting happily between her parents.

A bonus spin-off of all this had been Sally Eaglesfield, who'd come up to him earlier that evening, given him that nice shy smile of hers, and asked how he was feeling.

Only with Fred Calverley was there total failure. The one whole thing in his fragmented life had been his father's memory, and this Joe had inadvertently taken away from him. Willie Woodbine was delighted with the results.

'You've done it again, Joe,' he had complimented him. 'Fred's hurling all kinds of shit at his mum. Says she told him in the first place that Robbie was an impostor but could cause trouble about the estate so they had to get rid of him. Then she changed her tune and said they had to fix it up to look like he was Calverley's bastard so's they could get their hands on the Australian money. Then she said you were turning out to be one of those smart-ass kaffirs and they'd better fix for you to be taken out of the picture.'

'He's a druggie,' said Joe. 'Also, he's all mixed up about his dad. He's likely to say anything. Good defence brief will go to town.'

'With Mrs C. pleading guilty, he won't get a chance,' laughed Woodbine. 'She's putting her hand up for everything her boy is willing to lay on her. The chief's delighted.'

'I don't like this, not one little bit,' protested Joe. 'The woman's just letting her guilt talk . . .'

'Isn't that what we all want, Joe? To let guilt talk? Now you've done enough talking, I reckon, certainly more than enough to compensate for your own little bit of guilt . . .'

'My guilt? What's that?'

'Well, when I spoke to Greenhill, that Ozzie lawyer, he seemed to have this strange notion he'd already told most of what he knew to the chief constable. Natural mistake with a bad line. But you've done your bit, Joe. Now's the time to relax and get better. I'll be out there taking the flak and making sure nobody bothers you.'

Man who could be so magnanimous deserved all the promotion he could get, thought Joe. But what do I deserve?

'Why the shoot do I feel so bad about all this?' he asked Beryl when she came visiting. 'Mrs C. used me, Fred's a nasty piece of goods. So why do I feel like I left my fingers in the lathe?'

'Because you want justice without hurting people, which isn't generally possible,' said Beryl. 'Because you're fine for everyone else's good, but too nice for your own. I've been thinking about those photos, Joe, and try though I might, I can't see you getting deep into that stuff. So tell me all about them, the truth, I mean.'

He told her. She didn't say anything but leaned over him, her heavy breasts warm against his aching ribs, her full soft lips moist against his stitched-up face. It was all very painful but he didn't complain.

He glanced towards her now, her broad, handsome face very serious as she concentrated on the movement of the music towards the next soprano entry. Just before it came she suddenly looked his way, sent a huge affectionate smile, and then exploded into *'Awake the harp! The lyre awake! In shout and joy your voices raise!'*

Even without Joe's small contribution, the performance was a tremendous success, touching those heights which Mr Perfect had shown them were within their reach. The Rev. Tin Can had banned applause as out of character with the hallowed setting, but the silence which stretched beyond the last Amen was more eloquent than beaten hands and hoarse bravos! It was somehow part of the work, an extension of its magic so that for a while longer they all, performers and audience alike, remained in that world of joyful innocence before the Fall.

Finally, at a nod from the vicar, the verger drew open the great doors at the end of the church and let in the cold air of autumn and the traffic hum of St Monkey's Square, and with them the old imperfect world. The listeners began to rise, some to leave, some to move forward to congratulate their friends and family. Joe, watching the embraces and smiling handshakes and listening to the rising hubbub of happy voices, felt that perhaps after all, the old imperfect world wasn't such a bad place to live in.

'Not sneaking out of the side door tonight, Joe?' said Beryl.

'No way,' said Joe. 'First time, I found a body. Second time

222

I almost became one. From now on in, I stay in the bright lights and graze with the herd.'

'In that case, we'd better head on to the party,' said Beryl. 'Pity though.'

'Why's that?'

'I was going to suggest I take you home and light a candle and serve you up something special.'

Suddenly Joe's new suit began to feel as tight as the old. He glanced down the aisle where he could see Mirabelle and Rev. Pot standing like sentinels by the main doorway.

'But what would we say to Aunt Mirabelle and Rev. Pot?'

'Well, we could always sneak out by the side door,' said Beryl.

Joe thought once more of the poor boy who had come across half a world searching for truth and a father, and had found drugs and death.

Life was for being happy with what you'd got and joys that did not kill.

'Why not?' said Joe Sixsmith.

What's next?

Tell us the name of an author you love

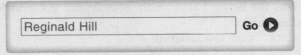

Reginald Hill   Go ▶

and we'll find your next great book.